SMUGGLER'S BRIDE

"Now what?" he muttered. He wasn't up to any practical jokes. He listened by the side of the shed and heard nothing for a few moments, then there was a muffled thud as something large fell to the ground, too big to be a raccoon. Rand walked over to the wood pile and grabbed a length of oak.

"All right, mister, I don't know what you and the Iveys are up to, but I want you to come out, real slow now."

There was no movement, but a muffled snort came from inside. It occurred to him that maybe whoever was in there wasn't in there of his own free will.

Still clutching the impromptu club, Rand put his hand on the latch and pulled hard, banging the door against the shed. He blinked into the darkness as dust and chaff swirled around, then looked down.

And grinned.

"Dang! I know I ain't got sugar on the supply list, darlin', so maybe you'd like to tell me what you're doing in my shed?"

PRAISE FOR SMUGGLER'S BRIDE

"4 Stars!…Marshall weaves historical facts into a well-written and highly captivating romance. The scene in which Julia and Rand find out that neither is what the other thought is humorous as well as poignant. The author ties up loose ends with a big bow and has an extraordinary way of setting the plot for her next book."

—Romantic Times Bookclub

"5 Cups!…Darlene Marshall has written a wonderful story filled with romance and humor. The sexual tension explodes between Julia and Rand. This book will keep you up late into the night. It is impossible to put down."

—Coffee Time Reviews

"8.5 Gargoyles!…A superbly written historical, the first book that kept me reading till the wee hours of the morning in a long time. I loved the characters and how they interacted with each other, they were vibrant and realistic. You felt for Julia and Rand, as things got more and more complicated for them. Her perfect blend of historical romance with a slight touch eroticism was a breath of fresh air. I loved the way [Marshall] made this entire book come together. I would most definitely read more by this author."

—In The Library Reviews

"There are so many 'forced to live together, she isn't who she says she is, he isn't who he says he is' stories out there, and I can usually find one that takes place in just about every time period. What's different about *Smuggler's Bride* is the twists applied to the intrigue, and the side characters like Ma Ivey that almost overshadow the main protagonists. It's as fun and light in tone as *Pirate's Price* and a pleasure to read."

—*Smart Bitches Trashy Books*

"*Smuggler's Bride* has it all, backwoods language, pirates, romance, thievery, secrets and lies all tied together for a wonderful tale of life in Florida and England long ago."

—*Roundtable Reviews*

"…A fast-paced, adventurous, passionate and thrilling plot that will please any reader loving a good mystery or romance novel. Again, Ms. Marshall has written a great yarn!"

—*The Best Reviews*

"…Full of romance and adventure. What's not to love about a tale with pirates, love, and pickled possums! There are definitely sparks between Julia and Rand, and the supporting characters are priceless. Ma Ivey and her sons are hilarious and very entertaining. Fans of Darlene Marshall will recognize some characters from *Pirate's Price* in this novel. You'll definitely want to give this one a read, as I think you will really enjoy this tale of love and pirates set in Florida Territory, 1843."

—*Romance Reader At Heart*

ALSO BY DARLENE MARSHALL

Captain Sinister's Lady
The Bride and the Buccaneer
Sea Change
Castaway Dreams
The Pirate's Secret Baby
Pirate's Price

SMUGGLER'S BRIDE

BY

DARLENE MARSHALL

SMUGGLER'S BRIDE

SMUGGLER'S BRIDE

This book is a work of fiction. All names, characters, locations, and incidents are products of the author's imagination, or have been used fictitiously. Any resemblance to actual persons
living or dead, locales, or events is entirely coincidental.

Layout and Formatting provided by: ElementalAlchemy.com

Published in the United States of America

I want to thank the Compuserve Books and Writers Community, especially the residents of Research and Craft. I also want to thank RWA Online for the encouragement and writing marathons.

Thanks to the Alachua County Library District staff for their help in obtaining books through interlibrary loan, and for the assistance of their Reference Desk. Additional thanks to Pam Williams at the University of Florida Levin School of Law Library for help on antebellum Federal crime and punishment. Librarians rock!

Thanks go to Steve Lopata for weapons assistance, again, and for schlepping his book on pepperbox pistols to WorldCon so I could see it firsthand, and for being a "beta reader."

Thanks also to my other "beta reader," Janice Gelb.

To Frisky the snake, for being there when I needed a good description of a corn snake. The mouse is on its way.

To Frisky's owner, Raphi, for encouraging all his friends to buy Mom's novel, and for help with chess, French, and economics (he said to be sure people know any mistakes are mine). Thanks also to Micah for the music and for offering encouragement when I needed it. I promise, one of these days I'll have a banjo-playing hero.

And finally, to my own hero, Howard. Thank you for being my number one fan.

AUTHOR'S NOTE

This is a work of fiction. That means the author elaborates on the truth. But much of what's contained in this novel regarding the Revenue Marine, a.k.a. the Revenue Cutter Service, later known as the United States Coast Guard, is true, including the quotes by Alexander Hamilton. Note: The uniforms described incorporate elements the Revenue Marine officially introduced in 1844, but some of it had been longtime USRM attire and appropriate to this story.

CHAPTER 1

Florida Territory, 1843

"Jumpin' catfish! You can't grab a woman and steal her, Frank. That ain't right!"

"Look, there she is now."

Franklin Ivey nudged his brother Benjamin. The woman they watched was bent over, her shapeless body swathed in layers of grimy homespun, a floppy bonnet falling over most of her face. She mumbled to herself as she cleaned.

"See? I told ya they got some tetched gal workin' here. No one'll miss her."

"I dunno, Frank. Cooper's goin' to be powerful angered with us if we take his woman."

Frank sniggered and spat a stream of tobacco juice through broken teeth, nearly making it to one of the spittoons ringing the tavern floor.

"Fancy boys like Cooper and Robin ain't got use for a woman. And she's no slave, so it ain't stealin'. Robin said she's just a used up tart from St. Augustine they brought here to clean."

Ben frowned and tugged at his long beard. "I dunno, Frank. I jes' don't think—"

"That's right boy, you don't think. You leave everythin' to me. I got a plan, and Washburn's goin' to be so grateful to us he'll take us along on his next job. And you know what that means," Frank said, rubbing two fingers together.

*   *   *

The "tetched" tart under discussion shuffled through the doors into the tavern kitchen, and after a quick glance around, straightened up with a groan of relief.

The cook and owner of Ganymede's Cup bustled over, wiping his hands on his apron, and peered at her anxiously. She gave him a reassuring smile.

"I'm fine, Uncle Robin. It's just a strain, staying hunched over and pretending."

He shook his head, his thinning blond curls jumping about. "I don't know what the world is coming to, when young ladies pretend to be servants. It is folly, sheer folly!"

"Do not frown, Uncle, it will cause wrinkles. And I was right, this is a brilliant plan! No one notices worn-out women. They fade into the woodwork where they can overhear everything," she grinned. "I have only been here two days and so far I've learned who is having an *affaire* with the lawyer's wife, who stole the Summerfields' cattle, and why Miss Jenkins left town suddenly to visit her auntie in Charleston. What a hotbed of gossip this tavern is!"

Lady Julia Anne Sanders Delerue was more cheerful than she'd been since she arrived in Florida, only to find Delerue-Sanders Shipping in disarray following the death of her Uncle Peter. A new factor would be coming over from the Bahamas to

10

manage the Florida holdings, but until he arrived the books had to be brought to order.

After poring over the ledgers late into the night, night after night, she was ready to chuck them into the Matanzas River for the pleasure of watching them sail away on the breeze. No matter how many times she tallied the figures and checked them against the documents she'd brought from England, the story they told remained the same: Someone was using her family's ships to skim cargo and smuggle contraband.

The shipping line remained profitable, but the Treasury Department watched ships with a hungry eye, capitalizing on the tariffs imposed by a Congress desperate for funds following the crash of the last decade. Running afoul of the United States Revenue Marine was *not* the report she wanted to give Lord and Lady Smithton.

Poor Aunt Suzanne could not help. Her father's sister was still frail, recovering from her own bout with yellow fever, and the loss of her beloved Peter. Going out in the backcountry to Ganymede's Cup seemed like a logical place to start looking for clues.

"Oh dear," Suzanne had said, wringing her hands. "You know I cannot like you going to that tavern!"

"Now, now, Auntie, the Cup is more of an *inn* than a mere tavern. A very respectable inn, frequented by the finest people. I will take the ledgers, and perhaps Uncle Richard can make sense of them. You know the uncles will take good care of me, and I can send a note today and they will drive into town to fetch me. And Uncle Robin has promised to show me how to prepare his special rum pudding. Just think, I might be able to make it for us by the time my parents arrive."

She hated to leave Aunt Suzanne at this point, but she knew she'd have better luck getting answers at Ganymede's Cup.

After all, what is the good of having former pirates for uncles if you cannot use them to track down smugglers?

"Did you learn more about who's using Delerue-Sanders' ships?"

She was brought back to the present by the former pirate's question. "I heard a snippet of something, two Crackers talking about a shipment of goods and a man named Washburn, but they moved off before I could get more. Does that name mean anything to you, Uncle Robin?"

Robin, an uncle by courtesy and longtime friend to her parents, tugged his lower lip while he thought. A sound from the kitchen entryway made him look up and he smiled, his aging cherub's face lighting.

"*There* you are! I was worried your leg would be bothering you so much you wouldn't make it down tonight."

The new arrival just grunted as he maneuvered in with his crutch, and once he was steadied he nodded to Julia.

"Good evening, Uncle Richard," Julia said, giving the gaunt man a smile. For as long as she could remember, her "uncles" Richard Cooper and "Robin, just Robin" had been a part of her life, visiting her family in England. When she had been a little girl, she'd babbled a mile a minute as she fished alongside the taciturn Richard, while Robin taught her the cooking skills that made his tavern a popular stopping place. The two old bachelors reminded her of the "Jack Sprat" nursery rhyme, for as ebullient Uncle Robin's waist broadened from his own good cooking, silent Uncle Richard seemed to get tighter and narrower every decade.

Richard hobbled now on a leg broken when a panther spooked his horse some weeks back, and he'd had to stay behind while Robin drove into town to get their niece. The leg was mending, but the break would take a long time to heal, and Julia was glad she could help out at the tavern until Uncle Richard recovered.

Besides, Ganymede's Cup, or "The Greek Boy" as the tavern had been known for years, was a favorite meeting place for the rivermen, soldiers, cattle thieves, and backwoodsmen who made up life on the Florida frontier. The Cup was known for the discretion of its owners. Tucked away as it was off the river, it provided a welcome spot for travelers of all stripes.

"Richard, you ever hear of a fellow called Washburn?"

Cooper looked at Robin for a moment, then shook his head.

"He seems to be quite the man of mystery," Julia admitted. "While most of the patrons out there enjoy bragging about their exploits, whenever Washburn's name comes up the whispers begin."

"I'm sorry, lovey, but that's a new one for me, too," Robin said. "But if he's up to something on the river, we'll hear about it. Everyone, just everyone, comes by here sooner or later!"

Julia looked at her uncle fondly, her smile peeking out from under the grime smeared on her face. "In that case, I'll go back out to slop some more tables. Uncle Richard, you sit yourself on that stool behind the bar and don't stand too long on that leg!"

Cooper grunted. After grabbing a bottle, he swung his crutch around and headed out the kitchen door to his usual spot behind the bar, where he could dispense alcohol and keep an eye on troublemakers.

"See? See?" Robin said. "Richard's just worried sick about your little scheme. It is all he can talk about!"

Julia rolled her eyes. "Uncle Richard hasn't said five words in five years, Uncle Robin, and most of those words were used up cursing the doctor setting his leg."

"Yes, well, *I* know what he's saying even when Richard is not putting it in so many words," Robin said. "And he's saying this is not a good idea!"

"You are beginning to sound like Aunt Suzanne. Where's that fierce pirate who terrorized Florida merchants?"

"I was the cook," Robin grumbled. "I never wanted to be a pirate."

Julia leaned over and gave him a peck on his round cheek. The tavern's other servants were returning after their evening break, and it was time for her to pull back into her rags.

"And a fine cook you are, Uncle. Now let me get back to my tasks, and I can leave you in here to do what you do best."

Julia hunched her shoulders down, pulled her bonnet further over her eyes, and followed Cooper out the kitchen door.

*   *   *

The stars were high when the last of the tavern's patrons staggered out the door. Cooper stumped around the room, putting out the lamps and eyeing the men cleaning up for the night.

Julia hobbled over to him. Leaning on the bar, she kept her voice low. "I'm off to bed, Uncle, and I will see you in the morning."

"Wait."

She shook her head. "It is not necessary. I will see you back at the house."

He gave her a frowning glance from under his gray eyebrows, but didn't argue with her as she went out the back door.

Julia took a deep lungful of the moist evening air. It cleared her head after the noise and smoke of the tavern, and she looked forward to washing off her dirt and settling in for the night. A rustling noise near the bathhouse made her pause, but she relaxed when a possum scampered out and ran across the yard. She turned back toward the big house. Suddenly, a black shape loomed over her out of the dark, throwing something heavy and soft over her head.

"Git 'er!"

She tried to scream, but the cloth that covered her mouth muffled the noise. She lashed out with her foot and only succeeded in throwing herself off balance as she was picked up by the shoulders and feet and bounced along for a few yards until she was hoisted through the air and laid down, not gently.

"C'mon boy, we got to get outta here!"

A wagon, Julia thought as the surface she was on began moving, and someone wedged her into a space between something soft, but lumpy. It was hard to tell through the cloth, but she thought she smelled…coffee?…as they bounced along.

Her arms were trapped close by the cloth covering her upper body, but she lashed out again with her foot and heard a soft grunt as it connected with something, or someone.

"There's no call to do that," she heard a rough voice say while more restraints were wrapped around her legs, trussing her like one of the Egyptian mummies she'd seen in an antiquities collection in London. "You jes' stay put there, ma'am, and we'll let you up soon as we're away from here."

"Don't go tellin' her nothin', boy. We need to get some distance between us and Cooper, and I ain't riskin' her yellin' her head off where someone can hear. When we get to Rand's place, it's soon enough."

Julia went still, knowing nothing could be done for now but to listen to her kidnappers and see if she could figure a way out of this. Were they holding her for ransom, knowing her family was rich? Were they part of the crew of smugglers using Delerue-Sanders Shipping?

Whoever was in the back with her patted her shoulder.

"That's right, take it easy, ma'am. I bet yer all worn out from cleanin' and what all. You jes' lay back and take a little nap in them quilts, and we'll be there by 'n by."

Julia grinned to herself and relaxed a fraction more. They thought she was the raddled hag she pretended to be, not a young heiress.

Then she frowned again. She could understand kidnapping an heiress, she could even understand kidnapping a young and attractive woman, but why would anyone snatch a cleaning drudge from a tavern? And what would they do when they uncovered her disguise?

Julia's thoughts ran in circles as the mules pulled the wagon and she struggled to stay calm and alert. It was clear wherever they were, they weren't headed into town. If they were on a road, it was at best a sand track. While she had no idea where they were going, they hadn't crossed the river, so they couldn't be headed too far west. There were isolated farmsteads off the St. Johns, and a few towns, but with enough distance between them that it was easy to lose oneself in the pinewoods. Even if she escaped from these two, there was no telling how far she was from civilization, or what passed for civilization in Territorial Florida.

She dozed despite her fears, the confinement and lack of air under the quilts making her sleepy. When she woke, she heard the morning birds calling and judged that it was dawn, or close to it.

"Let me out!"

There was some movement and a whispered conversation in harsh tones.

"I am afraid I might be ill if I don't sit up and get some air. Please," she added for good measure.

The wagon halted and within moments the covers were unwrapped from her upper body. She blinked in the early morning light and saw a man peering at her, looking much the same as the other Floridians she'd met at Ganymede's Cup. He was lanky and pale above the tobacco-stained beard covering his neck and upper chest. She took a deep breath and immediately regretted it, for her captor had not been in proximity to soap and water for some time. But she mustered up her best smile and said, "Thank you, that is much better."

He frowned down at her. Taking her chin in one grimy hand, he turned her head this way and that to examine her face in the light.

"Franklin, you had better put the brake on and come take a look at this." He scowled at her again. "How come you ain't an old woman no more?"

Julia stopped smiling. She'd been so anxious for air she forgot about her disguise. The other man jumped off the wagon seat and came around to the back, hauling her out and standing her upright in the road. The quilt they'd wrapped her in slithered down to her feet and her bonnet fell off. She stood there, blinking in the light but saying nothing.

"Well, if this don't beat all," the second man said in disgust, spitting a stream of tobacco juice to the side. "Who are you, missy, and why're you pretendin' to be somethin' you ain't?"

"I'm Julia Cooper," she said, having thought about her story while the wagon bounced through the night. "Richard Cooper's niece. My uncle thought it would be safer for me at the tavern if I looked less attractive."

The first man squinted at her. He looked enough like the other to be his twin, and Julia was guessing they were related.

"You don't look much like Cooper. An' ya talk funny."

"If you think I talk funny, it may be because I was raised in England, not Florida."

The one called Franklin scratched at his grimy neck.

"I dunno, Ben, this ain't what I had in mind. Maybe we'd best jes' leave her here. A half-wit biddy would be fine, but this gal's lookin' like nothin' but trouble."

Julia glanced around in a panic. They were in the middle of pinewoods and palmetto. Off in the distance a woodpecker hammered against a tree, a lonely sound in the wilderness.

"Take me back to Uncle Richard at Ganymede's Cup. I promise, he won't hurt you if I'm returned safely!"

The two men ignored her and went off a few yards to talk in

low voices. They didn't bother securing her, for where would she go?

When they returned, Franklin folded his arms across his chest and worked at the chaw bulging out his cheek, but the other looked more cheerful.

"Me an' my brother palavered and came up with an answer," Ben said. "He don't want to take you back to The Greek Boy, an' I don't want to leave you here for the panthers and bears, so we're jes' going to go ahead and drop you off at our friend Rand's place. Oh, and I'm Ben and this is my brother, Frank. Ben and Frank Ivey, Miz Cooper."

"It's a pleasure to meet you, Mr. Ivey," Julia lied. Ben beamed at her while Franklin scowled, but she plowed on. "Um, is your friend Mr. Rand a planter? Perhaps he can take me back to my uncle's inn."

"Who he is, is his business," Franklin said, spitting another stream of brown juice. "He's been poorly from the yellow jack and could use a woman helpin' around his place, keeping it neat and meals on the table and such."

"So he sent you to kidnap a woman?" Julia asked, outraged.

"Missy, you jes' worry 'bout keepin' our friend happy and you'll get out of this fine. Now…you goin' to ride quiet like in the back of the wagon, or do I have to tie you up again?"

"I will be quiet," It was hot enough back there without being under the quilts.

"You're a right smart gal, Miz Cooper."

Benjamin had wandered off to relieve himself against a nearby bush, unconcerned that he might have an audience. With as much dignity as she could muster, Julia told Franklin she would return shortly and walked away into the brush to do the same. When she returned, she scrambled into the back of the supply wagon unassisted, and put her bonnet on to shade her face. The men took up their places on the bench and started the mules, exchanging low bits of conversation as they jounced along.

"Are you going to stop for breakfast? I am hungry. And thirsty."

Ben rummaged in a bag at their feet and pulled out some parched corn and smoked mullet that he passed back in a grimy rag, along with a flask of water.

"That'll keep you until we get to Rand's," Franklin said. "Now hesh up. I need to think."

Julia "heshed up," glumly watching the countryside as they bounced along, waving away a fly attempting to perch on her nose. It was still a rough territory, sparsely settled between Jacksonville and Pensacola. Plantations radiated out from Tallahassee through the rolling hills of Middle Florida, but for the most part it was a wild frontier populated with poor Crackers, scratching out a living from the soil and supplemented by smuggling to get a little hard currency.

Law enforcement was mostly left up to individuals who settled their disputes with fists and eye gouging, or duels between "gentlemen" at the higher levels of society. With the end of hostilities against the Seminoles, the area became wide open for speculation and smuggling, and the absence of authority and control attracted all sorts to the area, from runaway slaves to runaway debtors. Newspapers and preachers regularly railed against the "rogue's paradise" of the Florida Territory.

Whoever was using Delerue-Sanders Shipping had to be tied in to the local economy. The scheme was a simple one: Each time a Delerue-Sanders ship left port, a copy of its manifest would be sent on to the offices in England. The papers from the ships arriving in Fernandina, St. Augustine, and Key West didn't match the copies in England, and either the smugglers didn't know a copy was sent on when each ship departed, or they were counting on the confusion in the months of Peter Marlowe's illness and death to cover their scheme.

Someone was forging signatures to the documents and making off with the goods underneath the noses of the Delerue-Sanders employees. No ships had arrived while she was in town, so she couldn't observe for herself how it was being done, or question the ships' captains.

If Reggie were here, she'd enlist his help, but he was still in the Bahamas. Reginald Whitehead had been part of the cadre of fast youngsters she had run with during her first Season, before an episode with a chambermaid had exiled him for some cooling off.

His parents took a chance and hired him as factor for Delerue-Sanders under Peter Marlowe's tutelage, never expecting Peter wouldn't be there.

Taking risks was nothing new to her parents. The Delerue family archives were vague on details, but told of how they had married and combined forces to defeat the notorious pirate Christopher Daniels and save Delerue-Sanders Shipping, winning the loyalty of the murderous pirate's crew. Now it was up to a new generation to save the family fortunes. As the cart jounced down the country road Julia daydreamed herself taking on that role, gaining her own place in the archives: "Lady Julia, who saved Delerue-Sanders Shipping from evil Florida smugglers."

On that cheering thought Julia settled herself more comfortably among the bags of corn and enjoyed the morning.

*   *   *

Rand Washburn made it as far as the chopping stump before he had to sit down and rest. He eyed the creek glinting through the trees, the water dancing in the morning sunshine. It wasn't far. Just a few yards if he wanted to go for a dip, or get some catfish. Nothing to a man who was strong and healthy. For one laid low by fever it might as well have been on the Gulf side of the territory.

He chuckled and wiped sweat off his forehead. Such a simple thing. Get up and walk. He could do it; heck, he'd been walking for most of his twenty-six years. His legs worked, but it was a question of how *long* the legs would work before the weakness set in and he had to sit down where he was.

But things needed to be done around here, and he couldn't put them off any longer. The woodpile was getting low and today would be a good day to see if he could swing an ax without cutting his leg off. Maybe it was the forced inactivity that was doing in his strength as much as the fever. He fetched the ax and after giving the woodpile a couple whacks to chase out any lurking creatures, began hauling sections of oak to the stump to be split.

It didn't take long to get into the familiar rhythm of the chore, and as the sun climbed higher he took off his cotton shirt to let the heat soak him. Sweat was pouring off his body, but it was a good sweat, a healthy sweat brought on by work, not fever.

He felt so good he went out into the woods after to see if his traps had caught anything that might be turned into supper. But it looked as if the raccoons had outsmarted him again, and he shook his head in bemusement. No sense getting worked up over it, 'cause he had food back at the cabin. If the raccoons were smart enough to take the bait without springing the traps, then they were welcome to it for their hard work.

He needed to rest again, but he could make it to the cabin. The sound of mules braying brought him up short, until he recalled this was the day the Iveys were due out with his supplies. He thought about asking them to stay on until he was back on his feet, but knew the Widow Ivey depended on her boys, and couldn't spare them for more than a day or two.

"Hey, Rand," Benjamin Ivey called out to him from his yard. "We was just finishin' up here. Thought maybe you'd crawled off into the woods and died from your fever or somethin', and we was goin' to come out there and look for you."

"Nope, I'm goin' to beat this, Ben. Can you and Franklin finish up for me?"

"You can count on us. You just go up to the house and sit a spell, inside outta the sun, and I'll be up there right fast."

"'Preciate it, Ben," Rand said, going up to the house to get a drink of water. He poured a cup from the jug in the kitchen and sat to drink it as Benjamin entered the cabin.

"You sure you're well, Rand? You still lookin' punky to me."

"I'm fine. Fever's broke, I just had a little setback yesterday. Tried to do too much."

"See? Now ain't that what we're always tellin' you? You

work too much. But we got somethin' to help you out."

"What?"

Ben pulled at his shirt collar and looked out the window of the cabin.

"Me an' Frank got to take off now to get home to Ma before dark. But don't you worry. With the supplies and the…other stuff…you gonna do jes' fine."

Rand sat for a moment and tried to gather his thoughts. The room no longer spun around him when he sat up, but it would be some time before he was back at full strength, and time was short. Another meeting was set in two days? Three days? How long had he been out with the fever this time?

"Ben, do you know what day it is?"

Ivey scratched at his beard and thought about it.

"Preacher came through and held a Sunday meetin' four, no, five days ago. That means today is…" He thought hard, brow furrowed.

"Friday."

"That's right." He looked impressed as hell that even while sick Rand could figure that out.

If today was Friday, the meeting was Tuesday. Four days to get himself together and ready to meet Brewer.

Rand stood, unassisted and pleased he didn't have to hold on to the table. Benjamin was backing toward the door and looked up at him warily.

"I gotta go now. Mebbe next time you need some help on a job, you'll think kindly a Frank and me, and remember how we helped you when you was sick."

"I am grateful, Ben." Rand said, and he meant it. The brothers were so dumb they'd cut down a tree to get a turkey, but they were reliable for all that, and like most of the backwoodsmen they were willing to pitch in and help out someone in trouble.

"Yeah, well, you take care a yourself. And, uh, you might want to check on those supplies in the shed right quick, make sure we got it all."

After he hurried out, Rand splashed some of the water on his face before drinking down another cup. The fever had wrung him dry and water was one of the things he craved. He'd worry about food later on, if he had the energy.

He stood in the doorway of the cabin watching Frank Ivey come out of the shed and latch the door shut. They were moving like the tide was running out on them. He frowned. Speed and the Iveys was something one didn't see together. The whole situation felt not quite right.

"You boys are in an awful hurry."

They looked at each other, and if anything, moved faster. Ben threw himself into the wagon seat, while Frank grabbed at the mules' reins.

Now Rand knew something was afoot. Had they left a raccoon in the shed? It would be the sort of stunt these two would consider funny. He began moving in their direction.

Franklin took one last look at Washburn's face, paled under his grime, and yelled at the mules. Startled, they began to move the nearly empty wagon along at a fast pace, with Ben holding on to his hat and jouncing on the seat. Rand leapt out of the way as the wagon passed him and Franklin yelled out, "We left ya a present, Washburn. You kin thank us for it later." The two brothers tore through the dirt yard, leaving nothing behind but their laughter and clouds of dust.

"Now what?" he muttered. He wasn't up to any practical jokes. He listened by the side of the shed and heard nothing for a few moments, then there was a muffled thud as something large fell to the ground, too big to be a raccoon. Rand walked over to the wood pile and grabbed a length of oak.

"All right, mister, I don't know what you and the Iveys are up to, but I want you to come out, real slow now."

There was no movement, but a muffled snort came from inside. It occurred to him that maybe whoever was in there wasn't in there of his own free will.

Still clutching the impromptu club, Rand put his hand on the latch and pulled hard, banging the door against the shed. He blinked into the darkness as dust and chaff swirled around, then looked down.

And grinned.

"Dang! I know I ain't got sugar on the supply list, darlin', so maybe you'd like to tell me what you're doing in my shed?"

* * *

Julia glared at the man staring at her while she was bound and gagged in the dirt. He was silhouetted by the sun as he pulled her up and steadied her with one hand under her arm, then made quick work of the knots binding her hands before kneeling down to get the rope around her feet. She yanked the cloth out of her mouth and took a deep breath. At least this one didn't reek like the Ivey brothers.

"I do not know what you and your friends think you are doing, but it will go easier on you if you take me straight to Ganymede's Cup!"

The man stood, slow and easy, and Julia took an involuntary step back. She was tall, but he topped her by a good head, and his shoulders filled the shed doorway. He cocked his head to the side and examined her, a long, insolent look that traveled from the top of her rumpled hair down past the shapeless dress to her boots. Then he backed out of the shed and motioned for her to pass.

She stepped out into the sunlight and blinked a moment, looking around and rubbing her wrists where the rope had chafed, then turned to look at the man silently studying her. He was barefoot, wearing only a pair of trousers, legs planted wide apart in the dirt and arms crossed over his broad chest. She felt the color flare in her cheeks as she met his gaze to avoid looking at all that near naked flesh. The sunlight picked out red tones in his tawny hair and while he wasn't full-bearded like the Iveys, he had enough growth on his square chin to darken his jawline without concealing it. His eyes were a color between hazel and true green with lines at the corners that would deepen if he laughed.

He wasn't laughing.

"So, you want to go to Ganymede's Cup? Now, what would a," his glance flicked over her again, "gal be doin' at a place like The Greek Boy?"

Julia fisted her hands at her sides, her temper rising as she drew herself to her full height. "My name is Julia Del—Julia Cooper. My uncle is Richard Cooper, the owner of Ganymede's Cup! He will pay you for your time and trouble when you return me to him," she added, looking around the rough farmstead. "Those louts kidnapped me and said they were taking me to someone who was sick and needed care. You do not look ill to me, and I demand you take me back immediately!"

A smile tugged at the corner of his mouth. "Would you stay with me if I was sick?"

"No!"

"Uh huh. Then we got ourselves a little problem here. I did have the fever, but I'm doin' better now, so I'll take you to the Cup, just not today." He put his hand to his forehead and winced. "Or tomorrow."

"But you must take me back today! It would be one thing if you were sick and needed nursing, but I cannot stay here alone with you."

"That's your choice. If you start walkin' fast down that road, you might catch up to the Iveys by sundown, and maybe they'll take you on with them so Ma Ivey can chaperone you. What I'm going to do now is head back to bed."

"Look here—who are you anyway?"

"Sorry, the introductions got kinda left behind. My name's Washburn. Rand Washburn," he said with a nod of his head. "My friends call me Rand. I don't care what *you* call me, long as it don't insult my mama."

Julia froze. *This* was the notorious Washburn? Something must have shown on her face, because he looked at her with an arrested expression.

She didn't know what Washburn's game was, but it might be connected to her family's troubles. Maybe she oughtn't be in a hurry to leave.

"I suppose there's nothing for it but to wait until you can return me, Mr. Washburn." She looked around her in dismay at the sunbaked property. "You are rather isolated out here in the woods."

"I like my isolation, I like the woods, and the sooner you're gone from here, the more I'll like it."

He turned and started walking toward the house, not bothering to see if she followed. She did, nudging some curious chickens out of the way with her foot as she passed through the dirt yard.

The cabin was an oak-shaded dogtrot, two pine log rooms raised off the ground, with a central breezeway. She'd passed cabins like this in her travels, but this was the first time she'd been in one of the backwoods residences. The front porch was deep, the overhang from the steep roof shading the rocking chair on the porch as well as the cabin's interior. As she stepped in, she saw through the breezeway to the covered back veranda and beyond to the separate kitchen.

The front room held a table and benches, a chair and some chests, but Washburn kept walking through to the back room. He held on to the doorway and looked over his shoulder at her. Sunlight poured through the opened windows and doors, and Julia could see the strain on his face as he struggled to stay upright.

"I wish we could talk more, darlin', but I 'bout wore myself out with all this excitement. Try not to burn the cabin down if you stay, and if you leave, shut the door behind you."

And with that he shuffled into his room and collapsed on the bed, still wearing his pants.

Julia cautiously came up to the doorway. "Mr. Washburn?"

There was no answer from the villain on the bed, except for a soft snore.

CHAPTER 2

Julia looked at the man sprawled on his belly. Asleep, he looked boyish, even with the beard, and she guessed him to be a few years older than she. His back was lean and muscled, with scars on his shoulders and along his ribs, evidence of encounters with bullets and blades in his life. And the hair curling across his neck needed a trim.

Julia's nose wrinkled. His hair wasn't the only part of Washburn that needed some work. He was sick, after all, and it smelled like the bedding could stand a change as well. There weren't any slave quarters at the farm, and from the bareness of the place it was clearly a bachelor establishment, so if anything was going to get done it would be up to her to do it. Her stomach rumbled and she put her hand over it. First things first, and that meant food for them both.

Out back of the kitchen shack was a woodpile, along with a corn crib and smokehouse, a chicken coop, and the shed she'd already seen. The necessary was on the other side of the back steps and someone had planted tomatoes and jasmine nearby to freshen the air. A well-worn path led down to the creek and the coldhouse where she found some of the supplies from the Iveys's shopping trip. Julia gathered wood from a pile that was high and fresh split. That, and the sad-eyed, but cared for mule in the paddock was evidence Washburn was on the mend. Maybe he'd overdone it and set himself back.

Julia soon had a fire going and she smiled to herself as she sat back on her heels, mentally thanking her mother for insisting that if her daughter wanted to spend time in Cook's domain at Rosemoor, or with her Uncle Robin at Ganymede's Cup, she'd learn like any other apprentice. Julia had started with the basics of scrubbing, chopping, and building the right fire, and had only then been allowed to try her hand at the sauces and baking.

There was rough lye soap and rags, and with the water heating in the kettle in the fireplace she started on the kitchen first. Soon pots of caked grits and congealed gravy were soaking for cleaning while she scrubbed at the table, sweat pooling on her body as the day heated up.

When she took a break, some oranges from the trees in the front yielded two tin mugs of juice, one set aside for Washburn with a rag over it to keep the flies out. She drank hers down while sitting on the front veranda, feeling the sweetness explode into every pore. It wasn't a bad piece of land, she thought as she looked around. The oaks kept the yard shaded, and the house was laid out to take advantage of the light and the breezes off the creek. There were figs and alligator pears and a grapevine, and she recognized some of the crops growing in the field—corn and squashes and new greens behind a fence where beans climbed.

Julia set her mug on the step and propped her chin in her hand as she looked out at the trees, listening to a mockingbird singing for its supper. Her uncles would be worried to death about her, Richard especially feeling frustrated by his inability to get on a horse and search. Having an adventure was all very well, but it could do a lot of damage to the ones who loved you.

If Washburn was true to his word, she'd be back at the Cup before her uncles could raise the alarm. If he was lying to her about that—

Julia stood and brushed off her skirts. Uncle Robin said nothing made people as mellow and agreeable as a good meal. She'd do her best to keep Washburn mellow and agreeable over the next couple days, but she couldn't rid herself of an image of a tawny pelted panther, content and drowsy when it had what it wanted, but deadly when its appetites weren't satisfied.

*   *   *

Rand knew he was dreaming, smelling heavenly odors and feeling a soft hand laid on his forehead. When he smiled, a sweet voice said, "You still look like something that ought to be buried, and if you don't want to end up that way, you had better get up and eat."

Rand's eyes popped open. In *his* dreams women begged for his favors, they didn't scold him.

That woman was still here, Cooper's niece. Or so she claimed, and he took his time looking at her as she leaned over him. The hair curling around her face was black as sin, and her brandy-colored eyes so thickly lashed it was a wonder they could stay open. He was reminded of a fawn he'd startled in the woods, and the way it had looked at him out of eyes deep and dark, seeming to hold all the secrets of the forest.

"Mr. Washburn? Can you make it to the table or shall I bring your soup in here? It will be getting dark soon, and you need to eat something."

He grunted and sat up, causing her to move hastily back. He felt better, and had a feeling if he ate whatever was smelling so delicious, he'd feel better still. Not getting food prepared while he was sick hadn't helped his recovery. He scratched his bare chest and watched his visitor turn bright red and back out of the room, mumbling something about corn. After her ragged skirts flitted around the corner, Rand smiled to himself and pulled on a shirt. She sure did spook easy for a gal who worked in a tavern like Ganymede's Cup.

He buttoned up the homespun shirt he'd traded Ma Ivey for and followed his nose out. The gal, Julia, was bringing a tin bowl to the table and steam was rising from its surface along with an aroma that made his mouth water. She set it down on the rough table where a spoon and a plate of corn pone was sitting, then went back to the kitchen for her own. Rand sat down at the table and started spooning it up before she returned. Chunks of vegetables and ham drifted in a rich broth and he poured cane syrup over a corn pone that was as tasty as could be.

Rand didn't stand when Julia came to the table, and she pulled a bench out from her side and sat, setting down her own food and pushing a tin cup of orange juice over to him. He took it from her without a thank you.

"So," he said, speaking around the food in his mouth, "what's your story, darlin'? You sure don't seem like you belong at Ganymede's Cup."

Her hand stilled as it lifted the spoon toward her mouth. "Why do you say that?"

"Maybe 'cause you're a gal. And you talk mighty fine for a gal whose uncle runs a tavern. You're English, too. I can tell from how you talk."

"My mother…my mother was a ladies' maid in a large house

in England, and spoke well, and I learned from her."

"And your papa?"

She crumbled her pone into a mess on her tin plate. "Oh. Well, to be honest, I don't know who he was, and my mother would not tell me."

"How'd you get from England to Florida?"

She looked like she was tempted to snap back "by ship," but answered civilly. "As I said, Richard Cooper's my uncle. After my mother died he offered to take me in. Since I had no family in England, it seemed the best course for me. Your friends, the Iveys, kidnapped me from the Cup and said you needed someone to help you out. And they were not interested in taking me back when I protested." She sipped her own soup. "And what about you, Mr. Washburn? What is your story?"

"No story," Washburn said. "I'm a farmer. Hogs and hominy, this and that."

"Have you lived here long?"

He shook his head, and took another bite. "This place was abandoned after the Seminoles started pickin' off the white people during the war, so I took it on 'cause of that 'Armed Occupation Act' they got to get folks to settle 'round here. Thought this was a pretty piece a land for growin'." He shrugged. "If it don't work out, then it's 'gone to Texas' for me."

He watched her stir at her soup as she thought. "It will be awkward, my staying out here with you, and I will try to make myself useful and not a nuisance until you can return me. Or send me to the Iveys. At the very least I can help with the cooking chores."

Washburn brightened. "There is that. This soup's mighty

tasty. Is there more in the pot?"

She stood to get him more soup, but paused, planting both hands on the table and leaning forward. She'd tied her hair back with a rag, but the humidity was causing curls to escape and corkscrew around her face. She was looking at him so seriously, he was tempted to smile to see if he could get her to do it back, but she started talking.

"Mr. Washburn, do you like chicken with dumplings so light they float off the plate? Baked turkey with pecan dressing? Rice that doesn't taste like paste?" She looked at him through her lashes and drawled huskily, "Sweet potato pie?"

He stilled, and gave her that slow, easy smile he'd been holding in. "You can make all that?"

She didn't smile back, but blinked at him. "Oh. Yes. Yes, I can make all those dishes and more. Of course," she said, looking down and fiddling with his dish, "I work best when I'm…left alone. Not worried about being bothered by…not when I'm bothered."

"Darlin', you cook up some good victuals and when you leave here, we'll both be smilin' and…not bothered."

His smile faded as she hurried out to the kitchen to get some more soup. She was lying. Not about the cooking, he hoped, but that tale about why she came to Florida. He'd worked too hard and invested too much into his plans to let a pretty face and a mess of black curls stand in his way. He didn't believe the story about the Iveys kidnapping her for a minute. Sure, maybe the Iveys *thought* they were kidnapping her, they were that dumb, but her story had more holes than a fishing seine. He didn't know which of his enemies had sent her, but he'd find out before he was done with her.

She was back at the table and quiet now, head bent over her bowl. He watched her as she ate. He idly wondered if, despite her concerns about being "bothered," she'd go so far as to bed him to try and get information.

Part of him thought that a splendid idea, but the part he kept buried, the part that had almost made him stand up when she'd come to the table rather hoped not. And at this point he wasn't sure which part of him would win the mental argument.

"Now," he said, drawing it out for two syllables until it became "naow." "Why don't I clear some stuff out of the other room so you can use it tonight, and you clean up these dishes in the meantime. 'Less you'd rather sleep out here with the fire."

She seemed startled that he'd give up his room for her, but he figured if he slept out front, he'd hear her if she tried to sneak out during the night.

"No, I would prefer my own room. With a door. That latches."

"Fine with me," he said, standing. "'Course, if you do get chilled, you'd be welcome to come on out and join me in front of the fire."

"That is not going to happen," she said crisply as she stood and gathered up the supper dishes.

*   *   *

Julia washed up the dishes by the light of an oil lamp and finished by taking a dollop of lard and rubbing it into her hands. If she came home with lobster claws, she'd never hear the end of it from her mother's most superior dresser.

Julia paused as she smoothed the fat into her roughened skin.

37

What seemed like an adventure on the road away from Ganymede's Cup was feeling more like a nightmare in the dense darkness of the Florida backwoods. She was miles from anywhere, trapped with a man whose intentions and words couldn't be trusted.

"Hey, gal."

She whirled around, startled, her hand going to her throat. Washburn stood on the breezeway at the entry to the kitchen, the night shadowing him from her. She didn't speak, and after a moment he said, "I put some beddin' on. There's net, too, to keep the mosquitoes out."

"Thank you, Mr. Washburn."

"Maybe you should call me Rand, since you're sleepin' here and all."

"Maybe I shouldn't," Julia said repressively. "And it would be best if you referred to me as Miss Cooper."

His lips curled up at the corners. "I'll think on that," he said, melting back into the darkness.

Julia blew out her breath and hung up the sack she'd used to dry the dishes, then took a tallow light and explored Washburn's bedroom. The bed wasn't soft with feathers or crackling from corn husks, and she guessed from the slight odor of dusty greenery that it was stuffed with Spanish moss. The bedding was worn, but clean, the quilt's pattern faded almost beyond recognition. A padlocked chest was at the foot and the table next to the bed held the pitcher and cup she'd seen earlier, as well as a small shaving mirror. She picked up the mirror and examined herself by the light of the candle. The curls she kept tamed by nets and combs had gone berserk and escaped from her scalp in an explosion of tangles and clumps. There was a smudge of greasy ash in front of her ear and she scrubbed at it, but then gave up with a sigh.

Julia stripped down to her shift and lay down on Washburn's bed, hands clasped atop the covers as she thought.

Washburn was lying. Even if she didn't already suspect him, he didn't look like the other Florida farmers—lank, whiskered men, sallow and malarial, but proud as Lucifer, with a goodly number of them missing part of an ear or a nose from the fights they were always getting into over some perceived insult. And he would also be the first Cracker she'd met, man or woman, who didn't chew tobacco.

Washburn, if that was his name, looked too good to be a piney woodsman. He was filled out and broad through the chest and shoulders. While his face was lined and brown from the sun, there was something about him, the way he talked and walked, that niggled at her and made her think he wasn't native to these parts, no matter how he sounded, or what story he told. If she could get back to Ganymede's Cup, or St. Augustine, she could pass on the information about his whereabouts to the proper authorities. Even if he wasn't directly involved with the smuggling at Delerue-Sanders, she knew he was up to no good hiding out here in the woods. Why else would he delegate the Ivey brothers to fetch him supplies? Most men would relish the opportunity to get off the farm, go into town, and let loose. It was more than valuing his privacy, or the illness.

Tomorrow she'd figure out a way to escape. But for tonight, she was stuck inside with Mr. Washburn.

Tired as she was from the work she'd done, it was a long time before sleep claimed her.

CHAPTER 3

A rooster absent from the yard the day before gave the morning call as Julia stirred eggs for breakfast, thinking about what had kept her awake during the night. This still had an air of unreality to her, but it was all brought into focus by the mundane tasks of starting the day's cooking, as promised.

"Is that coffee I smell?"

Washburn filled the doorway to the kitchen, a look of such amazed wonder on his face that she had to smile.

"Indeed, there was coffee with the supplies. Help yourself to a cup while I finish this up. The grits are about ready, and if you can wait a few more minutes, there will be ham and eggs as well."

"Bless you, darlin'. I'm beginnin' to think you an angel sent from above."

He poured a cup from the pot next to the fire and dumped in a generous serving of sugar before bringing it up to his nose. He closed his eyes and inhaled, then opened them and took a reverent sip.

"Ah," he said with feeling. "Hot and sweet, just the way I like it."

He was watching her as he said it, and Julia turned away to whip the eggs more fiercely before pouring them into the pan.

"If you had a milk cow here, then I could have my coffee the way *I* like it," she said, "and I could make some real corn bread and buttermilk biscuits as well."

"Milk cow's too much trouble. You'll have to make do with what I've got, but it smells like you're doin' just fine."

He topped off his cup and went out to the front room. Julia heard him out there putting up his bedding. Washburn may not have all the luxuries of city life at his cabin, but he kept his space clean and tidy, stowing everything away in its proper place as neat as a sailor.

That odd thought stopped her for a moment, but then she went back to her eggs and ham. He wasn't a sailor; there was no tar ground down into his skin. It must be her life spent around Delerue-Sanders that made her think of that.

When she brought the food out from the kitchen, he was seated at the table, waiting with an expectant look. He hadn't shaved, but was wearing a shirt and shoes. As he bent his head over the plate, the light coming in through the opened windows shone off his hair, picking out strands of gold amidst the darker shadings. Washburn's manners left a lot to be desired, she thought, as he started eating as soon as she put the platters on the table, and that helped to quell the urge to touch that hair and see if it was as soft as it looked in the morning light.

Julia served herself and moved the eggs around on her plate.

"Mr. Washburn, does that creek out back lead to a river?"

He studied her over his coffee cup and took a swallow before answering. "Why?"

"Because creeks often lead to rivers, and I thought it might empty into the St. Johns."

"Nope, that creek don't empty into the St. Johns."

He didn't say anything more but applied himself to his food.

"I thought I might be close enough to Picolata to catch the steam packet to Jacksonville."

"It's just a creek. No steam packet."

"But are we near Picolata?" she said in exasperation.

"No, we ain't near Picolata or anywheres else. Remember? I like being left alone, and that includes not havin' to answer nosy questions." He pushed himself away from the table and reached for his hat and rifle. "I got work to do since I fell behind yesterday. But I'll be back in time for dinner, darlin'." Touching the brim of his hat, he left the cabin, whistling as he went on a barely marked trail through the palmetto scrub.

"'Darlin' my eye," Julia muttered. She sat for a minute, drumming her fingers on the table before getting up to clear away breakfast.

After the kitchen was cleaned, instead of starting dinner Julia explored Washburn's cabin. There were two chests in the main room, secured by efficient looking padlocks. She deeply regretted not taking Uncle Robin up on his offer to teach her lock picking. The chest in the back room was now unlocked, containing nothing more than his clothing, rough and worn as the chest that held it.

The sun was high by the time Julia left the cabin, raising her arm to wipe the sweat from her brow and catching a whiff of why Washburn kept his distance from her. She thought of the countless baths she'd had over her lifetime, the footmen bringing water to her rooms, the maids laying out the linens and scented soaps. She'd never take hot water and soap for granted again.

Her enveloping drab's costume, nearly a rag to begin with,

was now beyond salvage. At least she had her own boots that she'd scuffed and scratched before assuming her disguise at Ganymede's Cup. If she had to do any walking to get to civilization, she didn't want to be doing it in her bare feet, and she wasn't sure she could handle the mule.

But there was a better way to get to civilization than walking.

Washburn's house was on a creek, and she was not about to take his word for where the creek led. It might feed into a river, and that river might be a tributary of the St. Johns, that north-flowing highway carrying the commerce and travelers of East Florida. If she could get downriver on the St. Johns she'd make it to Picolata, or Jacksonville, and could secure help and transportation back to Aunt Suzanne.

Whistling her own tune, Julia picked some ripe figs and a couple of oranges, then went back into the cabin to prepare.

The little boat on the creek had oars but no sail, a disappointment as she'd hoped for a skiff she could sail on the river. With this, the best she could hope for would be rowing to the river and catching the current north where she might hail a steamer. She loaded her supplies in the front of the boat and gave it a thorough inspection. It appeared sound, so she put her shoes and stockings in the bow, tore a strip of cloth off her tattered skits and bound the cloth around her hands to cushion them for the oars.

It was pleasant rowing, the cypress and sweetbays shading the creek against the rising heat. There was the flash of a deer's tail as it headed deeper into the scrub oak. A red hawk soared overhead, looking for breakfast, and when she saw a family of otters sliding down the mud into the water, she laughed aloud at their antics.

The creek widened and grew, joining with other waters until it was a small river. It was cool and restful in a way she'd never imagined Florida. Here was a side that showed itself like violets hidden in the forest, a face different from the mosquito-ridden, pestilent, humid sweat bath of the cities.

Julia was so captivated by the sights that she shipped her oars, letting the current take her, and daydreamed until she glanced over the bow of the boat.

And screamed.

A massive sea creature bobbed in the water off the starboard bow, gazing at her with limpid eyes while it masticated a wad of greenery in its whiskered mouth.

Julia's hand clutched the front of her dress as her heart raced, but then she shook her head and scolded herself for a ninny. It was a sea cow, large and cumbersome, but not dangerous.

It was, however, curious.

The manatee swam closer and bumped up against the boat, threatening to swamp it. Julia held on to the sides and rocked with the boat, but the manatee was not put off by the collision, and instead swam back a few feet and watched her placidly, looking for all the world like, well, like a large wet cow blocking her path.

"Shoo, shoo." Julia took off her bonnet and waved it at the creature. The manatee must have considered it an invitation, for it swam back to her and before she realized such a monster could move so quickly, snatched the bonnet out of her hand. Soon the calico was being chewed alongside the greens, a colorful sea salad.

"Aaargh! Go away, you beast!"

"Now, that's not a polite way to say good morning, darlin'."

Julia's heart lurched in her chest and her eyes rose from the manatee to the far bank, where a familiar figure leaned against a tree, hat pulled low over his eyes, rifle slung in his arms.

"Go away!" she repeated to the man. This time the cow listened, and dove under the water to head for the bank.

"Can't do that," he drawled. "You're stealin' my boat, and I want it back. But you're welcome to jump into the creek and swim down to Jacksonville."

"I'm not coming back. You can't keep me out on your farm, Washburn!"

He put the rifle up to his shoulder, aimed, and fired neatly across the boat bobbing in the sluggish water.

Julia was stunned as the report of the rifle sent small animals scurrying further into the scrub.

"You could have hit me!"

Washburn reloaded and sighted down the barrel. "That was the warning shot 'cross the bow. You bring my boat back or you won't like where the next round goes."

She believed him. As the manatee watched, she took hold of the oars and rowed for shore. Washburn walked over and climbed into the boat, planted himself in the bottom, and gave her a grin. The boat was lying dangerously low to the water and Julia's eyes narrowed as she stared at her nemesis.

"You wouldn't be thinking of whacking me upside the head with that oar, would you? I'd hate for this rifle to go off while we're squabblin'."

"Aren't you going to row?"

"Now why would I do that, with you already doin' such a fine job? 'Sides, I'm still plumb wore out from the fever. You go ahead and row for the both of us."

Julia didn't say a word. Grabbing the oars, she pulled back, moving the boat away from shore and into the creek. Washburn waited until he saw she was headed in the right direction, then gave a grunt and pulled his hat down, looking for all the world as if he were settling in for an afternoon nap, rifle secure in his arms. But after about two minutes he poked his finger under the brim and looked at her from river-green eyes.

"Does this mean there's no dinner waitin' on me back at the cabin?"

She didn't care about the rifle, she didn't care about the smirking baboon's bad reputation, she didn't care about killer manatees lurking in the waters. She grabbed an oar out of its lock, and hauled back in the form that made her the champion striker of her family's impromptu cricket matches.

Washburn moved fast for such an indolent bastard, leaning far to port and rocking the boat, with predictable results.

Julia flailed about in the creek before sputtering her way to the surface, wet hair falling in her face. She grabbed the fallen oar and held on to it while treading water. Something nudged her backside and she jerked around to find the manatee back, watching her like a puppy expecting another treat. There was no sign of her bonnet.

Washburn leaned over the side of the boat. "You want a hand?"

"No," Julia said calmly. "I have decided to follow your excellent suggestion, Mr. Washburn. I am going to swim to

Jacksonville."

His lips twitched. "Don't do that, darlin'. Maybe you're cranky 'cause you're hungry. Look, I've got dinner right here in this sack."

"I know that, you idiot, I packed that food!"

"It's all right, I don't mind sharin' with you, even though you stole my food and my boat," he went on cheerfully. He reached out his sun-browned hands.

Julia eyed him for a moment, then another nudge at her backside from her new friend convinced her the devil she knew was better than a cold night in the creek. For now.

He hauled her in, bracing himself against the boat's rocking, then reached down and fished out the oar.

"I think I'll row for a while. I'm not sure I trust you with a club in your hands."

She sat in the stern and ignored him, arms crossed over her wet chest while water ran off her in rivulets. At least she felt cleaner. She looked at the rifle he'd placed behind him.

"Don't even think about grabbin' that rifle. I'm fond of it and it wouldn't benefit from a soak in the creek." He pulled back on the oars, moving much more efficiently than she had, she couldn't help but notice. After a time he paused to remove his sweat-darkened shirt.

Julia tried to keep her eyes on the Florida scenery going past, but kept getting drawn back to the sight of Washburn's shoulders flexing with the oars, his hard chest rippling as sweat glowed on his sun-warmed skin, trickling through the light gold hair fanning across, and down his belly. His arms bulged with muscles moving like oiled snakes as he pulled the boat through the water, and he smiled when he caught her watching him. That smile deepened the creases alongside his mouth and made him look even better, damn his hide.

"Were you plannin' on rowin' all the way to Jacksonville?"

"If necessary. But I hoped I would find a boat on the river I could hail."

He stopped smiling. "There are dangerous men on the river. If you fell in with the wrong ones, you'd find your skirts tossed over your head and your throat cut, and if you were lucky, they'd cut your throat *first*. You need to stay put at the cabin and behave yourself, and like I said, I'll get you back to The Greek Boy in good time. Now, since I'm doin' all the work here, why don't you show me what you got in the feed bag and we'll take a little break."

Julia snatched the bag to her as Washburn made for the creek bank. She recognized the massive magnolia as one she'd passed that morning, and knew they weren't far from the farm. Washburn helped her out, then pulled the boat up on the sand. It was a pleasant spot, shaded and cool, with streams of sunlight coming through the lace of Spanish moss hanging from the trees. A fallen live oak stretched across the sand as if placed there for their convenience.

"Check for snakes!" Washburn barked as she was about to sit on the log.

Julia jumped back. "What? Where?"

He finished buttoning his shirt, sighed, and walked over to the wood, taking a stick and poking around at the base. Nothing flew up at him, so he sat down and motioned her to do likewise.

"You shouldn't mess with a log on the ground without

checkin' first to make sure there are no snakes nestin' there."

"What kind of snakes?"

"Unpack that bag and I'll give you a little nature lesson."

Julia pulled out the oranges and figs, a chunk of ham, and some leftover pone, sticky with syrup. There was also a bottle of water and Washburn had his own canteen, so they sat down on the log to eat. He pulled a nasty-looking knife out of his boot and gave it a swipe across his pants leg before cutting the ham in half and passing Julia a chunk. He chewed a bite off his own piece, brow furrowed in thought.

"Most of the snakes 'round here won't hurt you, but some of them are downright deadly and you should know what they are. The water moccasin and rattlesnakes can be troublesome, 'specially when it floods. If you smell ripe watermelons and there's nary a melon in sight, then stay back 'cause that's the smell of rattlesnakes. Most snakes'll leave you alone if you leave them alone. The moccasin has a white mouth inside, which is why it's also called a cottonmouth. And a cottonmouth is just flat-out ornery. It'll come after you for sheer meanness."

"I'm supposed to wait until I see inside the snake's mouth to figure out what it is?"

"Try using your charmin' ways on it. Now, the coral snake's tricky, 'cause he's got a cousin what looks like him, but ain't dangerous. There's a handy little way to remember which is which. If you see a snake that's got red, black, and yellow bands, say to yourself 'red on yellow, kill a fellow, red on black, friend of Jack.'"

He looked quite pleased with himself for remembering the mnemonic.

"If I see a snake I'm unlikely to be thinking of nursery rhymes."

"I was just tryin' to help. You goin' to eat all that?"

Julia sighed and passed him her remaining food. She'd lost her appetite anyway, after things had started out so well this morning. She washed off her hands in the creek, keeping an eye open for cotton-mouthed vipers and colorful killers, and when she returned, Washburn was pushing the boat back into the water.

"Climb in, darlin', and we'll head on back."

They rowed back to the farm with Washburn at the oars, and he beached the boat with Julia's help. She bent to pick up the food bag and slipped on a wet patch near the water, and his arm shot out to catch her, pulling her up against him before she could fall.

She expected Washburn to step back a pace, but instead he held her arm and frowned down at her.

"Look here, Miz Cooper, I meant what I said earlier about gettin' you back to your uncle's place. Don't go wanderin' off by yourself. It ain't safe and I can't be watchin' you every minute, so I want your promise that you won't take my boat again."

Julia looked up at him. There were strained lines around his mouth and she felt a twinge of guilt, remembering that it hadn't been long since he was down with the fever.

And he'd called her "Miss Cooper," not "darlin'."

"Very well, Mr. Washburn. I give you my word I won't take your boat."

They stood there a moment without speaking. He was still holding her, his fingers warm and dry. His long thumb was absently stroking against the tender underside of her wrist, and she wasn't sure he was even aware he was doing it.

But she was aware. Every nerve ending tingled from that small but vital connection. He was hard and solid as the oak trunk, and she thought she could feel the pulse of his heart where they touched.

"Hey, Rand! Where ya been?"

Washburn whirled around, his hand going to his waist as if he expected a sidearm to be there. He shoved Julia behind him, but then relaxed his stance as he recognized the shouter.

"Hey, Ben. We went for a boat ride on the creek. And a swim," he said.

Julia stood there, damp but dignified, as Benjamin Ivey loped down the hill to the creek.

"Afternoon, Miz Cooper," he said, ducking his head at her and giving her a gap-toothed grin. "Did you have a nice swim? Sure is hot enough for it!"

He seemed unconcerned that the last time he'd seen her had been when he and his brother were locking her in a shed and abandoning her at Washburn's farm. Further animosity toward the backwoodsmen seemed counterproductive, so Julia smiled back and said, "Good day, Mr. Ivey." Then she paused as a new thought struck her. "Have you come to take me back to Ganymede's Cup?"

Before Ivey could open his mouth Washburn said, "Let's talk up at the cabin, away from these gnats. C'mon, Ben." And without waiting to see if she followed—or offering Julia his arm—started walking up to the farm.

She grabbed her shoes and the bag and followed behind. A

two-wheeled mule cart sat outside the cabin, a diminutive figure perched atop the wagon gesturing at Franklin Ivey as he hauled parcels out.

Washburn stopped so abruptly Julia almost ran into his back. He looked over at Ben and said, "You brought Ma with you."

"She made us," he whined. "You know how she gits, and after she whupped on me and Frank for fetchin' that gal from The Greek Boy, she said we had to bring her out here."

Julia moved between the men for a better look, then glanced over at Washburn. Anything that left *him* discomforted couldn't be all bad, and she walked over to the wagon with a new spring in her step.

"You must be Ma Ivey," she said, holding on to the cart and peering up. "I'm Julia Cooper."

A floppy poke bonnet turned in her direction and Julia was looking up into a face sunken-cheeked and wrinkled with care, but unlike her sons, the raisin black eyes were bright and intelligent.

"So you're the gal causin' all the ruckus?" Ma Ivey leaned to the side and spat a stream of tobacco juice an impressive distance, coating a gourd plant growing near the fence.

Julia swallowed hard, and Ma looked at her and worked the chaw in her mouth a bit. "Tobac' juice kills the critters what eats the plants. You remember that."

"I will try not to forget," she said faintly.

Washburn and Ben came up beside her and with a resigned sigh, Washburn reached up and lifted Ma Ivey down from her perch.

He set her down in the dirt and she looked up at him like a

calico-covered raccoon at his feet.

"Thankee, Rand. I like havin' a handsome man to tote me about." She nudged him with her elbow. "Ah'd ask you to marry me, but mebbe you have other plans."

"Anytime, Ma, you say the word. You know you're the gal I'm dreamin' of."

Ma Ivey cackled. "Right now I want to talk to *this* gal. Ben! Fetch me that barrel. Frank! You take that perleu up to the house now! Rand, you put the wagon up! Gal, you tote that parcel and come with me!"

Having issued her orders, Ma Ivey marched off to the cabin, and Julia, Franklin, and Benjamin trooped behind. Franklin carried a covered kettle back to the kitchen, Benjamin put a barrel on the back step, and Ma Ivey rounded on them.

"Scat! You two fetch in that rocker from the front, then go help Rand with the mules."

"Yes, ma'am," the boys chorused, Benjamin with a grin and Franklin with a scowl, but after Ben dragged the rocking chair in, they turned and left the cabin, closing the door behind them.

"Now then," Ma said, setting herself in the rocker and spreading her skirts around her like a duchess, "you fetch me a spit cup, then tell me your story."

"Yes, ma'am," Julia echoed, and came back from the kitchen with an empty jar and two mugs of water.

As Ma Ivey listened, pausing to use the jar, Julia told her the same story she'd told the Ivey brothers and Washburn.

"Gal, you tell one fine story. 'Course I don't believe a word of it." Ma held up her hand when Julia began protesting. "You got your reasons for keepin' secrets, don't matter none to me.

But if you're goin' to stay out here with Rand, you're goin' to need what I brung ya."

Ma Ivey reached over to the table and passed the wrapped parcel to Julia, who undid the string.

"They were my Hannah's," Ma Ivey said quietly. "I had her for seventeen years afore the cholera took her."

Inside the parcel was women's clothing—skirts and blouses, a nightgown, stockings, and a shawl. They were off-white and indigo blue and the brown that comes from blackjack oak. There was even a piece of red calico used as a sash and a woven palmetto straw hat. Julia looked at the worn drab clothes and thought of the silks and satins she'd taken for granted in England, the fine muslins, the striped alpaca and crisp linens ironed by servants' hands. Then she stroked a blue blouse, soft and faded from many washings, sewn with love, embroidered with red flowers, and packed away in cedar for a child who would never wear them again.

"I thank you very much, Ma Ivey," she said. "These are lovely, and just what I needed. You could not have brought me a finer gift."

She glanced up at a noise from the doorway and saw Washburn standing there, looking on her with approval. She blushed, then frowned, for what was his good opinion to her?

"I will go try these on," and taking the clothes went to the back room.

She heard Washburn and Ma Ivey talking, but couldn't make out their conversation as she rid herself of her rags and pulled on Hannah's clothes. The shirt went over her head and had a lacing to close it in the front, a simple garment suitable for frontier wear. But it had been made for a younger, smaller woman and Julia had to work at the lacing to get it to close, and ended up having to leave it gaping open at the top with her lace edged shift showing through, a much finer garment than a girl of her station would wear. She chewed her lip and thought about an explanation if Washburn noticed, finally settling on it being a cast-off from the daughter of the house back in England. The petticoat and skirt were wider through the waist than she would wear, and ended well above her ankles, but there was nothing to be done for that now. She fastened the skirt tabs, pinched up a section of the waistband and tied the sash over it to hold it together. It was hard to tell from Washburn's shaving mirror, but she thought she would do.

"Now see, that looks right pretty on you," Ma Ivey said as she re-entered the front room. "Don't she look pretty, Rand?"

She didn't have to worry about Washburn noticing the quality of her shift. He was far too busy staring at her bosom, and he didn't look at all happy.

Julia smoothed down the brown skirt. It wasn't her fault Hannah's clothes were too small. She straightened up and scowled back at him. There was a knock on the door and Franklin and Benjamin entered the cabin. The two men also stared at her.

"Oh my, you sure do look fine, Miz Julia," Benjamin said with a grin. "You're as pretty as a speckled pup!"

"Oh yeah, mighty fine," his brother drawled.

Rand looked hard at Franklin, who held his glance for a moment before looking away.

"If we're all done here dishin' out compliments, I got chores to do," Rand said.

"That's why me and the boys are here. They're goin' to help you with the farm, and I'm goin' into the kitchen with this gal."

Ma hoisted herself out of the rocking chair and headed for the kitchen shed. Julia dutifully fell in behind her.

"You ain't from around here, I can tell that from how you talk."

"No, ma'am, I'm from England."

"Hmph. Only good thing that ever came from England was tea."

Julia didn't think it necessary to explain that tea came from China, for Ma Ivey was still talking.

"My Lemuel fought with Andy Jackson when we scuffled with the English, that was down in New Orleans. Ooowee, he said that New Orleans was somethin' to see, full of pirates and fancy ladies and Frenchies! In England did they teach you how to cook up victuals to keep a man satisfied, or did you just learn how to boil tea?"

"I am a good cook," Julia said without a trace of false modesty. "That's what I was learning at Ganymede's Cup, how to cook with local foods."

"Hmph. I heard about that Ganymede's Cup. Sodom on the river, that's what I call it! When those boys of mine said they stopped there, well! I gave them what-for, you can be sure. Bet you never baked a possum at that Greek Boy tavern."

Julia almost stumbled as she followed the tiny woman into the kitchen. "No, I cannot say I ever saw possum on the menu at the Cup." She could imagine Uncle Robin's shrieks if she suggested such a thing.

"That's what I'm here for, to larn you about real cookin', the kind that makes a man sit up and say howdy. Now git over here."

On the kitchen table was a cloth-covered basket, and a kettle had been placed back in the fire to stay warm. Delightful smells escaped from under the kettle's lid, but the widow ignored it and walked out to the back step, where she gestured at a barrel.

"We caught ourselves a pair of possums and you're darn lucky to git 'em, 'cause you can't eat possum in the summer. No ma'am, you have to wait 'til the weather turns, and the possum gets good and fat. Now here's what you do. Open up that barrel."

The barrel was sealed with a coating of lard around the lid, and Julia took a rag and wiped at it before prying the barrel lid off, almost dropping the lid on her foot as *she* stifled a shriek.

Peering up at her was a gigantic skinned rat.

"G'on, gal, reach in there and yank him out."

Julia stared at her in disbelief, but the widow just stared back, chewing away at her tobacco. Julia gulped, rolled up her sleeve and reached into the brine. Her fingers brushed against slimy cold flesh and she shuddered, but gritted her teeth and latched on, pulling the animal out by the tail where he hung upside down, brine sluicing off.

"After you shoot the critter you clean it, then hang it for a couple days so's you can skin it. They make a mighty tasty stew, but today I'm going to show you another way, 'cause any fool can make a stew, even some dang English fool. You ain't gonna puke, are ya?"

"No, ma'am," she said, and squared her shoulders, tightening her fingers to keep the possum from falling back in the barrel. She owed it to Britannia to stand firm in the face of these

American culinary challenges.

"Now, after you've killed 'n hung him, make sure your possum don't get away. Don't you smile at me, gal, I know what I'm talkin' about! They're sneakier than you think! A possum'll pretend to be dead and then he could be inchin' his way toward the door while you're cleanin' the potatoes and thinkin' 'bout how juicy he's goin' to be. So you skin him good, then he'll stay put.

"Best way is to let him sit overnight after you season him up. Get a pot with a tight fittin' lid, stick him in it, and make sure that lid's on secure so he don't get out. You get yourself some vinegar and molasses, salt and pepper, and you rub your possum all over, then put him away in the pot.

"Next morning you peek under the lid. If he's still there, then fine and dandy. You put that pot on the fire with some bacon fat, sear that possum all over and chop some onion to throw in the pot. Did I mention the potatoes? You got to have sweet potatoes with possum. You put that possum with the lid on tight in the oven and then go out and git your potatoes and after he's baked a spell you make sure he's still there, then toss the potatoes in the pot. Bake 'em some more 'til he's tender and juicy and you got some good eatin'!

"Bring him into the kitchen and we'll fix him up."

Ma sealed the lid back over the barrel and Julia repressed a small shudder. Cooking or eating large rodents didn't appeal to her, but she'd promised Washburn she'd cook for him, and if he wanted possum, possum he'd get.

"Are we having possum tonight?" she asked with some trepidation, eyeing the kettle on the fire.

"Nope, a perleu with chicken and some greens. Made it this mornin' 'cause while the weather's still warm you want to be doin' your cookin' early in the day afore the heat sets in."

That was a sentiment Julia endorsed, so she asked about the making of chicken perleu, and realized it was a corruption of "pilau," a rice and chicken stew she'd made before. The widow'd also brought crocks of buttermilk and butter, knowing Rand didn't have a milk cow. Julia thanked her effusively, because with the buttermilk she could expand her menus. Music may "hath charms to sooth the savage breast," but it was her experience with her father, her brothers, and the clientele at Ganymede's Cup, that the way to keep a man content was with a full stomach…barring other methods she didn't want to think about, and wasn't willing to try.

Julia rolled up her other sleeve and set the possum in her kettle, seasoning it as the widow directed, to be eaten the following day, then set to work making buttermilk biscuits while the widow watched her with a critical eye, chatting about life on the Florida frontier. The Iveys had come down from Tennessee by way of Georgia.

"Lemuel swore he loved me long as the water flowed and the grass growed, but he'd get an itch in his foot, so I'd pack up and follow along with him."

But Florida was Lemuel Ivey's resting place, and after that the widow had no desire to move on any more.

"I miss the mountains sometimes, but I don't miss the snow. And I like Florida 'cause we can get crops growin' all year 'round," the widow said, spitting out the back door before looking sidelong at Julia. "I got some money set aside for them boys when they marry, and that farm's doin' well enough. Got some cotton in the fields, hogs in the pen. Yes, ma'am, whoever marries my boys will be doin' right fine for herself."

For a moment Julia wondered if the widow meant to imply the brothers would share a wife. She was about as likely to marry one—or both—of the Ivey brothers as she was to marry Washburn. In other words, when the widow's hogs sprouted wings and flew overhead.

Julia made a noncommittal noise, and the widow went back to describing the joys of life on the Florida frontier. She listened with half an ear while she prepared a peach cobbler to stick in the oven after the biscuits finished. Snatches of the men's voices drifted in from outside, and the sounds became louder and angrier. The two women moved to the breezeway and looked out in time to see Franklin Ivey wave a hand toward the cabin and make a rude gesture. Washburn's fist lashed out, laying Ivey in the dirt, and his voice carried to the women standing there.

"I mean it, Ivey. You stay away from what's mine, and what's mine is everythin' on my property. Everythin'."

Ma didn't say anything but looked pleased, a strange reaction given it was her son lying there and staring up at Washburn, whose fists were still clenched. But a moment later Franklin picked himself up and dusted off, and that seemed to finish the discussion. They resumed the chores before the men adjourned to the cabin, where Julia learned another fact of life in the Florida backwoods, or at least this corner of it. Washburn's table manners weren't a fluke. The men expected the women to serve them before sitting down and eating their own supper. By the time Ma Ivey and Julia had the biscuits, perleu, sliced ham, greens, coffee, and cobbler on the table, the men had already worked through their first serving and were starting on seconds. It was a good thing Ma Ivey knew how to feed working men, Julia thought as she took a seat on the bench next to Washburn, otherwise she'd be licking the biscuit pan to get anything.

When she reached for cobbler to help herself to some dessert, Washburn had his hand on the plate, but he stopped and said, "You go ahead and help yourself."

"Since this is my first serving of dessert and your third, that's gracious of you."

"Let it never be said I don't know how to treat a lady right," he told her with a wink.

"Now," Ma Ivey said, stretching it out for two syllables. "When are you two gettin' married?"

Washburn sprayed coffee out of his mouth. But he recovered while Julia choked on her cobbler.

"It's rather sudden, Ma," he said as Julia gasped for air. He whacked her on the back one-handed, nearly sending her face-first into the perleu.

"Don't you lie to me, boy! I been sniffin' out falsehoods from men since afore you was hatched. Hah! You got no plans at all to marry this sweet young thing."

Washburn eyed the sweet young thing askance, but Ben said, "Why, I'd marry Miz Julia, Ma. She looks real nice now that she ain't a crazy lady no more."

Julia smiled at her backwoods admirer, but Washburn made a noise that sounded suspiciously like a snort. She wasn't the only one who thought so, for Ma Ivey said, "If you're done makin' noises like a piney woods rooter, maybe you'll answer my question, Rand Washburn. Tain't proper to live out here without bein' spliced together. The next time the circuit rider comes 'round, you two need to get right with God."

Julia found her voice at last. "I appreciate you looking out for me, Ma Ivey, but I am just here for a short while. It was all an unpleasant mistake, my being here, and I expect to be going back to my uncle soon. Very soon," she added, looking at the silent Washburn.

"Maybe Washburn ain't who you want. Those boys of mine ain't much to look at, but they're good boys for all that. You could do worse than to marry my Ben."

"Yeah," Franklin said, "It would be real nice havin' you out at the farm, missy. Real nice. You ought to think 'bout marryin' ol' Ben here."

He was staring at her too-tight top when he said this, and Washburn went very still next to her. Without thinking, she put her hand on his arm.

Benjamin frowned, confused by the tension.

"We thought if you didn't want her, we'd take her off your hands, Rand. Doin' you a favor. Maybe Ma would like the help out at the farm, that's all."

"She'll stay here," Washburn said flatly, not looking at Julia. "I like havin' a cook around. If you boys want to get help for Ma out at the farm, you're goin' to have to look elsewhere, 'cause this gal's stayin' 'til I get her back to town. And there will be no more talk of marriage."

"Wait!" Julia said. "Are you going back to your farm this evening, or are you spending the night?"

"We're headin' on back," Ma said. "We got animals need

tendin', but I thank ye for the offer. Right neighborly of you. I like this gal, Washburn," she said, pointing a bony finger at the man. "She's got grace and grit and plenty of it, even if she is English. And her biscuits are almost as good as mine. If'n you don't want her, my offer stands."

"I appreciate everyone offering to trade me away," Julia said. "But what I wanted to know is if someone might pass by your farm who could carry a note to my Uncle Richard Cooper, to let him know I'm safe."

"You don't need to be writin' nobody."

"Yes, I do. I'm willing to concede that you cannot take me back to the Cup for a few days, Mr. Washburn, but I must send a note to my uncle. I imagine he is worried sick about me by now. Do you have pencil and paper here?"

"Yeah, I got pencil and paper. Don't look so surprised, I can write. Read, too, long as I can move my lips."

"Samuel Ratchins will be riding by tomorrow to buy a couple hogs," Ma said. "He can carry your note, 'cause he'll be goin' by that tavern."

Washburn gave her a long, unreadable look. "Write your note, darlin'. Just remember, I like my privacy, and I'd hate to see anyone get hurt pokin' noses in what don't concern them."

Julia swallowed. "I understand."

Washburn fetched the paper and pencil, and she thought hard about what to say while Ma and the men cleared the table.

———

Dear Uncle Richard,

I am unharmed and well. I cannot tell you where I am, but I have been promised a safe return, and expect to see you in a few days. Please do not try to come after me, that would only cause more problems.

Your loving niece,
Julia Anne Cooper

———

Washburn took the note from her, read it without apology—or moving his lips—then folded the note and dripped some hot wax on it to seal it.

"It should get to Ganymede's Cup in a day or two. Maybe you'll be back afore the note gets there."

Julia watched him pass the note to Franklin to give to Mr. Ratchins, and she felt some of the day's tension drain from her neck. Her uncles would be frantic by now, and the note might help. She knew if he were not laid up with a broken leg, Uncle Richard would be scouring the countryside looking for her. She was almost grateful to Washburn for taking steps to ensure Richard Cooper didn't find them. If Washburn was as big a scoundrel as she suspected, the less her uncles tangled with him, the better she felt about it.

The Iveys packed up their kettles and hitched their mules to the wagon, lighting a lantern to guide them home.

"Not that I worry 'bout gettin' lost," Ma said. "The mules follow their nose to the barn, and we follow the mules. You want me to leave you some tobaccy to get you started on chewin'? Your greens'll be glad of it when the critters is gone."

"No, it's a lovely offer, but…no. You have already done enough for me today. The new clothes, the perleu—"

"And don't forget the possum!" Ma cackled.

"Believe me, Ma Ivey, I will never forget the possum."

To her surprise the little widow reached up and gave her a hug, then stepped back. "You don't look like my Hannah, but you look like you could use a hug from a mama. Now you take care of yourself, and if you don't want to stay here with Washburn, you walk down the road to our place. It's a fer piece, but you keep walkin', and you'll get there by an' by. And I'd be pleased to have a gal 'round the place, even if you don't want my Benjamin."

Moisture filled Julia's eyes. After the artificiality and posturing of British society, it was refreshing to find genuine caring from a stranger. It might be, as one wag said, that the Crackers "kept the Sabbath…and everything else they could get their hands on," but they pitched in when a neighbor needed a hand. Ma Ivey was nothing like Lady Smithton, but a mother's hug *was* appreciated, especially under these trying circumstances. She reached down and hugged the widow back, holding on a moment until a deep voice from the darkness said, "You're all packed up, Ma Ivey."

Julia stepped back, and Washburn hoisted the little widow into her wagon.

"Travel safely, Ma. I'll be seein' you by an' by."

"You take care of this gal, Washburn. Anythin' bad happens, you'll answer to me."

Washburn didn't say anything, but waved Benjamin to start the mules on their way. He turned in his seat and waved at Julia.

"Good night, Miz Julia! You made some fine biscuits!"

"Good night, Mr. Ivey," Julia called, and waved Benjamin and his sullen brother on. She watched until the cart was swallowed by the darkness and she could no longer see the lantern bobbing in the night, then sighed, and turned back to the cabin. The Florida night closed in on her, the darkness and moisture oppressive. It reminded her once again she was alone with a man who had secrets, and was prepared to do anything to keep them.

CHAPTER 4

Washburn was finishing up the dishes when she entered the cabin. She took a towel and silently helped, drying and replacing items. His kitchen was well stocked for a frontier cabin, and she must have said something aloud about it, for he chuckled.

"I like my privacy, but I like my comforts, too. I've lived rough, and I've lived soft, and soft is better."

She reached up to put a jar away, the movement tightening her blouse against her body. He came up behind her, silent as a panther, and plucked the jar from her hand, reaching up to put it on the high shelf. Julia tried to move, but his body blocked her, one hand resting on the counter alongside her hip, locking her in place. She went stone still, feeling the heat of his body, the room silent except for the whine of a mosquito outside the window.

His hand came back down, his long fingers brushing against a lock of her hair worked loose from its tie. He tucked it behind her ear. At the warm touch of his fingertips she jerked back, coming into full contact with his body.

"Shhh…" He soothed her like a skittish mare, but didn't move. He also didn't release the hair he was holding. She could feel him rubbing it between his fingers like a mercer testing the quality of fine silk.

"Very soft."

"You said you would not bother me," she said in a low voice, looking straight ahead. There was a tin of saleratus in front of her, and a box of salt. She tried to focus on them, not on the shivery heat his fingers were sending through her as they moved from her hair to the tender skin at the nape of her neck.

"Am I botherin' you? We're just standin' here, in the kitchen. It's a nice night, an' I ain't got nowhere else to be."

He moved a fraction closer and she could feel his breath on her neck…she could feel him. All of him, hard and muscled and trapping her there by pinning her with the lightest of feather touches stroking her neck.

"What could happen in the kitchen, that you don't want to happen?" His hand moved down her back as she held herself still, dreading and anticipating his next touch.

His lips brushed the back of her neck and she gasped, that brief contact sending fire skittering along her nerve ends. She shivered, but she didn't feel cold. Just the opposite. His fingers left the spot on her neck and moved down her arm until they rested atop her hand on the counter, his thumb rubbing over the pulse beating at her wrist.

His left hand moved in front of her and settled on her waist, again like he was afraid of spooking her, but she felt every cell of him through the thin fabric of the worn skirt.

"I'd make it worth your while," he said huskily. "I can pay more than Franklin Ivey would ever be able to pay you, darlin'. More than you'd earn at the Cup. And I'd make sure you had a good time, too."

It was like being doused in the creek. She stood there, stunned and frozen. He was offering her money to lie with him. A whore's fee.

She almost turned and slapped him, but hesitated. That would be the response of Lady Julia Anne Sanders Delerue. "Julia Cooper" worked in a tavern. A woman who worked in a tavern, even if she wore a disguise, wouldn't be offended by that kind of talk, indeed would expect it from a belly-crawling snake like Washburn. She straightened her back and brought her head up, avoiding a collision with his nose as he pulled back and stepped aside.

A tiny, overheated corner in the darkest recesses of her mind wondered what a guaranteed "good time" with Washburn entailed, but she refused to think about that as she turned and faced him.

He was watching her, his eyes darkened and heavy, the green a bright flash from beneath his lids. She licked dry lips, a mistake as his gaze zeroed in on that small movement of her tongue.

"That is an...intriguing offer, Mr. Washburn. But we already have an arrangement. I am here to cook and I am going to leave, as soon as I can. Any further complications would...it would just complicate things. Step back please. You *are* bothering me."

He watched her for a moment, his gaze unreadable, and then he smiled, a false gleam of his white teeth that did nothing to reassure her.

"Here I was thinkin' that maybe we could make a little change in our arrangements. There's a storm comin' and it could get mighty cold tonight. Wouldn't want you to be all alone in that big bed, shiverin' away."

"How generous of you, but I will pass on that offer, thank you," she said dryly.

He stopped smiling at her and two lines furrowed his forehead.

"You're not thinkin' on what Ma Ivey said, are you? What she said 'bout bein' married?"

Now it was her turn to smile. "Why? Are you going to make me an offer of marriage? How unexpected! Will you get down on one knee and swear your undying devotion? Make pretty speeches about my face and form? Offer me," she waved her hand around the kitchen shack, "all your worldly possessions if I'll be yours? Why, Mr. Washburn, this is so unexpected!" She put her hand over her heart and fluttered her eyelashes at him.

"Yeah, well," he said, shifting his weight uneasily, "I didn't want you to get the wrong idea 'bout what's goin' on here, that's all."

"Believe me, I have no illusions about the situation here. Now, if you are done, I would like to wash up for bed."

He barely moved in time as she stomped past him into her room and slammed the door shut.

*   *   *

Julia thought it was the thunder and lightning that woke her. The anticipated storm roared in, lashing the cabin with hard-driven rain. But the cabin stayed snug and dry, and Julia lay there in the dark, smelling the rain on the rushing air.

Then she heard the noise again. The moaning wasn't the wind in the branches, but came from the outer room. The room where Washburn slept.

Julia wrapped the shawl around her and unlatched her door, peeking around the corner.

The embers from the fireplace gave an edge of light, and she saw Washburn's pallet near the door. He was thrashing about on it, muttering.

"No! Stop! Stop shooting! The children!"

Maybe his fever had come back. He had worked hard today. Julia chewed her lip in indecision, but when he cried out again, she clutched the shawl around her and tiptoed out to where he slept.

Washburn's face shone with sweat and his eyes twitched, but he wasn't awake.

"Mr. Washburn?" she whispered.

He moaned and tossed again, throwing off the cover. He was bare, at least the part she could see. She knelt down next to him.

"Mr. Washburn, wake up!" She grasped his shoulder, giving it a shake.

She had a sensation of flying before her back and head connected with the floor. A form loomed above her, a long-bladed knife catching the lightning as the sky tore apart in another thunderous volley.

"Don't!" she screamed. She couldn't move, his muscled body pinning hers beneath him. He was a dark mass in the night, and she felt his body quiver with suppressed tension.

"Julia?" he said in a dazed voice, and then looked at his own hand as if it were some stranger's that happened to be filled with a foot of lethal steel.

"Hellfire!" He threw the knife from him. It hit the wall and stuck there, quivering in the fading echoes of the thunder.

Washburn rolled off her and sat on the floor, turned away from her, head in his hands, his naked back silhouetted by the fireplace embers. She didn't say anything as she tried to get her breath back and stop the tremors wracking her body. He reached for the cover and she thought he was going to wrap it around her, but instead he pulled it across his lap, then looked over his shoulder.

"Did I hurt you?"

"No, I don't think so." She touched the back of her head. Her fingers came away dry and she gingerly sat up, too, hugging herself as she watched him.

"I heard you cry out and thought you might be sick again. You were having a nightmare."

"Was I?" He looked out the window. "I don't remember it."

"You said something about 'shooting' and 'children.'"

He froze in the dark. "Ah. *That* nightmare." He took a deep breath. "I am sorry I woke you. Go back to bed, Miss Cooper. It will not happen again."

She looked at him steadily. "Are you sure you are well, Ra— Mr. Washburn? I do not mind staying up if you need anything."

He turned from the window and looked at her again over his shoulder, propping his hand on his blanket-covered knee as he appraised her. The rest of the cover had slipped low around his hips, and she quickly brought her eyes back up to his face, but not quickly enough.

"Well now," he drawled. "What did you have in mind? Rockin' me back to sleep?"

The thunder rumbled in the distance as the storm moved on, leaving a steady rain behind.

"No, Mr. Washburn," Julia said repressively as she rose to her feet. "Our agreement covers my cooking skills. I was offering to make you a hot posset."

"Oh, darlin', what you could do to help me sleep involves a lot more than a hot drink."

The slam of her door cut off his laughter. As she climbed back in to bed something about her conversation with Washburn stuck at the back of her mind and almost kept her awake. The day's events caught up with her though, and she soon fell back asleep to the sound of the rain on the roof.

*   *   *

In the wake of the storm, the morning air was cooler as what passed for autumn in Florida took hold. Instead of fog shrouding the farmstead, the air was crisp with a sunrise so spectacular Julia paused on the kitchen porch just to enjoy the sight.

She dabbled at watercolors, as did most girls of her class, but the colors in Florida were bolder than at home, as if a watercolor of the English countryside were painted over in oils. The land was awash with shades of green ranging from pale sage to vibrant emerald, the sky was an intense ultramarine that made her blink, and flowers exploded in a profusion of fuchsias, golds, and reds, preparing for their second season.

Her mother would get a wistful look in her eye when she'd talk about her home, but to Julia she seemed content with her life in England. Lord and Lady Smithton worked side-by-side running Delerue-Sanders, and as a youngster Julia had loved playing in her parents' study. They had matching desks at opposite ends of the room, the earl's neat as a pin, the countess' a jumble of papers and journals, and the flotsam and jetsam of shared voyages. A conch shell from the Florida Keys held pride of place as a paperweight, and Julia loved to hold it up to her ear.

"Do you hear it, poppet?" her mother, the former Miss

74

Christine Sanders of St. Augustine would say. "When I miss Florida, I listen to the sea, and it reminds me of home."

"But Devonshire is near the sea, too, Mama," Julia said in puzzlement.

"Ah, but the English sea is not like the Florida sea." She'd smile, and when Julia was small she'd thought in the English sea the fish sat around drinking tea and eating Cook's jam tarts, while the Florida fish had parties with alligators and served pecan pralines.

Now she was beginning to understand what her mother missed. A chorus of mockingbirds and sparrows welcomed the fresh-washed day, and a blue heron strode majestically under a sweet gum, looking like a long-legged vizier surveying his subjects. She picked some unripe persimmons, setting them aside for their color to deepen to the red orange that marked them as fit to eat. Having once tasted an under-ripe persimmon, it was a mistake she'd never make again, but Uncle Robin's ripe persimmon cake was a treat.

Thinking about cooking and Ganymede's Cup brought back memories of the episode with Washburn during the night. Rock him to sleep, indeed! She wasn't such an innocent as all that! Her mother had talked to her in depth, to Julia's great embarrassment, about the mechanics of the relations between men and women. While she felt a certain fascination for the hydraulics and sheer engineering of the endeavor, she never imagined it would involve the kind of playful nonsense Washburn exposed her to. If any of the young men back home had dared to try such a maneuver....

But of course, none of them would have, for they were

gentlemen, unlike her lowborn captor, who was even now emerging from the cabin with a rifle in his hand. Julia didn't bother to greet him as she plucked fruit off the tree.

Ma Ivey'd made mention the preacher wouldn't be around on circuit this Sabbath week, so she knew she couldn't use that leverage to get Washburn to take her off the farm. Instead, he said he was headed out to try and bag a turkey.

"But you ought to go ahead and cook the possum for tonight, darlin'. Them turkeys are wily and might outwit me."

"That wouldn't be too difficult," Julia muttered under her breath, devoting herself to getting the cabin in order. She felt a small surge of satisfaction when Washburn returned turkeyless, but he had managed to bag some mourning doves. Their yard chickens were safe from the pot, at least for another day.

The baked possum wasn't at all unpleasant, she found. In fact, its tender meat most resembled duck, and Washburn promised to keep the brine barrel filled with possums if she'd continue to cook 'em so fine.

"You might want to try your hand at coon, too," he said, sucking some meat off a bone. "They're gamy but still good eatin'."

"I don't know how comfortable I would be eating a raccoon," Julia admitted. "I have seen them at the water and they look so intelligent, the way they wash their food in their little hands. I saw one yesterday who looked just like the vicar bowing over his Sunday supper back home."

"Your vicar wears a bandit's mask?" Washburn smiled. When he smiled like that it was hard to remember why she was here, and what she hoped to accomplish. Of course, that was likely his goal—to keep her off balance while he plotted whatever it was he was plotting.

After supper he surprised her by helping her clean up, then pulled out a knife and whittled at some dark wood while she mended her clothes before the fire. When Washburn saw what she was doing, he went to his chest and brought out some clothes of his own that needed tending.

She looked at him, and he gave her that big grin that showed off his fine white teeth.

"Our agreement was that I would *cook* for you, Mr. Washburn."

"I'm sharin' all my things with you, and I even gave you my own bed to sleep in. You wouldn't begrudge a man a little mendin', would you? 'Specially seein' as how that's my thread and needles you're usin' on your own things."

Julia scowled and took Washburn's mending to add to her own pile. First the cooking, then the mending, soon she'd be doing his wash and hoeing his garden. And he made it sound as if she'd chosen to be out in this godforsaken place with him.

At least the weather'd turned for the better. The cooler nights brought fewer mosquitoes and that was a comfort, but there was still something in the air. Not the weather, but a tension growing in Washburn as one day followed another at the farm, and he put off her demands to return to Ganymede's Cup, saying he'd take care of it after he finished his other business.

Julia thought about it when she went down to the creek late the next morning while Washburn was out tending to something unspecified. The weather had warmed again, but she knew winter was coming and wanted to take advantage of being able to bathe in the creek while she could.

She lathered up with Brooke's almond soap, enjoying the rich scent of a product she knew was sold in the finest apothecaries. The man *did* love his comforts.

That made her pause. What was the source of the money he used to purchase these comforts? She'd seen nothing yet to disabuse her of the idea that Washburn was a smuggler, maybe the smuggler connected to the Delerue-Sanders thefts. The thought of breaking the locks on his chests fleetingly crossed her mind, but she was certain that would just make him angry, and she wasn't sure she could get away fast enough. As long as he thought she was ignorant of his business, the safer she'd be.

*   *   *

Rand came through the trees and headed down to the creek for a wash before returning home, but found someone had beaten him to the site—and it wasn't a raccoon washing its supper. No, Miss Julia Cooper was sitting jaybird-naked in the creek, washing with his soap. He settled back to admire the show. She was long and lean, but rounded in all the places a man liked a woman to be round. Those legs of hers would feel like heaven wrapped around his waist. He reached inside his pants and adjusted himself, something he'd been doing far too often over the last few days. She was some kind of treat, sashaying around his cabin, sticking her little nose in the air and twitching those hips in front of him while she did her chores. A man could grow real used to that kind of entertainment, but he also knew she was doing it on purpose, trying to keep him from finding out what she was really up to out here. The more time he spent with her, the more he heard her talk, the more unlikely that story about her being a poor little orphan seemed. The instincts that had kept him alive so far were telling him he dare not take his eyes off of her.

Not that that was hard. The only thing that was hard at the moment was his cock, and it was stiff enough to be used for a belaying pin. He moaned, but she was too busy to hear it, working that soap into a fine lather, rubbing it all over her arms, up her neck...

He wiped the sweat off his brow, but didn't take his eyes off of her as she dropped the soap and bent over at the waist, affording him a view of a bottom as rounded and perfect as a peach.

If he didn't do something, he was going to have to go change trousers. A *gentleman* would turn his back and walk away.

Yep, that's what a gentleman would do.

"It's down by your foot, darlin'."

She screamed and dropped into the creek, arms crossed over her bare chest. Rand chuckled. It wasn't as good as the show a moment ago, but it was still mighty entertaining.

"How long have you been standing there?" she snapped.

"I just got here and saw the soap fall," he said with wide-eyed innocence. "Though I have to admit, I was a bit concerned about the gators takin' a bite off that pretty butt of yours."

"There are alligators in this creek?"

"Not now that you've screamed your head off there ain't. Ooowee, I thought a bobcat could screech, but you got them beat all to hell and back! I imagine there's not a gator within twenty miles of here now, but it's no problem, I'll stay here 'til you're all done and protect you. You take your time."

"I am not going to bathe with you watching, Washburn! Turn around so I can get out of here."

"I dunno, this is a mighty fine show here."

Her eyes narrowed to two black slits. "For dinner, I have fried catfish, corn fritters, baked squash, white biscuits, and a sweet potato pie. Unless you want all of that to float down this creek while I serve you this morning's leftover grits, I suggest you turn around *now*."

He turned around. Dang, that woman did not fight fair at all.

CHAPTER 5

The moon was low in the sky, rich and golden as it hung half seen through the Spanish moss dangling from the trees. Washburn gathered his rifle, pistol, and ammunition, and checked his supplies as Julia silently watched.

"I'm goin' out," he said to her. "You bar the door tonight and stay around the cabin tomorrow. When I return, I'll take you back to Ganymede's Cup."

"Where are you going?"

He looked at her, his face blank of expression. The grinning backwoodsman was gone, replaced by someone who she suspected more closely resembled the real Washburn.

"You don't need to know that. All you need to know is tonight you stay in the cabin."

She raised her chin, wanting to goad him into revealing more information that might tie him to the missing cargo.

"It is a lovely night out. Maybe I will take a stroll in the moonlight instead."

He put down the gun and advanced on her, never taking his eyes off hers. She wanted to stand her ground, but found herself stepping back as he moved closer, until she hit up against the rough log wall. He kept coming and bracketed her with his hands alongside her head, trapping her between his arms.

"I don't want there to be any confusion 'bout this, so I'm

goin' to tell you straight: If you're outside tonight, you won't be around to see tomorrow's sunrise. If you want to make it back to your uncle's tavern in one piece, you be smart and stay in. You don't hear nothin', you don't see nothin', you don't know nothin'. It's better for your health that way."

He leaned in until he was so close she could see the flecks of gold in his eyes as` they drilled into hers.

"There are nasty things in the dark. Predators who would enjoy feastin' on a tasty morsel like yourself."

She licked her lips and the light in his eyes flared. For an instant she thought he would close that space between his mouth and hers, exposing her to all the danger of rousing the hunters that walked the night.

"You are deliberately trying to scare me. I am not a child afraid of the dark." Her own voice came out shaky, belying her words, but she raised her head and stared him in the eye.

A long, silent moment ticked by before Washburn pulled back. "You stay locked in here tonight." He walked away from her, pausing in the doorway to look back.

"Sometimes it's right smart to be afeared of the dark." He turned and closed the door behind him.

The mule brayed out as Washburn walked past the corral. Wherever he went, he was going on foot, and that strengthened her resolve. She waited until she thought he was gone, grabbed her shawl, and set out after him.

The light of the harvest moon cast the woods in sinister relief, and the high-pitched squeal of a rabbit was abruptly cut off as an owl caught its supper. Julia clutched the shawl tight around her as she moved along, hurrying, but staying far enough back to not give herself away. She didn't know how far she'd gone from the cabin, but kept walking, and tried not to think about what would happen if she was lost. Every thicket seemed to hide glowing eyes, the hungry eyes of the real rulers of the Florida pinewoods, who fought tooth and claw to survive. In the distance, a large cat coughed and the birds stilled as the heart of the night beat with the struggles of predator and prey, but Julia moved on, rightly fearing the two-legged predators most. She yanked her skirts free of a gallberry bush, and when she looked up Washburn's light was nowhere to be seen. She went still, fighting a rising panic that clawed inside her chest. A wet mist had settled over the ground, blocking her sight, and she closed her eyes, straining her senses, listening for clues. There—faint, but identifiable off to the right—the sound of voices and the smell of water. She opened her eyes and saw a slight glow reflecting off the mist, the flicker of firelight, and she leaned against a cypress as her body sagged in relief.

She stood there for what seemed like an eternity, finally roused by a mosquito taking a drink from her neck. She slapped at it, then raised her skirts and tied them up at the waist to keep from rustling against the palmetto fronds as she hunched down and crept through the scrub.

The noise led her down to the river, where a fire roared like the flames waiting to roast sinners. A group of men were gathered on a sand beach, laughing and passing brown jugs around. Her eyes watered from the light after the darkness of the deep woods, but as they adjusted she picked out more details. There were boats pulled up on the sand, open boats with poles for navigating through the cypress knees, some boats with oars, and even a sloop further out on the water. She'd been within walking distance of the river all along, but Washburn hadn't seen fit to share that information with her.

The anger she felt drove all thoughts of backwoods dangers out of her mind, and for one mad moment she was tempted to stand up and confront these ne'er-do-wells with their crimes, but common sense took over when she picked one all too familiar voice out of the hubbub.

*   *   *

Rand dipped his finger in the white powder and brought it up to his tongue, letting the crystals dissolve before he spoke.

"Liverpool salt. I can move this for you. What else you got?"

Daniel Brewer looked at him and scratched the stump on his face, all that remained after one too many nose-biting tavern fights.

"The salt's the best of it, Washburn. And there's plenty of it. They used it for ballast on this last trip of the *Manticore*."

"How'd you unload it before you hit St. Augustine?"

Brewer snickered. "The revenue cutters can't catch all of us, Washburn. Hell, they're lucky if they pick up some Cuban bringing in sugar without a tariff stamp, much less catch on to our operation."

Rand grunted in acknowledgment. The salt was a good haul. Even with the nearby salt ponds at Key West it was a valuable— and highly taxed—commodity prized by westerners who needed it to preserve and ship meat. There was fighting in Washington over protective tariffs keeping New England and Virginia salt factories competitive, while the westerners wanted cheap salt any way they could get it.

"Yep, it's easy pickin's and with our folks in place we can pretty much just waltz in and take what we like."

"You have someone workin' with you in St. Augustine?"

Brewer went stiff. "What'cha need to know that for?"

He shrugged. "I like to know who I'm dealin' with, that's all. I don't like surprises."

Brewer guffawed, his good humor restored. "I know what you mean, Washburn. Most surprises are bad news for someone! Hey, Thornton, let me get a kiss from ol' Hannah there!"

Brewer reached out his hand for the black bottle of home-brewed corn liquor and took a long swallow, then passed the bottle to Rand, who tilted "Hannah" back for his own drink.

"What else you got, Brewer?"

Brewer licked his lips, his little eyes shining with greed over the haul. He wasn't the head of the operation, but he could get Washburn where he wanted to be, dealing with the larger and more valuable cargoes.

"French brandy, China silks, coffee. What can you take?"

Rand scratched his chin as he thought. The coffee he could handle without a problem and he'd be a fool not to take the brandy. The silk might be more difficult.

"How much silk?"

Brewer looked at some papers in his hand, his lips moving as he puzzled out the words.

"Here, let me help you with that." He reached for the papers and Brewer hesitated, but being unable to read much more than his own name, he reluctantly gave them over.

Rand skimmed down the sheets, a copy of the *Manticore's* manifest. It was as he'd suspected. Most of the Delerue-Sanders ships came via Cuba, and they'd stop to take on water at Cape Florida or Mosquito Inlet before moving up the coast. The cargo would be unloaded there, with or without the captain and supercargo's knowledge, and be picked up later. Not all of the cargo, just enough to turn around without difficulty. When the ship entered port in St. Augustine or Savannah or Fernandina, the tariffs would be paid on what was in the hold, with the smuggled cargo being shipped in for no fees.

Fifteen hundred dollars worth of coffee coming in duty free meant a tidy profit. A simple plan, but one that worked all too well given the poor state of the Revenue Marine. The revenue cutters couldn't begin to cover all of the coast, not when the ships were spread thin with surveying, rescue operations, and winter cruising between Charleston and Key West. Underfunded, understaffed, looked down on by the regular navy, despised by the merchants who paid the tariffs, the Revenue Marine was no one's darling.

Well, except maybe Alexander Hamilton, he'd loved his revenue cutters that brought money into the Treasury, but look what happened to him, Rand thought. Irritate the wrong people and there you are, worm food.

"I figure you got other manifests for when you reach port?"

Brewer snickered. "Good enough to fool the customs agents."

"All right, I can buy the silk, too. Bring me the salt, silks, coffee, and brandy, and I'll take them off your hands."

"That's going to take a heap o' cash, Washburn. You sure you can come up with the silver?"

*   *   *

Julia watched from the woods, fists clenched, nails digging

into her skin. She couldn't understand all that was said, but she recognized the Delerue-Sanders markings on the crates well enough. She was right. Washburn was a low-down thief, a liar and a smuggler, no better than any of these other malefactors. She felt a prickling at her eyes and swallowed hard as she watched him in the firelight, drinking and bartering away her family's property.

Moving away from the tree, she crouched down and inched along the rise over the river bank, trying to get closer without being spotted. There were no guards posted up here. If they were expecting trouble, they were expecting it from the river, where armed men stood near the boats.

She stretched forward to grasp the root of a sweet gum to pull herself up. Her boot dug into the sharply angled ground, but when she put her other foot before her, it was in leaf mold. Her leg shot out from under her with a painful twist, and she felt the still wet ground give way beneath as she tumbled down to the riverbank, her arms wrapped around her head to protect her from the jutting stumps and rocks.

She landed with a thump and all was stone quiet as she lay there, waiting for the ringing in her head to stop. With a groan, Julia tried to push herself to her feet, only to be stopped. A boot pinned her skirt to the sand. She turned her head and through the tangles of hair falling around her face looked up a long leg clad in butternut, past a familiar wool jacket, to an unsmiling face lit from beneath, giving it a satanic cast in the flickering light.

"You just couldn't listen, could you?"

Washburn reached down and hauled Julia to her feet as the men gathered around, keeping a firm grip on her upper arm when she tried to move back from the gathering crowd.

"Oooweee," Brewer said. "This belong to you, Washburn?"

In a low voice for Julia's ears alone he said, "You keep your mouth shut and do as I say, no matter *what* I say, and you might survive this."

He looked at Brewer and shrugged. "Yeah, she's mine. I told her to stay put, but the gal ain't well furnished in the upper story," he said, tapping at his forehead.

He gave the girl's arm a slight squeeze when she made to open her mouth, and she closed her teeth with a snap.

"Well now, ain't that a shame," Brewer said. "See, we got ourselves a little problem here. No one can know about this meetin' tonight who ain't a part of the operation. Why don't you give that gal over to me, and I'll make sure no one ever hears about what happened here."

"She *is* a lot of trouble, but she's my problem to deal with. I'll take care of it."

Dear heaven, they were talking about killing her. She swayed on her feet, but Washburn's grip on her arm kept her upright. She could feel the heat of his hand through her sleeve, branding her, as he discussed disposing of her like a troublesome dog that wouldn't hunt.

"Do it here and now, Washburn, so we know you won't go soft on us."

"I said I'll take care of it, and I ain't goin' to do it for your entertainment."

His hand slipped into his coat pocket, where Julia'd seen him stash a pepperbox pistol back at the cabin. Some of Brewer's men saw the gesture and reached for their own weapons, and the mutterings from the dark took on an ugly tone.

"There's 'nother way," a voice said drunkenly from the fire. "You don't have to get rid of her."

They turned as a group to where Squire Reynolds was half collapsed over a jug of scuppernong wine.

"Marry her. You can fetch her back if she runs off, you can even lock her in the attic and forget about her. Happens to crazy relatives all the time." Reynolds spit a brown stream of tobacco to the side. "A woman and a man become one when they marry, and that *one* is the man. Coverture, they call it in the courts. An' that means if she's your wife, she can't testify against you."

In the silence that followed this pronouncement, Julia heard the sounds of the night insects as they buzzed around the fire and the burble of river water lapping up against the boats. It was all too unreal, and she prayed any moment she'd awaken from this nightmare and find herself back in bed in England, thinking of nothing more pressing than what gown to wear that day.

But that was not an option. Washburn turned his head and looked down at her. She couldn't read his expression as he stood backlit by the fire, but he finally said, "There's nothin' for it then. Next time the preacher comes through, we'll get hitched."

"Why wait?" Brewer sniggered, wiping his hand across his wet mouth. "You can get spliced tonight and take care of this problem, or we can take care of it for you. But if that gal leaves here, she's leavin' here as some man's property. If'n you don't want her, Washburn, I can take her off your hands. I got ways to make sure she don't talk to nobody 'bout nothin'. Hell, I'll marry her myself!"

He ran hot eyes over Julia's form and clutched his groin.

"How 'bout it, gal? Y'want to marry Washburn, or mebbe you'd like to marry a man with a little more fire in his belly?"

Almost unconsciously, Julia moved closer to Washburn.

"Nobody's goin' to get married tonight," he snapped. "Do you see a preacher here?"

"Don' need a preacher," Reynolds said. He drew himself up in drunken dignity until he stood, waving slightly in the breeze off the river. "Sir, I am a justice of the peace. I can say the words and write the paper, and you'll be married pas' redem—redempsh—you'll be hitched.

"But I can't marry two people together when one of 'em's unwillin'," the magistrate continued. "Gal, do you want to be married to Washburn—or Brewer—'til death do you part?"

"Wait a minute—" Julia started to speak, but Washburn, who was still holding her arm, pulled her in front of him so he could look her in the eye.

"It's that 'til death idea you want to think on. You do not have a great deal of choice here, in case that's slipped your notice," he said quietly. "You brought this on yourself by sneakin' out after you was warned. Answer the squire's question."

"Give her a kiss from Hannah, maybe that'll help her decide!" One of the men laughed, and a black bottle was passed to Washburn, who pressed it into her hand.

"Drink. It'll help."

She took a long swallow of the whiskey and almost fell to her knees as the raw liquor hit her.

"Well? What's it to be, gal?" the squire asked.

Julia looked around her. The men stared back, hungry looks

in some eyes as they muttered suggestions about using her before her throat was cut. She saw compassion in others, lasciviousness writ large on Brewer. The one she couldn't read was the man who held her, and she looked up into his eyes for a long, long moment.

Then she drew herself erect, generations of Delerue ancestors strengthening her spine.

"I am appreciative of the great kindness and honor you do me by asking me to be your wife, sir," she said in flat tones, never taking her eyes off Washburn. "I accept your suit."

She saw the quick gleam in his eye before he responded in equal tones, "Thank you, my dear, you have made me the happiest of men."

He raised his voice. "Gather 'round, boys—looks like there's goin' to be a weddin'!"

He took the bottle from her and raised it. "To us, darlin'. Lord help us both."

Then he took his own long drink, not his first, or even his second of the evening. He wiped his mouth with the back of his hand and made to pass the bottle on, but Julia took it from him. The whiskey went down easier this time.

He helped her to a fallen log and sat her down, then joined her, not looking at her. She dazedly watched the mood change from fatal to festive. The smugglers were joking about how they always expected Washburn to be the one getting married with a gun at his back, and they called out lewd suggestions on how he should keep his nosy bride in line.

More wood was tossed on the fire, and the flames leapt, throwing sparks high into the night sky. Some meat cooked over a spit, and when the wind blew the odors over, Julia swallowed against sudden queasiness. A shudder ran over her frame and she felt a slight squeeze from Washburn's hand on her shoulder, an oddly comforting gesture. He wouldn't talk to her, or even look at her, but she was pathetically grateful for his presence among these men, even knowing he'd been willing to cut her throat not more than a half an hour back.

"I need paper and ink," Squire Reynolds said, and a boat was sent out to the sloop, returning soon with ink, a pen, and some ragged handbills advertising the appearance of Mrs. Letty Lacroix, directly from Paris, France, appearing at McCall's Playhouse in Savannah and performing selections from Shakespeare's *As You Like It* and *The Taming of the Shrew*.

"We're just about ready here. Rand, you stand on the right. Gal, you're on the left."

Washburn extended his hand, and Julia rose to her feet, staring ahead as she was led before the magistrate.

Squire Reynolds cleared his throat dramatically, and brushed off the front of his coat.

"My dear friends, we have assembled here in the sight of God and in the presence of you all as witnesses, to unite in holy matrimony Rand Washburn and—" He peered at Julia in befuddlement, breathing alcohol fumes into her face. "What's your name, gal?"

"Julia Anne De—" She swallowed. "Julia Anne Cooper."

"Rand Washburn and Julia Cooper," he continued. "If you, or any of you here have, or can show just cause or impedi— impedimen—just cause why this couple should not be lawfully joined together," he paused again, this time for effect, "after

God's ordinance in the holy estate of matrimony, I charge you to speak now or else forever hereafter hold your peace!"

There was no sound from the assembly in the aftermath of these ringing words, and the night itself seemed to hold its breath waiting for the next act of the performance. The squire was enjoying his moment of glory and he looked sternly at the couple who stood before him.

"I charge you both, as you will answer on that great Judgment Day, if either of you know of any imped—reason why you can't be married here today, to confess it now. Otherwise, your marriage will not be legal in the eyes of God or man!"

Julia closed her eyes in relief. She was using a false name. It wouldn't be a real marriage. So she said nothing as Reynolds swayed before her, and she did not look at the man standing at her side.

"Julia Cooper, do you take this man, Rand Washburn, as your wedded husband? Will you obey him, and serve him, in sickness and in health, and forsaking all others keep yourself with him as long as you both shall live? If so, answer 'I will.'"

Julia swallowed hard, but said, "I will," knowing all the time that she was swearing falsely, for there was no Julia Cooper.

"Rand, take Julia by the right hand."

He turned and took Julia's hand, and she looked down at her red, work-roughened hand swallowed up by his. Visions of St. George's in London, white lace gloves, and the smell of roses were blown away on the dank river air, and when she looked up, she saw Rand Washburn watching her as the magistrate said, "Do you, Rand, take this woman to be your lawful and wedded wife, to love, cherish and honor her in sickness and in health, forsaking all others, cleaving to her only, as long as you both shall live? Answer 'I do.'"

There was an uncomfortable pause, and Julia heard someone shift and cough, before Rand Washburn said in a clear and carrying voice, "I do."

"Hey, what about a ring!" yelled out a voice from beyond the fire.

"Yeah, can't get married without a ring, can ya?"

He looked at her for a moment longer, then said, "I have a ring."

He worked at his right hand, finally freeing a ring from his finger, and taking Julia's hand in his placed it over the ring finger of her left hand. The gold was still warm from his skin, and a ruby winked up at her in the light. When he slipped it past her knuckle, it hung there loosely. She cupped her hand to keep it on.

"Then by the powers vested in me by the territory of Florida, I pronounce you husband and wife. Kiss 'er, Washburn."

The magistrate finished saying the words that bound her to the piney woods smuggler, Rand Washburn, whose face filled her vision as he leaned down. She braced herself, but he kissed her chastely on her closed lips before turning back to the magistrate, who was using the pen and handbills to write out their marriage papers.

"I will file these in St. Augustine, my boy," Reynolds started, but Washburn put his hand on the papers.

"No. I'll hold on to this for now, Squar'. I'd as soon everyone in St. Augustine not know my business."

"I could be fined a sizable amount if this license doesn't get filed."

A flash of gold shifting from Washburn's hand to his stilled any further objections the justice of the peace might have. Washburn folded the papers before stashing them in his pocket.

Reynolds looked at Julia, shrugged, and said, "You *are* married to him, Mrs. Washburn. All these men are witnesses. And I may be a drunken old reprobate, but I *am* a justice of the peace."

Julia was still too worried about surviving among the smugglers to focus on the legality of the wedding or the fate of the marriage papers. Washburn was sticking close to her, deflecting the demands of the men who wanted to kiss the bride, using quips and laughter that never reached his eyes, the cold flat blankness still there, even as he joked about his altered status.

"Here," she said, passing back the ring. "It is too loose and will fall off my finger."

"You keep it, Mrs. Washburn. You've earned it."

Julia glared at him but said nothing further, instead turning her back on him and ripping a ribbon from her chemise. She tied the ring around her neck and tucked it inside her dress.

Someone produced a fiddle, and someone else brought out a flute, and the smugglers celebrated Rand and Julia's wedding with dancing and music by the river. A plate of the pig roasting over the fire was pressed into Julia's hands and she pushed the food around on her plate, not eating it, but when a jug of wine made the rounds she downed it. She wanted to maintain this feeling of numbness.

And she didn't want to think at all about how the wedding night would end.

Julia upended the jug, the sweet wine spilling down her throat and running out at the corners of her mouth, dampening her bodice in sticky patches.

Washburn watched her out of the corner of his eye and she passed him the jug as she swiped at her mouth with her hand, smearing pork grease across her cheek. A grimace of distaste crossed his well-formed features and she was tempted to slap him. How dare he find fault with *her*, a woman whose name was discussed as a matrimonial prospect for some of the finest families in Britain. He was just some no 'count smuggler, and as soon as she could she'd get away from him and send the entire British navy after him to hunt him down and hang him high…

She frowned woozily. Maybe the Americans wouldn't want the British navy hunting down one stray Floridian, but she'd make sure her papa straightened it all out. Tears filled her eyes. A girl wanted her mama and papa on her wedding day, and here she was, sitting on a log and getting chigger bites, instead of enjoying a wedding breakfast in the great hall at Rosemoor or their London townhouse. It wasn't fair. She took another drink to console herself, hugging the jug for comfort.

"Looks like you've had enough of that wine, Mrs. Washburn," Rand said as he took the scuppernong from her loosened grasp.

"Don' call me that!"

He just grinned at her unpleasantly, and lifted the jug to his own mouth.

Brewer and some of his men had left the bridal couple to their supper, but they returned now in high spirits, hooting and hollering.

"It's too late in the evenin' for you to set out for your place, Rand," Brewer said. "So we prepared a spot for you and your bride right here."

"We'll head on back. I don't plan on spendin' the night here."

Brewer shook his head and the men around him snickered.

"See, now I thought you'd say that. But remember what I said earlier? That gal ain't leaving here unless she's good and proper married, and the way we see it that ain't goin' to happen without a good and proper weddin' night. So you'll stay here."

Since the men with Brewer were armed, Julia stood when Washburn gestured at her, and she joined the party of drunken smugglers as they marched up the riverbank, banging pans and shooting their guns into the air in a noisy shivaree.

There was a hut on stilts out on the edge of the river, a ladder leading up to its single room. Julia stood looking up the ladder at the dark entrance to the river shack.

"You need me to carry you up to our honeymoon hideaway, darlin'?"

Julia looked over her shoulder and gave him what she hoped was a quelling glance, then hitching up her skirts climbed the ladder, to comments from Brewer's men over her ankles and backside.

When she reached the top, she paused and looked back. Washburn was watching her from the bottom, and his eyes glowed in the firelight like a panther watching a doe. She hurried up through the opening into the shack.

Someone had lit a tallow stump and it flickered its light on a plank table and bench. A pile of musty smelling and suspicious looking bedding spilled across the floor, and another door opened onto a covered veranda leaning out at a precarious angle over the river. She stood out there, gauging the distance down to the water. It was too far to jump without risking hitting one of the cypress trees, and besides, she could hear Washburn and Brewer and a couple of the men climbing up behind.

"See? Jus' like I told you, a real cozy little nest for you and the missus."

This set the others off into paroxysms of laughter. All except Washburn.

A jug of wine was passed up and he drank first, then the men drank off it before leaving it on the table. Washburn watched, arms crossed over his chest, that empty expression on his face. She would have rather put up with the baboon backwoodsman than this cold, silent automaton.

The smugglers vacated the shack, and Julia slumped down against a wall, watching the man who watched her in the near dark. He sat in a corner, drinking, while the sounds of drunken revelry floated up from the river. Washburn stared out the veranda, finally turning to look at his wife, who huddled with a quilt around her shoulders, shivering in the night breeze.

"Come here," he said. "Don't look at me like that, you're cold. Sit over here next to me, and bring that quilt. It's going to be a chill night, and there's no reason for us to suffer more than we already are. It's a long time 'til mornin'."

Julia crept over to him, but when she kept her distance, he snorted and grabbed her by the arms, hauling her to sit across his lap. She was so stunned at being manhandled this way she couldn't speak, and he shook his head and chuckled.

"You sure are skittish for a tavern gal." His movements were loose, his speech slower. He pressed the jug into her hands, but she set it aside unsteadily.

"I thin' we've both had enough, Mr. Washburn."

When she turned back, his lips were inches from her own, and she smelled the tang of wine on his breath.

"Rand," he whispered.

"What?"

"Call me Rand. After all, the squar' says we're married, so maybe it's time you called me by my name, 'specially seein' as how this is our weddin' night and all." His hand was on her back, and when she tried to wiggle off his lap, he sucked in his breath, and moved his leg over hers, trapping her there.

"I didn' know you was so eager," he said thickly, and brought his head down close to hers. For a moment she thought he'd kiss her, but he hesitated a fraction above her mouth, and instead placed his lips below her ear, on the sensitive spot just beneath her jaw. Her protest came out as a breathy gasp, not the strong words she wanted to say.

In fact, her entire mind seemed to have come disengaged from the rest of her body as Washburn's mouth slid across her neck, nibbling and licking his way 'round to her other ear. He also had more than two hands, she was sure of it, because they seemed to be everywhere, roaming over her back, her arms, and now on her bodice, plucking at the laces. When she feebly moved her own hand down to stop him, he held it and rolled them both down and over, cradling her head with one of those extra appendages until she was on her back on the quilts.

Julia looked up at the thatched roof, the wine she'd consumed spinning the room around her. How had this happened? One moment she was sitting shivering, and the next moment a silver-tongued devil was using that tongue to rob her of her ability to think. That same devil sighed in satisfaction as he pushed apart the opening of her bodice, his own liquor consumption not impairing him as he plucked open the ties of her chemise and stared at her breasts. He touched the ring on its ribbon, and it bounced against her skin.

"Oh yeah," he murmured. "These beauties looked wonderful down by the creek when you was bathin', but they're even better up close. Bet the drovers down at the Cup pay a pretty penny for this sight. And tonight they're all mine."

Julia opened her mouth to explain that no one at the Cup had ever seen her breasts, but lost her ability to speak, because his long-fingered hands were on those breasts and they felt wonderful. No boy or man who'd ever shared a kiss with her had ever presumed to try such a thing. A smooth-talking smuggler dared, and instead of throwing him off her body, she gave in to the instinct that arched her back, each gentle squeeze and touch of his fingers across her swollen mounds stoking the fire building deep inside her body.

"Does that feel good, darlin'?"

"It feels wonderful!" she gasped, the honest admission torn from her.

He chuckled. "Well then, maybe you'll like this, too."

He leaned down and she saw the light reflect off his golden hair before he put his mouth to her breast, and then she saw nothing except stars behind her closed eyelids. His tongue swirled around and around, raising her nipples to where they stood out at just the right height for him to grasp between his callused thumb and forefinger and roll gently. All Julia could do was moan and clutch at Washburn's jacket as he said, "See? I told you you'd have a good time. You'll enjoy it, I promise. It'll be fun, not like sellin' it at the Cup."

This statement set off a small alarm bell in the recesses of her mind not yet completely befuddled by drink and sensation, but any protest Julia would have made was stilled as his mouth returned to her breasts and his hands continued their devilish magic.

She heard the rustle of clothing being undone and then a breeze shivered over her bared legs before Washburn settled his length across her, and she was grateful for the warmth of his body until she felt his fingers probing down at the apex of her thighs. He must have been satisfied with what he found, because before she realized what he intended, he had her legs up over his hips and she could feel his bare skin. She only had a moment to wonder where his trousers had gone to before he grinned at her, said, "Hold on, darlin', an' we'll have a real fine time," and thrust himself into her.

Afterward, it would have been difficult to say who was more stunned. Julia yelped and froze, all the good sensations wiped out by the pain of Washburn's entry, while he went rock still, bracing himself on his forearms. His expression became almost comical as shock widened his eyes.

"Julia? You have done this before, haven't you?" he asked in a strangled voice.

"How could I? I have never been married before!" she whispered. She moved her hips to ease the discomfort and he bit back an oath and said, "Don't do that!"

His face was covered with sweat and he swore again, but instead of pulling himself out of her he pushed further in, and she blinked up at him. The pain was receding now. When she hitched her hips forward, she felt more relief, and something else, an echo of what had gone before.

He groaned and began moving within her, the friction of his skin against hers rubbing at her and rekindling the heat that had been burning through her veins, but within the space of few moments he tensed and swore and jerked himself out of her. She felt him convulse against her belly before his movements stilled and he collapsed across her body, breathing harshly.

After a lifetime he raised himself up on his elbows. Julia blinked up at him owlishly, a frown between her eyes.

"That hurt. You told me it would be fun. That wasn't fun." She frowned again. "Get off of me. I'm going to be sick."

He rolled off to the side and helped her to the edge of the hut, just in time as she lost her supper into the river. Her last thought before her mind blanked out was that she hoped he'd consider it a commentary on his skills as a lover.

CHAPTER 6

"You should'a told me."

"It is not exactly the sort of thing that comes up in casual conversation, now is it? 'Pass the grits. Oh, by the way, I'm a virgin.'"

They were walking through the woods back to Washburn's farm, the bright sunlight stabbing her eyeballs, the beautiful day mocking her mood.

After the fiasco of their wedding night Julia passed out on the floor, the wine exacting its price for her overindulgence. But not its final price, that she was paying now, forced to tromp through the brush with a head feeling as if it had been pounded into her shoulders with tent pins. She was also sure someone had coated her mouth with possum fur while she was unconscious.

When she woke, Washburn was on the veranda of the hut, leaning against the wall and staring out over the empty river. The smugglers had departed in the night, and a foraging raccoon scampered away from the garbage they'd left behind as embers from their bonfires smoked in the morning mist.

They didn't say much, and avoided each other's eyes while they gathered their gear and began the long walk back to the cabin. Julia glanced now at her companion. For his part Washburn looked, if not daisy fresh, at least capable of dealing with a normal day's routine, including the complications of having a wife. He stopped and took her by the arm, turning her to face him.

"Look, I didn't ask you to come out to the farm. All I asked was that you stay put and I'd take you back to your uncle. But you had to do things your own way, didn't you?" He jerked his hand away and kicked at a tuft of grass. "There're things goin' on you know nothin' about—"

"I know a lot more than you think!"

He looked at her for a long moment.

"Now, that's part of the problem, ain't it? You know a lot more than's healthy for you to know, and until this business gets squared away, we're goin' to have to put up with each other."

"The first thing we need to do is get this marriage dissolved."

His jaw tensed, but he said nothing, and Julia looked at him in disbelief.

"You cannot seriously be thinking we are really married?"

"We are married. You were there, you heard the magistrate."

"Yes, and you took the wedding papers from him so he could not file them! I saw you pocket them." She thought about it for a moment. "But that was before you knew I was a virgin, wasn't it?"

"That makes a difference."

"How is it different?"

"It just is, that's all!"

"I see. So if I were some tavern girl from Ganymede's Cup trying to get by as best I could, then it would be all right for you to…to have relations with me. What's one more man, after all? But if I am a maiden, it all changes? I am a totally different person? I am not the same woman who gets up each morning, and fixes your breakfast, and wants to get out of here and never see your smirking face again?"

This last was said on a rising note that brought a glare from her "husband," and Julia thought it would serve him right if she had a screaming hysterical fit right here in the palmettos. But knowing Washburn, he'd probably shoot her to shut her up.

"Don't be naïve," he gritted.

"Ooooh, big word for Mr. Cracker Washburn! I'm impressed!"

He threw his hat on the ground, then kicked it for good measure, startling a covey of quail out of the nearby brush.

"Goddammit, what you was before don't matter! Not anymore. As of last night there ain't no Rand Washburn and Julia Cooper, there's only Mr. and Mrs. Rand Washburn, so you'd better get used to it, *Mrs. Washburn*." He took a deep breath and bent to pick up the abused hat, slapping it against his pants leg to shake it out. Instead of putting it back on his head though, he shoved it at her.

"Here, put this on. You're gettin' red."

She opened her mouth to argue, but at the look on his face jammed the hat over her dusty curls, then poked a finger under the brim to keep the too large hat from flopping forward over her eyes.

"Look…" He stared off at a scrub jay raucously chasing after a thrush invading its space, "You don't want to be married to me no more than I want to be married to you. For now we'll leave things as they are, and when my business here is done we'll figure out what to do."

"You can destroy the papers. No one will know we were

married, and we can go our separate ways. What happened last night was a mistake. A mistake I want to forget and I have no intention of repeating!"

He just looked at her, turned, and started walking down the trail.

She clamped her teeth so tight her jaw hurt, because she knew if she opened her mouth again, she'd tell him who she really was, that Julia Cooper never existed. If the marriage was legal she was, in fact, Lady Julia Washburn. She could imagine how he'd take *that* bit of news!

Even with all her anger, something tugged at her chest. Something poignant. This backwoods smuggler seemed honor bound to make the marriage real, because he'd taken a young woman's virtue.

It wasn't what she expected of him. And she told herself she didn't like it.

They kept walking and after a while the tension in Julia's head eased and she could enjoy more of the sight of a Florida she hadn't seen, the busy autumn world of returning northern birds and squabbling natives, staking their claims to the insects and nesting areas of the pinewoods. Washburn walked through the woods with confidence, but kept his rifle cradled in front of him. When she came up beside him, she saw his eyes were moving over the terrain, scanning it for danger. The trail was wider here and they could walk abreast rather than with Julia trailing behind.

"How much did you hear last night?" Washburn broke the companionable silence.

"You mean before I fell off a cliff and ended up married?"

"Yep."

"Would you believe me if I told you I did not hear anything, but fell as soon as I showed up?"

"Nope. And if you're goin' to tell me lies today, at least make them entertainin'."

Julia thought about how best to approach this conversation. At least now that it was out in the open, she could see about securing more information on his involvement with the smuggling from Delerue-Sanders.

"Very well, Washburn. I have to tell you I was suspicious of you from the beginning and thought you might be involved in activities...outside the law. But I have learned from my time at Ganymede's Cup that such activities are quite common around here, so it was not a complete surprise."

He grunted at this, and Julia continued.

"You have a farm that is not producing much more than subsistence items. You have a mule I have never seen pull a plow. You do not even have a cow, much less cattle, or cotton, or slaves, yet you have a pantry well stocked with comforts and plenty of gold. I would have to be quite stupid not to have noticed this."

He smiled at that, but didn't look over at her. "You may be many things, darlin', but I never thought you was stupid. Even though I told Brewer you wasn't furnished in the upper story."

"Thank you, I think. So when you left last night I was curious." An idea began blossoming in her mind, and Julia decided to see where she could take it.

"I figured if I knew what you were up to, maybe I could make myself useful to you in some way and get a share of whatever it is you are involved in. After all, I do not want to spend my life working at a tavern! I want to return to England, where I belong, not live out here slaving for my uncle. If there is money to be made, I would like to be in on it."

"Go on."

"I could see from the activity at the river that you are a smuggler, involved with some kind of ongoing operation. I heard you negotiate with Brewer over a shipment of goods. But what happens next—I don't know. I slipped, and, well, you know what happened after that."

"It don't bother you none that I'm involved with smugglin'? You don't have a problem with stealin' other folks' stuff and keepin' the revenue from collectin' customs duties?"

"Not at all," Julia said breezily. "I do not give a fig for whether the United States gets its money. And I will wager that shipping company you are robbing—Delerue-Sanders?—can afford the losses. That is why they have insurance, and if they cannot keep track of their own goods, well then, bad luck to them, I say!"

Washburn chuckled and shook his head, then looked at her with an intrigued glint in eyes the changeable color of the pinewoods. The warming sun picked out threads of gold in his hair and the stubble on his face, highlighting its planes and hollows. Julia tightened her shawl around her as a shiver raced down her back.

"Dang, you're just full of surprises, Mrs. Washburn. Who'd've thought I'd be fortunate enough to end up married to such a larcenous soul?"

"We are two of a kind. And do not call me Mrs. Washburn. I

do not mind being your partner in smuggling, but I am *not* going to stay married to you."

"But, darlin', we're so well matched!"

"No, we are not. After I get my share, I want to go far away, back to England, and never have to see you again, Washburn."

"Aw, now, honey, is that any way to talk to your husband?" he said, putting his hand over his heart. "And don't you think you should call me Rand, since we're married and all?"

Julia kept her eyes straight ahead, and heard the bray of the mule in the distance. They were almost back at the cabin.

"No. Let us keep this straight between us. I am leaving here as soon as I am able to. If you took me back to Ganymede's Cup today, I would wave good-bye and never think about you again."

"Now you *are* lyin'."

"Do not assume what happened last night is going to bind me to you," Julia said through her teeth. "I will stay until we can get this fixed, and I will stay to make money smuggling, but I will not stay because I was forced to marry you to save my life! In fact, the fewer people know we are married, the better. I have no intention of telling the Iveys or anyone else about it."

"Won't do no good. Everyone who was there last night knows, and I wouldn't be surprised if word is already filterin' out over the river."

"There has to be a way out of this!"

He scratched his chin.

"Could be done, but it would take a powerful lot of money for lawyers and what all. The lawmakers in Tallahassee can be bought, but they don't come cheap. A couple over to Alligator got unhitched. I do recall that happenin'. 'Course, she was tossin' up her skirts for the soldiers and drovers that came by, so people knew he had cause. Not sure we have cause, here."

"We will find a way to resolve this. In the meantime, if you are so set on thinking of me as your wife, don't you also think you should tell me about your smuggling operation?"

"Nope. What I think is, we're home, Mrs. Washburn, and you should get yourself into the cabin like a good wife, and fix me some victuals. That walk gave me a powerful hunger…'less there are some other wifely duties you'd care to perform?"

Julia just sniffed and walked past him to the cabin.

*   *   *

Rand watched his *wife* stalk away from him, the inky curls flopping from under his hat bouncing in time to the sway of her hips. He took care of the mule, then retreated to the woodpile to work off some of his mad even as mouthwatering smells began drifting out from the cabin.

The steady motion of the axe swinging down to section oak sweated out the last of the alcohol. Each thwack of the wood mocked him, the homely chore reminding him of what was at stake in this game. If all worked out, he'd never have to see this dirt farm again, never have to split logs, or feed chickens, or husk corn the rest of his life. But first he had to figure out what to do about that woman in the cabin.

A thieving wife who wanted to join his smuggling operation was a complication he didn't need. It gave him little satisfaction to know he'd been right to suspect her, and he was still sure she was lying about why she was out there, but he might be closer to the truth with her confession that she wanted the easy money and a return to England. Maybe there was someone there waiting for her? Someone who'd sent her to ferret out information?

He paused to take off his shirt as the sun rose and the work warmed him, then began swinging the axe again, a wave of self-disgust rippling from his midsection through the arms that last night had been so eager to hold that girl. He'd done some low-down things in his life, but he'd never gotten drunk and deflowered a virgin. Never mind he'd been forced into the marriage at gunpoint, or that she seemed to know what she was doing. Rand Washburn wasn't yet such a cad that he could turn his back and walk away from this situation. Despite her denials, he was married to Julia Washburn *née* Cooper, and she'd have to deal with it and with her American husband, 'cause he wasn't taking off for Britain!

Rand paused to wipe his forehead, and smiled mirthlessly, remembering the eligible young women who'd once thrown themselves in his path. But that was in another place, when he had been a different person than Washburn the smuggler.

He pulled another log out to split and propped it up, but paused as random bits of the previous night filtered through his consciousness. Then it had seemed like being married to Miss Cooper was a *fine* idea. Her breast filled his hand as if designed for it, the ripe tip peaking and swelling at a touch. Her skin was soft as egret down, her lips like sugar in the cane, waiting for the right person to suck the sweetness out. It *had* been good, right up to that disastrous moment when he broke through her maidenhead and they'd stopped having "fun."

A noise made him look up. Julia was standing on the veranda, watching. Her eyes followed the movement of his arms over his head as he raised the axe, and he knew she was watching the muscles bunch and flow in his chest and shoulders.

And he was vain enough to appreciate it.

He split the log, then smiled and rested the axe alongside his foot. Sweat trickled down through the hair across his chest and he scratched at it idly, never taking his eyes off her face.

"Do you want me?"

"What?"

"You was standin' there, so I thought maybe there was somethin' you wanted me for, darlin'."

She cleared her throat, but that did nothing to erase the high color in her cheeks. "I made breakfast. Come and eat," she said, turning on her heel and fleeing back into the cabin.

Rand pulled on his shirt and thought about how having a wife would complicate his life. And wondered, too, what the sleeping arrangements would be later.

If he were a prudent man, he would leave her alone.

But if he were prudent, he wouldn't be out here in the backwoods waiting for smuggled goods now, would he?

CHAPTER 7

Julia's tension increased as the day wore on and Washburn did nothing to decrease it, sidling up next to her, finding little excuses to touch her hand, her shoulder, the small of her back. When she jerked away from him, he smiled as if tormenting her were the most amusing thing in the world. It was all a game to him, one more comfort he was looking to enjoy out in the piney woods.

After supper, when she thought she'd go insane if there was one more suggestive glance or innuendo, Washburn went to his chest, unlocked it, pulled out a box, and relocked the chest. The box was painted pine and he took it to the table and opened it, revealing a well-worn chess set. The hinged box acted as the board and he set the pieces up, then studied them.

"What's that?"

Washburn looked up, startled out of his concentration.

"It's a chess set. You never seen one before?"

"I do not believe I have," Julia said. She picked up a white knight. "Why, this is carved like a horse's head! How adorable!"

"I could teach you to play, darlin'. It would be a nice way to while away the nights this winter."

"Is it hard to learn how to play chess?"

"Naw, anybody can play. Why, I bet you could beat me after a game or two." He rotated the set until the white pieces were in front of Julia.

She sat down at the table and Washburn explained all the pieces to her, their moves and their rankings.

"So the queen is the most powerful piece on the board? I like that!"

"Yeah, she's powerful and has lots of moves, but it takes capturin' the king to win the game. And when you win, you say 'checkmate.'"

"And the horses are the ones that do the funny jumping, correct?"

"Not horses, knights. Now let's play a game to see how well you learned. White goes first."

"It does? Oh, that's going to give me an advantage!"

He beat her in fifteen moves.

"Remember to use those pawns, and be prepared to have casualties, Julia. Sometimes you have to give up somethin' now to win later."

She frowned at the denuded board. "Can any piece be lost to win the game? Even the queen?"

"Even the queen can be sacrificed if it means the game."

He rolled a rook between his fingers. "Care to try again? I think you've got a real talent for this, darlin'. In fact, let's make a little wager."

"Wager? What kind of wager?"

"I'll give up my queen. And two pawns," he added generously. "I think you can beat me. And let's make this the wager… If I win, I get to spend the night back in my own bed with you. If you win, you can stay in the bed and I'll join you there." His lips tilted up at the corners and he waggled his eyebrows at her.

"Oh, very droll, Washburn. How about this instead? If you win…" She thought about it for a moment, tapping her lip. "You sleep in the bed, and I will sleep out here on the pallet. But if I win, I get to stay alone in the bedroom, by myself. Every night."

"That's a hard bargain," he sighed. "And now that we're married and all, I could insist on takin' my bed back. With you in it. But I'm a gamblin' man, so I'll take that wager, even though I like my way better. And you'd like it better, too."

She beat him in twelve moves.

He stared down at the perfectly executed trap, dumbfounded, as if he expected to see blood dripping from the vanquished black king.

Julia stood and stretched, then tapped the board with one dainty finger. "You should not feel bad you did not see that coming, Washburn. But just so you know, the knight fork was what finally did you in. Good night! Do not forget to bank the fire," she called cheerily over her shoulder.

Julia closed the bedroom door behind her and laughed to herself when she heard the rueful chuckling from the next room as he put up the chess set.

The queen was indeed the most agile and powerful player on the board.

*   *   *

"When is Brewer coming back with the goods? And how will you transport them out of here?" Julia asked the next morning as she stirred batter for griddle cakes.

"You don't need to worry your pretty lil' head about that." Rand poured himself a cup of coffee. He sighed after the first

115

sip. "I feel like it was almost worth gettin' married, just to have someone make the coffee in the mornin'."

"That's something we need to talk about, Washburn." She poured the batter onto the hot griddle and turned to him for a moment, hand on her hip. She had no idea the picture she presented, warm and rosy from the heat in the kitchen shack. He leaned against the doorframe and took another swallow. She was wearing one of his shirts, the top two buttons undone, and the long sleeves rolled up past her elbows.

"You may have noticed I am wearing one of your shirts this morning."

"Oh yeah," Rand murmured. He'd noticed. Looked like she had two puppies in a sack in there, tusslin' when she moved.

"The reason I am wearing your clothes is because the laundry needs to be done and you have not done it."

That statement took him out of his contemplation of how much fun it would be to undo the rest of the buttons on his shirt and give those pups some air.

"What?"

"I said, you have not done the laundry, Washburn." Julia turned back to the grate to squat down and flip the cakes.

"Yeah, well, that's your job. You're the wife."

She turned her head and looked up at him with raised brows. "Is that what you thought? That because that magistrate pronounced a few words over us I would take over all the domestic chores? Who did your laundry before you had a wife?"

Rand shifted and ran his free hand through his hair. "I did my laundry. But I didn't like it!"

"No one likes it. Here is what I propose... I will continue

with the chores I have been doing, the cooking and tending the garden and keeping the cabin neat. I will even do the mending. But you will do the laundry. After all," she said dryly, "it's not like you have a lot of acreage to plow out there."

"No, but I do have to hunt and fish to keep food on the table. I can't be spendin' all day doin' women's work!"

"If it is women's work, it is not work *this* woman ever did. At the estate where I lived there were laundresses who did the cleaning for the entire household. I can cook better than you can, but it seems to me that if you have experience doing laundry, then you can continue to do a better job than I would. Not to mention that if I am spending all my time doing laundry, then I won't have time to make the pork pie I was planning for dinner. With persimmon cake for dessert."

There was something wrong with this logic, Rand knew it, but he couldn't come up with a good argument. It became even harder to think about it when Julia waltzed past him into the house carrying a plate and leaving behind an aroma of griddle cakes, syrup, and woman.

He retrieved the coffee pot and followed her into the house, brow furrowed. "All right, I'll deal with the laundry. But it will need to be today. Tomorrow we might have company."

"Brewer?"

He grunted and sat down at the table. When he reached for the plate of cakes, a spoon came down sharply across his knuckles.

"Ow! What was that for?"

Julia glared down at him. "Mr. Washburn, while I have every intention of making this mockery of a marriage as temporary as possible, it would still be nice if you observed some of the amenities of polite society while I am here."

Rand cocked his head to the side. "What'd you say?"

She sighed and seated herself. "When a lady comes to the table, a gentleman rises and waits for her to be seated."

"Oh yeah?" Rand said, grabbing the plate before he could get rapped again. "Don't that make it harder for her to serve him his victuals? And do all the men have to rise? 'Cause if not, I can see how you could end up real hungry if they snatch all the ham off the plate while you're bobbin' up and down like a fish float."

She just looked at him and sighed again.

Some perverse devil prodded Rand to continue. "Only people I know like that are those officers durin' the war. Saw some naval officers at a do in St. Augustine, dancin' and carryin' on with the ladies. Oooweee, some a' them boys looked so starched they'd flake into pieces if they moved wrong! I suppose the men in England spend all their time jumpin' up and down waitin' on ladies?" He snickered. "No wonder we kicked their asses outta America. They was too busy observin' amenities to do anythin' worth doin'."

"The men I knew in England were *gentlemen*," Julia said, taking a sip of coffee. "Really, Washburn. You act like you were raised by wolves. Don't you have any family?"

"Not that you need to concern yourself about." He softened as he remembered what brought her to America. "I know you're an orphan, Julia, but believe me, you're better off not meetin' what's left of my family. You wouldn't like them."

He could imagine what his family would make of *her*, and suppressed a shudder at the thought of that meeting.

"Now eat up, gal. I need to go tend to Victoria if I'm goin' to do the laundry."

Her coffee cup paused before it reached her mouth. "Victoria?"

"That's what I call my mule," he lied. He'd just that moment decided on the animal's name. Judging from the way his wife's eyes bulged, he knew it was the correct decision.

"You named your mule after the *queen*?"

"Don't you think she'd be flattered? The queen, that is, not my Victoria. She already feels pretty special."

"Why did you name your mule after the queen?"

"I think it was the way she flicked the flies off her rump that made me think of it. Not the queen, the mule. There was something kinda, I don't know, *regal* and *British* about it. But if you're jealous I'll rename her 'Julia darlin'.' I'd be happy to do that for you."

His darlin' wife just shook her head and went back to her coffee. Rand was rather pleased with himself. It didn't make up for being hoodwinked during a chess match—and sleeping alone—but it was a start.

*   *   *

True to his word, Rand strung a line between two trees, then built up a fire outside and filled the kettle. He stirred the wash stick through the clothes, his and hers together. Julia smiled, wondering if Rand was thinking of his shirt getting more intimacy than he was, rubbing up against her shift in the wash water.

"Here, I brought you a drink from the well."

Rand stepped away from the heat and lye fumes of the kettle

and took the jar from Julia, gulping down the water. He removed his hat and rubbed his forehead, his hair matted to his head. It was a clammy, heavy day and it didn't look like it was going to improve as the sun rose higher.

Julia looked around the farm yard. "You could make a go of this place, Washburn, if you put some effort into it."

"Think so?" He put the hat back on.

"Mmmm. The land is sandy, but there are some crops that would grow here. Sea island cotton would do well, and you could ship it downriver to Jacksonville and sell it out from there. You can grow it on less acreage than short cotton, and you will get a higher price for the crop as the cloth it produces is better quality." She tapped her lips as she thought. "It would take a while, and you would have to hire workers. The workers could also be doing other tasks around the farm, since the cotton can be picked over a period of months, unlike the short cotton—"

She stopped. Washburn was watching her, and she took a small step back, feeling suddenly like she was being sighted down the barrel of a gun.

"Now that's a right interestin' plan," he said softly. "You learn all that waitin' tables at The Greek Boy?"

Her hand rose to her throat. There was no way to explain she'd learned about cotton production at her mother's knee, since Florida cotton was a frequent cargo of Delerue-Sanders Shipping.

"Oh, well, we get cotton planters and factors stopping by the Cup, and you can't help but overhear the conversations while you are waiting on them."

"Uh huh. Like I said, an interestin' plan, but it would take slaves to make it work and I ain't buyin' any."

She looked at him in interest. "You don't hold with slavery, Washburn?"

"Nope," he said, stirring the kettle again. "Too much trouble. You got to make sure your people have shelter, and food, and clothing, and what all, and it's a whole lot of work I don't want to take on. Like I said, I'm happy with being alone out here in the woods." He watched her as he stirred the kettle. "What about you? Good money to be made in buyin' slaves and rentin' them out. Is that what you want?"

The question was casual, but the way he was watching her was not. Julia thought about the slave market in St. Augustine, and shuddered. Her Aunt Suzanne had house slaves and had lived in Florida long enough that she'd become used to the idea, but Julia couldn't stomach it, and neither could her parents. Lady Smithton was active in the anti-slavery society in Britain, inspired partly by the British publication of fellow Floridian Moses Levy's "A Plan for the Abolition of Slavery."

But Julia knew Levy's views were so unpopular back home in Florida that he'd never acknowledged his authorship of the tract, and the Territorial laws discouraged emancipation and rights for freemen. So she picked her words carefully.

"I intend to return to England, as I said, and have no need myself of slaves or the responsibility for them."

Julia paused to wipe her own sleeve across her forehead. It was still morning, but the air pressed down like wet cotton wool, until you felt you couldn't breathe in any more without drowning. Washburn seemed less bothered by the heat, but Julia didn't think she'd ever become accustomed to it.

"Rain's comin'," Washburn said, looking out to the west. "Guess I didn't pick the best day to do the washin', but we can always dry some a' this in the cabin, front of the fire."

Julia helped Rand hang the wash, then he headed out to the woods to do "man's work" as he termed it, checking his traps and bringing back something for their pantry.

The heat worsened as the sun rose to its zenith. The smell in the henhouse was ripe enough to make her head spin when she gathered the eggs, and Julia breathed in small gulps, taking in as little of the fetid atmosphere as possible.

She wanted to be back in England, where the weather now was cool and crisp, autumn as it should be. Tears filled her eyes as she brushed more flies away from the front of her nose.

She wanted her mother.

*　　　*　　　*

When Rand opened the cabin door he spied Julia up on the center of the table, skirt hiked up in her hand.

"Snake!" she whispered, pointing with her shaking free hand to a darkened corner of the cabin.

He dropped his bag and fetched the lamp and the broom. When he raised the lamp and peered into the corner, there was a faint susurrus—a sound like sand falling on the floor. Looking closer, he set down the lamp and broom and said, "C'mon outta there, fella." He crouched down and waved his fingers in front of the snake, and when it coiled to leap he grabbed it behind its head. The snake wrapped itself around his arm, but Rand didn't let go of the snake's head.

He straightened and turned to Julia, the snake clinging to his arm, tongue darting in and out in agitation.

"This ain't nothin' but a corn snake, darlin'. He's likely more scared of you than you are of him." He held the snake up, admiring the red, gold, and brown stripes and chevrons patterning the reptile's body as the snake squirmed in his grasp. "This is a frisky one, too. Bet he could help with those rats in the corn field. C'mon, fella, let's put you to work out back."

When he returned from releasing the snake into a friendlier environment, Julia was still sitting up on the table, cross-legged, staring out the window. Her hair had come undone and was falling down her neck and back in ringlets that clung to her skin, and large circles darkened her blouse under the arms.

"What are you doin' up there?"

"I hate this place. I hate Florida. I hate living where giant beetles fly into your hair and where snakes come into the house. I hate breathing in wet gnats and I hate the mosquitoes and I hate the damp that keeps my clothes sticking to me. I hate that it is autumn and it is still hot enough to raise bread. And I hate you for keeping me here," she finished conversationally.

"Come down," he said, reaching up his arms.

"No. I am going to stay up here until I die, and they will find nothing but my bones in a moldy mound on the table."

He reached up and slid his hands under her skirt, moving them against the tender flesh around her ankles and at the backs of her knees.

"That tickles!"

"Then you'd better come down before you squirm right off. I want to show you somethin'."

"Oh, I bet you do want to show me something, Mr. Washburn!"

"Yeah, that, too. But come down for now and I'll show you somethin' else that's special. You'll like it."

She looked at him and sniffed, but allowed him to lift her off the table and set her down. He took her by the hand and led her down to the creek, telling her to be careful of her bare feet, then he helped her into the boat.

"Where are we going?"

"Trust me, darlin', you'll like it."

She sniffed again. Trusting Washburn was not on the agenda for the day.

He poled up the creek, away from the juncture with the river. The small tributary narrowed and soon they were both ducking under low-hanging cypress and oak branches. She saw a bull gator sunning itself on the bank, lazily watching them go by and ignoring this midday incursion into its domain. When Rand could pole no further, he tied up the boat and jumped into the shallow water, lifting Julia and following the creek down along a sandy strip.

"What is out here? It seems like the middle of nowhere."

"That's what makes it special."

Despite the poling he showed no strain carrying her and since her feet were bare and the ground was rough, she didn't encourage him to put her down. Besides, she rather enjoyed it, though she'd never tell him so.

He walked into a hammock of live oak sprawled out like a dowager who'd loosened her stays and emerged on the other side to a pool fringed by sand and boulders on one side, bushes bright with yellow berries and more oaks and laurels on the other side. Rand carried her past a pair of mossy-backed turtles sunning themselves on a fallen log, over to the boulders and set her down atop one flat as the table she'd stood on earlier. The sun shone hot on the pool, an open patch in the thickness of the woods. The stream they'd followed ran from it, water rushing rapidly through. When she looked over the lip of the boulder into the pool, she saw why.

The water was crystalline and turbulent, gushing up to fill the pool and overflow into the creek. She could see grasses waving on the bottom as if whipped by a heavy wind.

"Does it look shallow?" Rand asked.

"It must be shallow. I can see individual blades of grass on the bottom."

He grinned and taking a rock off the ground, tossed it into the pool. It took a long time to hit the bottom.

"It's deeper than you think. It's the clear water that makes it look shallow. Fools the eye."

"What is it?" Julia asked in fascination.

"It's a spring. Lots of lakes and rivers 'round here start from springs. Why don't you get in? It's shallower over near the sand, but you could jump off here if you want. It's plenty deep enough."

He was already shucking off his boots and undoing his shirt. Julia looked at him and bit her lip. He was going to get naked and go swimming whether she joined him or not. And it did look inviting. Her shirt was sticking to her back, her hair felt like it was plastered to her head in lanky lumps, and she didn't want to think about how long it had been since she'd washed her entire body.

And, as he kept reminding her, they *were* married.

Julia paused in removing her own clothes to watch Rand strip. She'd seen statues in London, brought home to museums and estates from Greece and Rome. He looked like a statue of Apollo she'd particularly admired, long limbed and sculpted with an eye for male beauty.

He dove off the lip of the boulder into the spring, then shot to the surface, tossing his head back and showing her a gleaming mouthful of teeth.

"Quit thinkin' about it and c'mon in, the water's fine and cool."

Julia stopped thinking and finished removing her outer clothes, but left her chemise on. It barely fell past her hips, but even so she felt better having something between herself and his slick, wet body, even if it was just a thin layer of fabric.

She took her own stance on the edge of the spring and dove in, slicing the water with barely a ripple.

When she surfaced, Rand was watching her. "Nice dive, darlin'. Where'd you learn to do that?"

Julia pedaled her feet and moved her hands through the water, working against the power of the springs that wanted to shove her down the creek along with gallons of fresh water.

"Just something I learned when I was young," she said. Her brothers had taught her in self-defense, when she insisted on following them around Rosemoor and getting into the same situations they did.

"Uh huh." He rolled on his back and pushed himself toward the sand, stroking easily through the water. She held on to a branch and found a patch of sand to stand on without getting swept away. Washburn wasn't making a move toward her, and she found herself relaxing, not realizing until that moment how stiffly she'd been holding herself, ready to fend off an attack in the water.

Speaking of attacks in the water…

"Are there alligators here?"

"They like it better where the water's still and they can be undisturbed. Look for them further down the creek."

"I would as soon not, thank you. But I do wish I had some soap with me."

"I can take care of that." He climbed out of the water and walked across the sand to the bushes, the sunlight gilding all of him. He was most definitely more *lifelike* than those Greek statues. One might even say larger than life.

And getting larger.

"Would you stop that!" she snapped out without thinking.

Rand stopped in puzzlement, branches bright with berries broken off in his hands. Then he saw where she was looking, and he had the nerve to grin and scratch himself.

"Darlin', there are some things a man can't help. Itchin' is one of them. The other is sayin' howdy at the sight of a good-lookin' gal. But don't act like you got a poker up your butt now, 'cause I brung you a present."

He jumped back into the water and glided over to her, the foliage in his hands like an olive branch.

"I didn't bring soap, but I got me some soapberries. Here, try 'em."

He showed her how to take the yellow berries and crush them, rubbing them together to make a lather.

"An' if you want, I'll even wash your back for you, and I

hope you'll wash mine."

"No, to both offers, Mr. Washburn. But I thank you for the berries." She gave him a real smile this time, and he paused, the expression on his face changing.

"Julia…"

She knew what he was asking. But it was not a question she was prepared to answer, so she ducked beneath the surface and swam away from him, to the safety of the bank.

CHAPTER 8

Victoria brayed in the yard and Julia paused with her hands in the basin of soapy water. Washburn was gone this morning when she woke, taking the mule with him, and now she felt some of the tension ease out of her shoulders. She didn't believe he'd abandon her but they weren't talking much these days.

Washburn would sit by the fire, whittling or cleaning his guns, and sometimes she'd look up from her mending and see him watching her. She was grateful for the never-ending work—hoeing the garden, preparing their meals, putting up preserves from the extra fruit and vegetables they couldn't eat. She did her chores and went to bed, the chess set in the corner mocking her as she'd take her candle into her empty bedroom. If not for the chores, she knew she'd toss and turn all night, wracked with worry over her family and the troubles at Delerue-Sanders.

And listening for every little noise from the next room.

At first her arguments and retorts were all lined up like cannonballs, ready to fire off when her husband would try to assert his rights. She'd be in the kitchen, stirring soup or kneading dough, thinking about each slicing, scathing response she would give him if he tried to seduce her.

But he didn't try. Oh, he'd still make rude remarks and suggestions, but he didn't push her. Julia frowned as she poured water over her hands and dried them on an old sack, then stepped out onto the breezeway.

There was a dance going on at this isolated farm, a pavane of lies and deceits, half truths and evasions. Despite his insistence that he was her husband, she could not be sure how far he'd go to protect his schemes. Where Brewer might kill her cheerfully, Washburn would kill her with a great deal of regret, but she still feared he'd kill her if she stood between him and his comforts.

He was putting away the mule cart, dirt streaking his forearms where he rolled up his shirtsleeves. More dirt caked his boots, and when she saw the soiled cloth covering what appeared to be a box near the fence, she figured out what he was doing. If Brewer brought the stolen merchandise today, he'd expect to get paid.

Was Washburn a middleman for a larger distributor? What was the source of his gold—capital from previous smuggling operations, or money from someone staking him?

She wasn't particularly bothered by Washburn not trusting her enough to let her know he was off digging up gold this morning. From his point of view, there would be no reason to trust her. She understood that. She didn't trust him, either. But she shuddered, thinking back to the wedding night and Brewer's offer to marry her. Bad as Washburn might be, she'd take him over Brewer any day.

She heated a pan to fry eggs and was whipping up some redeye gravy when she heard steps on the back veranda, the sound of him washing up.

The light dimmed in the kitchen as Washburn blocked the doorway, water dripping off his head and bare chest. He was barefoot and wearing his trousers, his soiled shirt in his hand.

"I brought a couple squirrels for supper, and a possum I'll clean later. Do I have a clean shirt?"

"I borrowed one of your shirts while my clothes were drying, but I folded it and put it back on top of your chest."

He grunted and walked past her into the house, and even though his passing allowed more sunlight to stream into the shack, it seemed colder and darker in his absence.

Washburn returned, pulling the shirt over his head, but paused. When his head popped through, he had a smile on his face, a smile she hadn't seen much of lately. He held his sleeve-clad arm up to his nose and took a long sniff.

"It smells like you," he said, the smile reaching all the way up to his eyes. A stray beam of sunlight danced across his hair, shining threads of gold glinting back at her.

Which brought her back to the day's business, as she shook her head to clear it of his charm and influence. She cracked three eggs into the pan alongside some sizzling ham, and cut a square of cornbread.

"That for me?" He sniffed again, and *she* almost smiled at the thought of how a man's mind could jump from scented ladies to food without missing a beat.

"To tide you over until dinner. From the looks of you and your cargo, I take it Mr. Brewer is coming?"

"Yep, I expect him today, and you don't need to invite him to stay to supper. I want Brewer to unload his cargo and burn the wind leavin'."

He tucked his shirt into his trousers and buttoned himself up, and she turned away from him, annoyed that the sight of a man's unbuttoned trousers could bring heat to her cheeks. He gave her that smirking grin she was coming to despise, and while her hand tightened about the handle of the frying pan, she didn't smash him with it, tempted as she was.

"There is coffee," she said brusquely. "It is not fresh, but it is still hot."

"That's good enough for me, darlin'." Washburn brushed past her into the house. He returned with a cup in each hand, and she took it from him with thanks, adding enough sugar to make the aged drink more palatable. She was learning to drink her coffee without milk, and one thing she fast realized was when coffee was good and fresh, it was very good, but without milk to soften its flaws a bad cup tasted that much worse. She peeled an orange to have with her coffee while Washburn shoveled in the late breakfast.

"I want you to stay in the house while Brewer's here. I don't expect trouble, but I don't believe in lookin' for none neither. I don't know what kind of mood he'll be in when he gets here, if he's been drinkin' or what, so it's best you stay put. And I mean it this time," he said, pointing his fork at her for emphasis.

"Do not worry, Mr. Washburn, I will stay out of your way."

He looked at her, one eyebrow arching upward. "Why is it I worry more when you agree with me than when you're argufyin' with me?"

"I have no desire to try and figure out how your brain functions. You will have to work this one out for yourself. Are you done?"

She rose and took his plate, walking back to the kitchen shack to confront the dead squirrels.

*   *   *

The sun was moving toward noon when Rand heard the jingle of harness and a mule's bray, answered by Victoria in her corral. He was on the porch in the rocking chair, his knife and a chunk of sweetgum in his hand, a small mound of shavings curling around the rocker. Despite the midday heat he had his coat on. He folded his knife and with a final, "Stay here," over his shoulder, stepped out into the yard to meet the smugglers.

Brewer came through the woods with a couple of men driving the two-wheeled mule carts useful for navigating through the tough brush. The carts were piled high with bales and boxes and the mules looked longingly at Victoria's trough, but Brewer made no move to care for his livestock.

"I brung ya the merchandise, Washburn," Brewer said, spitting tobacco juice at a skink scuttling across the yard. He missed. "Where's that pretty wife of your'n? You decide to keep her, or did she have an accident out on the river when you was done with her?"

"Let's see the goods," Rand said. He was standing casually, his legs apart and hands in his coat pockets. A noise from the cabin distracted him, but when he looked over his shoulder there was no one there. For once that girl was doing as she was told and staying put.

"I got it all. The silks should do you real good. Last I hear, cotton was shippin' for two dollars a bale and selling for ten up in Boston, and the silk's doin' even better. But before I tell the boys to unload, let's see the color of your money."

Rand watched Brewer's face a moment more, then turned and fetched the chest from the veranda. He set it at his feet, opened it, and showed Brewer its contents, then shoved his hands back in his coat pockets.

"There it is, and no banknotes, just as you said."

"Mighty nice." Brewer wiped his hand across his mouth. His small eyes narrowed even more as he looked back at Rand and his lips pulled back from his broken teeth.

"Seems to me, Washburn, that mebbe I don't need you after all. I thank you for the gold, and I can take it and the goods back to St. Augustine and sell it my ownself."

Rand smiled at the smuggler. "I got a nice double action Allen pepperbox here in my pocket. Now, it could go off all at once and blow a hole the size of Pensacola through your guts, or I could shoot you down and still have enough left for your men there. Though I got to tell you square, Brewer, this beauty and I saw a lot of service durin' the war and she was real reliable. It's your call how you want to play this out."

Brewer sniggered. "I got an ace up my sleeve, Washburn." He looked over Rand's shoulder. "Jeb! Fetch that gal outta the cabin!"

He kept his eyes on Brewer, but heard a man's voice behind him. "She ain't here, Dan'l!"

Brewer frowned, but kept *his* eyes on Rand.

"You keep your gun aimed at the back of ol' Washburn here, Jeb. Smiley, you check the privy and down at the creek. Find that gal and haul her up here. And, Jeb, if Washburn tries anythin', do him in!"

"I would not do that, Mr. Brewer."

Rand was almost as startled as Brewer as he heard Julia's voice coming from somewhere above him. They both turned around and spotted the top of her curly hair, and the barrel of his rifle, poking over the cabin roof.

"The view from up here is excellent, gentlemen. Mr. Brewer, please tell your man sneaking around the back of the cabin that if he does not join you at once, I will blow your head off. And I will shoot your men next. I assure you, I can reload faster than they can run."

"Big talk, gal! I got Jeb here with a gun aimed at Washburn's head. If you don't come down, I'm goin' to kill him!"

"Oh, would you, please? You kill Washburn, I pick off you and your men, and I leave this pesthole a wealthy widow. It sounds like a good plan to me. But if you do not like that plan, you do as *I* say and you leave here alive."

Brewer looked at him and Rand scratched his chin to hide his grin, though he wasn't a hundred percent sure Julia didn't mean every word she said.

"That woman's crazy as a coot and mean as a rabid raccoon, Brewer. Mean enough to shoot you down for the fun of it. Hell, I *know* she'd enjoy shootin' me! From here it looks like you're ten feet above the high-water mark on dry land, 'less you do what she says."

Brewer's eyes grew wide and he nearly swallowed his wad of tobacco.

"Don't shoot, Miz Washburn! I was jus' funnin' old Rand here!" He looked back at him and whispered, "Dang, boy, I'm sure glad you married that woman 'stead o' me!"

"Yeah, I sleep with one eye open. You'd best water the mules and get yourself outta here."

"You said it, cousin. Jeb! Smiley! Get this unloaded!"

"Have them put it on the veranda, Mr. Brewer, but you stay

right where you are," a call came down from on high.

"Yes, ma'am. You heard Miz Washburn, get to it!"

The men made short work of piling the haul at the cabin, loaded the chest onto one of the carts, gave the mules and themselves a drink from the trough, and turned back for the woods.

"Brewer!" Rand called out as the smuggler was leaving.

"Yeah?"

"Tell your....supplier...there's more where this came from. But next time, I want to meet with him personal. I ain't happy with how this went today, and I want to make sure there are no misunderstandin's next time. You hear me?"

Brewer looked at him and spat some juice to the side, then scratched his nose stump. "I hear ya. I'll be in touch."

"Good-bye, Mr. Brewer!" came the call from the roof.

Brewer just looked up, squinting at the figure backlit by the sun and spat again before heading into the brush.

Rand watched until they were well away, then looked up at the roof himself. He couldn't see Julia, so he walked around to the back of the cabin where there were boxes piled on barrels to make an impromptu staircase. A pair of slender ankles and dirty bare toes appeared over the side of the roof and there was some rewarding butt-wiggling as his wife backed down and sought her footing on the precarious perch.

"Don't worry, darlin', I'm here and I'll catch you. You can let go."

The wiggling stopped and she levered herself over and up, sitting with her legs dangling off the edge. Her hair had escaped from its tie, the curls breaking free to fall with abandon around her face and neck. Julia brushed some hair off her forehead and paused to look out back of the cabin, her hand shading her eyes from the midday sun.

"It is a nice view up here."

"It's nice from down here, too," he said, admiring the trim ankles and rounded toes. "Would you have shot Brewer and his friends?"

"Of course," she said calmly. "They were going to rob you and kill you in the bargain. I don't imagine they would have left me as a witness either. I was tempted to eliminate them anyway so we could keep the gold and the goods, but I was afraid you would be killed in the fracas and I would have a difficult time disposing of the silks and coffee on my own."

Maybe he'd spoken more truth than he knew when he told Brewer about sleeping with one eye open.

"I can see the creek from here. Why don't you get the ladder instead of me jumping down?"

"Now that wouldn't be near as much fun for me, would it?"

"Do not make me use this rifle, Washburn."

"I suppose you learned to handle that rifle at that English estate where your mama worked?" he drawled.

"No, my Uncle Richard taught me."

"And you've become an expert shot in these past months?"

"Care to find out?"

"Aw, I don't believe you would shoot me. But why don't you pass that rifle on down so I can put it away for safekeepin'?"

She just smiled at that, but passed him down the rifle and shot bag. He put them up and came back to where she sat, swinging her legs.

"No ladder? How can I be sure you will not let me fall?"

"You're going to have to trust me, Julia."

She looked down at him and stopped swinging her legs. "I cannot trust you. And you do not trust me."

He opened his arms and waited, and she looked down at him, into his eyes, her own dark and serious, then launched herself off into the air.

He caught her and she slid down his body until her feet were on the ground. Without her shoes she had to tilt her head back to look up at him. "You can let go of me now."

He could, but she still had her arms around his neck where she'd grabbed on, and he still had his hands resting on that rounded bottom, so instead of letting her go, he pulled her closer until they were so tight against each other a piece of paper would've had problems slipping between them.

She was all sun-warmed and soft and fit in his arms like she'd been made for him.

"I didn't thank you for savin' my life, darlin'," he said huskily, showing his gratitude in the most natural way he knew how. He lowered his head to hers, his lips moving across her mouth, lulling her lips into openness, anxious to taste all that sweetness she kept inside her prickly shell.

Instead of pulling away, she tightened her arms around him and kissed him back, and when his tongue made a foray between her luscious lips, she opened for him, a slight moan of acquiescence signaling her approval of this maneuver. A lifetime later she broke off, her eyes dazed and dark as she looked up at him, her lips red and moist.

"Dang," she whispered, and pulled his head back down.

He moved her back against the wall of the cabin, bracing her there without breaking that endless kiss, a kiss that tasted like oranges, and honey, and Julia. He moved slowly, languidly, knowing now that she was inexperienced. A rush of possessive satisfaction flared through him. No matter what else she was, or had been, or what she planned to be, she was new to the ways of love and there was so much he could teach her, would teach her, because right now in this place, she belonged to him. She was Rand Washburn's woman, and he was going to show her how good that could be.

*   *   *

Julia was confused. Hot and confused. Burning hot and confused about why her arms were tightening around Rand Washburn, and why his tongue was inside her mouth, and why it felt better than just about anything she'd ever felt before. Ever since she'd climbed up on the roof and hauled the rifle up after her, she'd felt the blood racing through her, all her senses heightened by the danger. And now when it was over, instead of thinking rationally of all those wonderful reasons why she should be slapping his face, and all those wonderful lines she'd prepared for when he'd force his attentions on her, she was trying to swallow his tongue and taste all of his mouth and absorb the scent and feel of him—his hard muscles, the rasp of his whiskers against her chin, the silky feel of light-kissed hair she clutched in her two hands.

It should frighten her, alone out in the woods with a man who clearly meant her no good, but at this instant of time all that seemed important was Washburn's lips, and how they felt on hers, and his mouth, its beautiful shape molding to hers as if they were two halves of a whole finally brought together, and the strength of his sinewy arms, wrapping around her and pulling her up against his length.

He was everything she'd ever been warned about, and at that moment, everything she'd ever wanted. She wanted to feel his weight on top of her, she wanted to feel his arms banding her, she wanted to wrap her legs around him and take him inside her, where she could feel the pulse pounding deep, deep inside that untouched softness that made her want to press against him, grind against him. And then thought was action, and he moaned and pinned her to the cabin wall, his hips thrusting at her through her skirts, letting her feel how much he wanted her.

The wanting was a sweet madness that drove her to spread her legs wider, cradling him and rocking up against him, her hands moving down to his hips to pull him even tighter, trying to ease that ache that kept growing as his hands moved down to her breasts.

"I knew you'd come around," he muttered thickly as his lips moved down her neck.

Julia froze, his words breaking the spell. What was she doing, out in the middle of nowhere with this Cracker smuggler? Where was the cool Lady Julia Delerue who'd eased her way out of so many inappropriate or distasteful encounters with gentlemen in England?

This is different. You want this.

She shook her head to clear it, and pushed against Washburn's chest. "No."

He went rock still, but pulled his mouth away, moved his hands off her breasts, and leaned his forehead against the wall.

He braced his arms alongside her, his head next to hers, and she heard his breath coming in like a bellows working.

Julia stared up at him as he turned toward her. Rand's eyes were jet circled by jade and a muscle worked at the corner of his jaw. In that instant she was as frightened of him as she had ever been, but she took a deep rush of air and shook her head again.

"No."

He pushed himself off of her and she leaned back against the rough logs, otherwise she would have puddled down to the ground on legs that wouldn't support her. Her hand came up and touched her own swollen lips.

"It is because of the danger," she whispered. "Brewer and his men. I have heard that when you have been in danger, or in battle, and you survive, all you want to do afterward is prove that you are still alive. That is all this is, a reaction to the danger. You don't want me, you are only reacting to what happened."

He grabbed her hand and pulled it up against his groin. If he'd been any harder, she'd have thought he'd stashed the pepperbox in there. And from the feel of it, it was primed to fire off all barrels.

"Does *that* feel like I don't want you?" he snarled. "There's a lot of things a man can pretend, but this ain't one of 'em. Believe me, *darlin'*, all I want to do is throw you down on the ground and bury myself so deep inside you they won't be able to separate us with a crowbar!"

She swallowed, his hot words bringing an answering rush of heat from inside her body. But she shook her head again.

"You don't want *me*, Washburn. Right now you want any woman who's handy. I happen to be the one who's around. You are the one who said your body is merely reacting to a good-lookin' gal."

He stared at her with eyes that burned like green fire. "Are you so sure of that? You can crawl inside my head and tell me what I'm thinkin' right now?"

She nodded. "I am sure," she said in a low voice. "I am sure because of the way I responded…it is just a reaction to the events. It is not about us."

"Huh. So what you're sayin', and let me make sure I understand this, is that a minute ago when you was tryin' to climb all over me like a vine all over a porch, and rubbin' up against me like a dog with an itch that won't quit, it wasn't *me* you wanted, I just happened to be handy. So to speak."

"Yes."

"You would'a done the same thing with, say, Frank Ivey?"

"Y—No!"

"So you wouldn't be shovin' your tongue into *his* mouth like you was diggin' for gold?"

Julia drew herself up and straightened her shirt. "I do not have to stand here and listen to your crude talk. I have dinner to get on."

Washburn said something rude under his breath and spun on his heel, headed away from the cabin.

"Where are you going? Dinner will be ready soon."

"Hang dinner," he yelled back over his shoulder. "I'm goin' to go take a dip in the creek."

"The water will be freezing!" she called out.

"That's what I'm countin' on!"

*   *   *

When Washburn returned, he seemed in better spirits as Julia dished up the squirrel stew and greens.

"There are times when I'm out checkin' traps, and you'll be here alone at the farm," Washburn said as he chased the last of the stew out of his bowl with a chunk of hot corn pone. He popped it into his mouth and swallowed. "You sure do have a way with squirrels. That was mighty tasty. Anyways, I want to be sure you can handle that rifle, and the pistol, too. After we get this cleared up, let's go out into the yard and you can show me what you know."

"Then will you show me what is in the crates Brewer brought?"

Washburn frowned. "I'll show you, but it's not for us. Maybe I'll keep a bottle of the brandy, but the rest of it will do more good bein' sold than stayin' here."

"How will you get it away from the farm?" Julia asked, propping her chin on her hand.

"There are some men comin' in a few days. And I don't want you shootin' any of 'em," he added dryly.

They moved out into the yard in the late afternoon, the sun slipping far enough behind the trees to give some relief from the muggy heat. It was past the season where it rained each afternoon, but the days still felt liquid as the autumn grew into a pattern of weather that would be warm, then hot, then hotter and humid, until a thunderstorm would roll through dropping the temperatures and bringing crisp air in its wake for a few days, and the cycle would begin all over again.

A jay hollered from a branch overhead as Washburn pulled some gourds from the garden and set them along the fence. Julia was standing across the yard with the rifle cradled in her arms and Washburn headed back toward her, taking his hat from his head and wiping the sweat off his forehead.

"Now, this rifle ain't fancy, but it does the job. It's a common rifle..."

He droned on, and Julia watched with what she hoped was an interested expression. She'd had an eclectic education for a young English lady, growing up with parents who felt women should know how to use a variety of weapons, and from her uncle, who'd started teaching her to fire a rifle when she was eleven years old. This was a .54 caliber flintlock, likely from Derringer's in Philadelphia, or one of the Connecticut foundries. It was a rifle she'd shot before, being Uncle Richard's favorite, though he also kept a Hall breechloader out at the Cup.

But when Washburn pulled the next weapon out of his bag, she showed real interest.

"Is that one of the Colt revolvers?"

He looked at her. "How'd you know that, darlin'? I imagine there ain't too many Colts floatin' around English manors."

You'd be surprised, Julia thought, annoyed at letting the knowledge show, but raised her voice and said, "I heard about it at Ganymede's Cup, and having an interest in firearms, I remembered the discussion."

Washburn grunted. "You're right, it's one of Mr. Colt's. A .34 caliber Patterson, to be exact, five shots in a revolvin' breech."

"I'm surprised you don't carry it instead of the Allen," Julia said. "Surely it weighs less?"

"It does." Washburn chuckled. "And it's less wearin' on my

pockets. Maybe that's why they call this one the pocket revolver. But like I told Brewer, the pepperbox and I go back a ways and I'm right fond of it. Know its quirks and all. But if you can handle this Colt, I'll leave it with you when I'm not around. Let's see what you can do with the rifle first."

He stepped back behind her and Julia examined the flintlock. Washburn kept all his weapons in top shape and this one shone with the care and handling it received. She took the ammunition bag and slung it over her shoulder, positioning it for easy access to reload.

Then she demolished some gourds, exploding them in short order.

Washburn whistled through his teeth. "Not bad, not bad at all. I've seen men who can load faster, soldiers mostly, but I've seen few who can match you for accuracy. You weren't bluffin' when you were aimin' at Brewer."

"I do not bluff, Washburn." Julia flexed her hand and blew cool air on the heel, stinging from where she'd rammed the ball and patch into the rifle.

"Here, let me see."

Before she could protest Rand took her hand in his and traced the red marks with one long finger. Then he raised her hand up to his mouth and kissed the red area so softly it felt like a hummingbird had brushed against it.

Julia yanked her hand back and nearly fell off balance.

"What was that?"

"I was kissin' it to make it feel better."

"You do not give up, do you? I have told you, repeatedly, I am not interested in playing games with you!"

"We been playin' games from the moment I found you in my shed," Washburn said with an easy smile that didn't reach his eyes. "I'm tryin' to figure out what the rules are with this game here. After all, you did offer to shoot me today, along with Daniel Brewer and his men."

Julia looked at the scraps of gourds on the ground. Moments ago they'd been whole, now they were shattered beyond repair.

"I don't know how this is going to work itself out, Washburn, but we are bound together until we can free ourselves from this entanglement. In the meantime, I will guard your back. I owe you that much for saving me from Brewer the other night."

He watched her with an intent expression that convinced her there was more in his head than eating, bothering her, and smuggling.

But all he said was, "You want to do the pistols another day?"

She went along with the conversational switch.

"No, let's get this done now. Besides, it's good for me to get a feel for your firearms."

After she cleaned and put up the guns, Julia retired to the house but found herself drifting from the kitchen to the front. The boxes on the veranda seemed to call to her, especially the ones with the Delerue-Sanders markings on the side.

She went to the front doorway, but a voice floated over from the mule's corral, "Leave those boxes alone. We'll move them into the house in case it rains, but don't go messin' with them."

Sure enough, Washburn washed up and with her assistance moved the parcels in the late afternoon. The days were shorter now, not like a winter day up north where darkness came midafternoon, but even in Florida the change of seasons could be felt and seen in the changing light.

Acorns rained down on them as they worked and squirrels raced around gathering up nuts. The pecans were plentiful enough that there was a constant supply of tarts and nut-filled biscuits, pecan dressings, and some for cracking and eating in the cool of the evening.

Maybe a pecan-persimmon tart would be good, Julia thought, and then stopped. It seemed like all she did these days was cook and take care of the cabin. Well, and fend off armed smugglers, but she hoped that wouldn't be a common occurrence. When was the last time she'd seen a newspaper, or picked up a book, or paged through a journal? Isolated out here at the farm, it was easy to forget there was a much larger world out there, a world where nations went to war, sometimes over seemingly small issues. She needed to stay focused on her goal, the goal of uncovering who was smuggling her family's goods.

And then what? The little voice in her head nagged at her. What would become of Washburn when this was done? Would he have to give her a divorce from his prison cell? Would she go back to England and slip into her old routine of balls and luncheons and shopping and house parties in the country?

Somehow she didn't think it would be that easy.

CHAPTER 9

After supper Washburn cracked open a bottle of the smuggled brandy and poured them each a cup, then went through the bales and packages checking them against his list. There were luscious silks and more brandy and huge bags of salt. But when he uncovered a metal box wedged inside a bag of coffee, his eyes lit up.

"There you are!" he muttered, and Julia looked up from the silk she was caressing, thinking he'd talked to her.

Washburn caught her movement and looked at her, an arrested expression on his face. But then he sat back, and she could tell from the slight glitter to his green eyes that the brandy was relaxing him.

"What is that?"

"I'm not sure, darlin'," he said, watching her. He seemed to be expecting her to react at the sight of the box. When she didn't, he opened the lid and whistled.

Inside were banknotes, bundled and new looking.

"Dear Lord!" Julia breathed. "Did you know that money was in there?"

Washburn said nothing, a smile turning up the corners of his mouth. He broke the seal and took out one of the banknotes, holding it up to the lamp to examine it. Julia didn't recognize it, which wasn't unusual. Five years ago there were over thirty thousand varieties of notes in circulation in America, issued by state banks and private institutions. She'd heard some of her aunt's friends discussing the failure of the Union Bank in Tallahassee, and the Panic of '37, how land speculation and shady bond deals brought ruin to investors left holding worthless bits of paper.

"I suspect this banknote's not worth a Continental."

She looked at him quizzically.

"It's an old American expression datin' from the war of independence. So much paper money was printed by the new American government without anythin' to back it, the notes issued by the Continental Congress were considered useless, 'not worth a Continental.' Now, let me ask you a question. Is this money?"

"Yes, of course it is."

"How do you know? It's a piece of paper. You believe it's money, because you believe there's gold behind it, right? If people stop believin' that this piece of paper is money, then this note don't buy what it did last week. It's worthless paper, like a Continental. If you got more paper in circulation than there's gold to back it, then the paper is seen as worth less. Or worthless. So why use paper at all?"

He was looking at her like a teacher waiting for a promising pupil to supply the answer and Julia found, to her surprise, she was enjoying the discussion. In all the time she'd spent working with Delerue-Sanders and listening to her parents talk business, she'd never thought about the properties of the money they handled.

"You can use coin for some amounts, but if you were

spending a great deal of money you might not want to carry around that much specie," she said slowly as she thought. "Gold and silver are heavy, and obvious."

"That's right. What you want to do is keep your gold and silver somewhere safe and get a piece of paper that you can pass on, that represents your gold and silver. But the person receivin' that paper has to believe it's worth what it says on its face. Now, our friend Brewer, he don't want to take banknotes 'cause he trusts what he can see and shove in his pockets. But other folks like banknotes just fine, long as they believe in them."

"What about those banknotes?" Julia asked. "Do you know the bank that issued them? And why were they hidden inside that bag of coffee?"

"All excellent questions." Washburn poured her some brandy. He looked down inside his own cup and without looking at her said, "I'd like to know those answers my ownself. The coffee was part of the haul from Delerue-Sanders. An English company. Now, why would English shippers be hidin' American banknotes inside a bag of coffee?"

Julia was dying to know the answer to that herself. Whatever was going on with the altered manifests and missing cargo, it looked bigger than some occasional pilferage. And what was Washburn's stake in this? He seemed to know a lot about the properties of money for a piney backwoodsman.

"Delerue-Sanders? Are they a large company?"

He shrugged. "Large enough. Some English lord owns it, though I hear the Sanders part came from an American he married.

"You're English, darlin'. Y'ever meet these folks while you

was growin' up on that fancy estate?"

Julia swallowed, and hoped the sweat trickling past her ear couldn't be seen in the dim light.

"England's a big place, Washburn. I do not believe I ever crossed paths with the owners of this company."

"England's a big place all right, but not as big as it would like to be. Couple a years back they was all fired up over there 'bout Canada rebellin' and the U.S. givin' them an assist. There was English ships burned on the border lakes, and it looked like war all over again."

Julia knew this, but didn't let on to Washburn, keeping a polite look on her face. The brandy made him garrulous and she wanted to keep this narrative going, to find out as much as she could about her smuggler husband. He didn't need to know Lord Ashburton had been a guest in her parents' home, and the state of affairs between the two nations was of acute interest to the Anglo-American owners of Delerue-Sanders Shipping.

"Down here we was havin' our own problems with you Brits."

Washburn examined the brandy in the light of the lamp and took a reverent sip.

"Dang, that's smooth. Anyways, while Dan'l Webster and that Lord Ashburton was discussin' Canada, the Georgians were all in a hissy fit because England built up its colored troops in the West Indies. Those Georgians and South Carolinians and Louisiana folks was sure they'd wake up one mornin' and find black regiments from Jamaica camped on their doorstep, tellin' their slaves they was free if they'd throw their lot in with England."

"Could England invade the southern United States that easily?" Julia asked with real interest.

"The navy thinks so. Or at least that's what they've been sayin' to the southern politicians, who are now behind fundin' them. The navy secretary says over half the United States trade passes through the Gulf of Mexico, and the Gulf of Florida could be blocked by two steam frigates. The British navy has a couple of new steam warships with a shallow draft that would do the job nicely."

He grinned. "I think what convinced them was when Mr. Upshur said the only question that needed to be asked, was whether the United States wanted to meet the enemy on the ocean, or landing upon our shores? That woke those Washington layabouts up and got them movin'…and diggin' into the public coffers to improve the navy. But as usual, those poor boys in the Cutter Service was left behind, makin' life easier for you and me." He hoisted his glass in her direction.

"You mean the Revenue Marine?"

"Cutter Service, Revenue Marine, it's all the same. They can't even decide on a uniform, much less a name for themselves. They ain't got a regular station between Savannah and Key West, and that leaves an awful lot of Florida coastline unwatched."

"But the threat of war with England is past! Even I know that Sir Robert Peel has been working to maintain more cordial relations between the two nations."

"Well, now, if that's so," said Washburn softly, "then why is some English lord and ship owner bringin' in counterfeit banknotes, which are sure as hell goin' to stir up a hornet's nest of trouble?"

She didn't know the answer to that, but she knew there were some hard-line politicians in England who still saw the United States, or parts of it, as territory to be regained. Sir Edmund Whitehead was one of the most vocal in this camp, insisting that a strong Canada and a British presence on the American continent would help check the growth of a potential economic and military rival.

"What do you think I should do, Julia? Should I keep the banknotes?"

His idle question brought her back to the current crisis. He watched her, gauging her reaction, and she chewed at her lip. She knew what Lady Julia would say. But that person wasn't in this cabin tonight. Not if Julia Cooper wanted to stay alive.

"Keep them. Brewer didn't know they were in there, otherwise he would have made mention of them. As far as I can see, it is found money in every sense of the word. And if they look to be real, you should have no trouble passing them off."

"Whether or not they are real banknotes?"

"If they are good enough, you can pass them on."

"That's what I expected you to say, darlin'," he drawled and Julia turned her face away from the light so he wouldn't see her flush of shame at being taken for a liar and a counterfeiter and a thief. Even by one such as him.

She stood and headed for the bedroom, pulling her shawl close around her, though it wasn't cold in the cabin.

"Good night, Mrs. Washburn."

Julia stopped at the doorway and turned. He was watching her, but she couldn't read his impassive face as he sat there surrounded by the stolen goods.

She said nothing as she closed the door behind her.

*   *   *

It was the yelling that woke her, again.

"The children! Don't shoot!"

Julia pulled her wrapper off the bed and tiptoed to the front room, navigating around the stacked bales. His pallet was near the door as he slept guard over the goods, but in the glow from the low fire she could see him moving, twitching in his nightmare.

She knew better now than to wake him by touching him, so she called sharply, "Rand! Wake up! Wake up this instant!"

He jerked awake and stared at the beams overhead, sweat covering his face and neck. Julia walked over to the bottle of brandy left on the table and poured out a measure for him, and some for herself, too.

She knelt beside his pallet and held the cup out. "Sit up and drink this. You were dreaming again."

He blinked up at the ceiling again, and a shudder wracked his body.

"Rand!"

"I'm awake," he said hoarsely and sat up, his head in his hands.

Julia sat cross-legged alongside him as he rubbed his eyes.

"I'm awake," he said again. "Go back to bed."

"No."

He turned his head, and Julia took a sip of her own brandy, hoping he couldn't see the slight tremor in her hand. She remembered the last time he woke yelling.

154

"I am not leaving. Tell me about your nightmares."

He looked away from her, staring at the fire. "Go back to bed, Julia."

"No," she said again. "And do not try to fob me off, or distract me with your feeble attempts at seduction."

As she'd suspected, this brought him around, the corners of his mouth bracketing.

"Now, that hurts. No one's ever called my courtin' feeble."

"They weren't bound to you in marriage. I am serious, Rand. I will not leave until you tell me why you have nightmares."

"You called me Rand," he said. "When you're angry it's always 'Washburn' this, and 'Mr. Washburn' that, but when you're bein' sweet, it's 'Rand.'"

Julia frowned. She'd think about the implications of that later, for now there were more important issues.

"Tell me," she said implacably.

"I don't know any entertainin' bedtime stories," he said, looking down at the cup he turned 'round in his hands.

She leaned forward and put her hand on his arm, stilling his motion. He felt as tense beneath her fingers as a cable drawn taut and ready to snap.

"Your nightmares are hurting you. If you talk about them, it may ease your sleep. And I am a good listener," she said softly. "Why do you cry out that children are being shot?"

He sat still so long she thought he would not answer, but she said nothing more. Soon he started speaking, his low voice carrying in the quiet of the cabin.

"It was durin' the war. There was this Dr. Motte who said Florida was 'a perfect paradise for Indians, alligators, frogs, and loathsome reptiles' and he couldn't understand why in the name of common sense we just didn't let the Indians keep it. Most days I thought he was a right smart fella for sayin' that.

"Seven years we spent bleedin' and dyin', more from dysentery and fever than bullets, but men have to have land, and the Indians were in the way, raidin' farms and keepin' crops from bein' planted. So the government made promises, and broke promises, and made more promises, but by the time Major Dade and his troops was massacred, we knew there would be no peace for the Indian if he stayed in Florida.

"They wasn't particular who served in the volunteer militia, long as you could fire a gun. Militia, soldiers, sailors—everyone was brought in to drive the Seminole from Florida. But it was almost as if the land itself tried to keep us out. Down in the southern swamps, the saw grass cut our legs like razors, tearin' through our clothes. It was either too wet to walk, or too dry for boats."

He took another drink, then looked down at his hands holding the cup.

"But you stayed," Julia said.

"We stayed. We had orders to 'harass and terrify' the savages, and we did follow orders. Even when those orders got confusin'. You had the army, the navy, the marines, and the Revenue Marine, all thinkin' they knew what they was doin', and none of them talkin' to each other, and no one with a strategy worth a damn. The navy would send in gunboats to fire on villages on the coast, and the Indians would pick up and move further back into the swamps. Some of them are still there, bidin' their time, waitin' for us to pack up and leave.

"If that wasn't enough, the Spanish from Cuba was smugglin' arms to the Indians, the British was off the coast raisin' black regiments in the Indies and scarin' landowners with fears of a slave revolt, and it was just one damn thing after another.

"One night, we was sent to the Withlacoochee to bring in some Seminoles so they could be transported west. This group included runaway slaves, and slaves owned by Indians, and free negroes, and maroons who was mixed black and red, all livin' together. Major General Jesup stirred up a hornet's nest when he said Seminoles and their property, their negroes, could all go west. But blacks taken in war who didn't freely come in for relocation, they didn't have those protections."

He stared at the fire.

"It was hot that night, the mosquitoes so thick you could swing a cup and catch a quart, and we caught the Seminole by surprise. The warriors surrendered right away 'cause the camp was full of women and children. The women was screamin', the children was cryin', and a couple of the Georgia Volunteers saw this as a great opportunity. They killed the warriors after they surrendered, then told the commandin' officer the women and children must be escaped slaves and besides, since they hadn't come in of their own will they had no protection under General Jesup's rules.

"The commandin' officer saw the reasonin' behind this, and told those Georgia boys they could do what they wanted."

"Didn't anyone protest?"

"You mean besides the women and children wailin' for their dead? Yeah, one youngster protested, but he was outranked, and he was from Boston, so those Georgia boys didn't pay him no mind. This was back in '37, a couple years after the war was underway. Those scruples got whupped out of 'em after a few years in the swamps."

"Did the war change you?"

"War changes everyone," he said flatly. "You don't forget what you see, or what you did."

Rand took another drink.

"The women, some of them *had* been slaves. They told the children to run into the woods, and the older ones started runnin', and the women grabbed the little ones and started runnin', too."

She felt the words hovering over them, pressing down like a swamp miasma. "What happened?"

He turned his head, and she knew looking at her while he spoke was one of the hardest things he'd ever done.

"The men opened fire to make sure those dangerous negroes and Seminoles didn't get away."

She swallowed the nausea rising in her throat. The silence stretched between them until he said, "Aren't you goin' to ask me what I did?"

"I think in your own way you are a man of great honor, Rand."

"Honor is one of the first casualties of war. Along with truth."

Staring into those haunted eyes and not flinching from what she saw there was one of the hardest things *she'd* ever done. But no matter what lies lay between them, he deserved the truth from her now.

"No. No, Rand Washburn, I do not believe you shot down fleeing women and children."

Rand watched her, and his eyes caught a gleam from the firelight, flashing like a panther's in the dark. "I should not have told you about this. I have never talked about that night to anyone. Never."

"That is likely the reason why you have nightmares. When you confront the things that frighten you in the dark, they lose their power over you."

Time slowed in the silence broken by the call of peeper frogs out in the night. He set down his cup and reached forward and took hold of her hair, his fingers sifting through the curls around her face.

"What about you, Julia? What frightens you in the dark?"

He was frightening her. Frightening her with the power he had to make her body react, to yearn toward him. To forget who she was, and what he was.

"So soft," he murmured, tracing his finger across her brow, down past eyes that dipped half shut, to lips that parted without volition. Julia leaned into that touch, the heat rising from his bare chest, the tang of the sweat drying on his skin.

"Rand," she whispered, but didn't know what she would have said, for his mouth covered hers, cutting off all speech. It was a gentle assault against her defenses, a skirmish that breached her barricades and caught her off guard. The more the sensations flowed through her, the more she realized this was what she'd wanted all along, this exploration of the senses, the darkness pressing in around them, the smell of the smuggled spices and brandy seasoning the tension because even now, she knew, she knew she shouldn't be doing this.

And she didn't care.

Lady Julia Anne Sanders Delerue had been searching for something more than the conventions and hidebound rules of London society, and she found it in the arms of a Cracker smuggler, a man whose rough hands made her nerves sing, whose bristled face scraped at her tender skin as his kisses moved down along her throat, bringing the blood flowing to the surface, heating her in places untouched.

Rand laid her back on his pallet, brushing her hair out around her face, framing it as he stared down into her eyes. His hair fell around his head, shadowing him, making him appear even more alien in the dying firelight because she couldn't see his expression, but she could read it in the tension of his body above her.

"Lord, Julia, you are so beautiful," he said, and leaned down to place a tender kiss on the corner of her mouth. She made a small noise in the back of her throat and he kissed her on the pulse that beat there, even as his fingers undid the buttons of her nightgown.

She closed her eyes when Rand opened the cloth. He did nothing at first, then she felt a touch, light as a leaf falling past her, as his fingers traced the curve of her breast, stroking in from her ribs, so delicately. She sighed and relaxed, letting the touch flow over her skin, warming her and fanning the embers that had been smoldering inside her for so very long.

He was touching her body the way he talked, slow and easy, unrushed, because what was the point of rushing when the nights were warm and long, the air heavy and moist with the evening mists?

She tentatively raised her own hand to touch his bare chest

and he stopped, and she looked up and saw the flash of his teeth in the dark.

"You go right ahead, darlin'. It's all yours."

He settled himself next to her, his head propped on his arm and he held still as her hands roamed over his shoulders, up his corded neck, through the unruly hair that fell past his brow. Her fingertips skimmed down his throat and he made a sound as her roving hands moved lower, across the light hair sprinkling him, but when her fingers grazed the nipples standing up off the muscles of that hard chest, he swore and grabbed her hands, his grip hot.

"My turn, now. Too much of that and we're goin' to be done too soon."

He held her hands in one of his, and with the other he covered her breast, rubbing his thumb across the rigid tip, and her back arched off the pallet.

"Like that? You'll love this," he said thickly before his head blocked the light and he took her nipple into his mouth, sucking deeply while he released his grip on her so he could busy his hand on her other breast.

Julia closed her eyes again because it was more than she could bear, the tug of his mouth echoing in the tug of sensation deep in her womb. All of her body was connected to that bundle of nerves he laved with his tongue, sometimes rough, sometimes smooth, but always escalating the sensation.

"Sit up."

Blinking, she pushed back with her hands to comply. Rand was now astride her legs, and he grabbed the nightgown rucked around her hips and pulled it over her head, covering her mouth with his, and wrapping his arms around her as he lowered her back to the pallet. He was nude and she felt him, the length of him throbbing against her mound and belly, but her legs were trapped between his, and when she tried to move he tightened them, trapping her further.

"Be still," he ordered. "Tonight it will be *my* way, no fightin', no backchat."

She opened her mouth to protest this high-handed treatment, but before she could say anything he was kissing her again, deeper this time, more urgency, more need evident in every move. After a moment it didn't matter because there were no more protests she cared to make.

"Tonight, darlin', I'm going to take you to the stars," he said as he glided his mouth along her jawline, down her throat. But she remembered the riverside shack.

"What if it hurts?"

"It won't hurt," he muttered, his kisses moving down her body, across her ribs, her rounded belly. Her hands clenched in the covers and he was still kissing her, moving lower yet.

"But the last time…"

"It…won't…hurt. Goddammit, Julia, you're goin' to enjoy this if it kills me!"

And then he kissed her in a place she never expected to be kissed. He was holding her thighs apart and she struggled to sit up, but the heat flowing from where his mouth worked its magic sapped her strength. With a moan she lay back on the pallet and let him do his worst.

And his worst was very good indeed. With his fingers and his tongue, Rand sought out each nerve that could be stroked to new heights, each iota of pleasure that she was capable of experiencing. Julia's mind was overwhelmed by her body's response and as if from a distance she heard herself asking, begging for more pleasure.

"Whatever you want, darlin'," he said thickly, and eased his finger inside her.

She gasped and pushed back against the invader, her body welcoming his touch with a rush of moisture. He bit out an oath and slipped another finger inside while he lowered his head, and gave a final lick to the hard button of nerves he'd stimulated so effectively.

Julia shattered.

Her body dissolved into a million fragments of feeling, rushing out into the humid night. When she regained her senses, Rand was next to her, his head propped on one hand, looking quite pleased with himself.

She would have slapped him if she'd had the energy.

But when he lowered his head to kiss her again, and she tasted her own passion in his kiss, and felt the tension of his own need, she was willing to overlook his attitude. She wrapped her arms around him, pulling him down to her even as he maneuvered his leg between hers and entered her as easily as an oak leaf drifting down into the creek. He glided into her like they'd been made for each other, a thought that thankfully didn't go any further as the feelings began to build again in her body, embers blown to life by the stroking of his shaft, every withdrawal and return firing her nerves. She hitched her legs higher around his hips, wrapping them around him and pulling him even deeper inside her. Rand groaned and began moving harder, faster, kissing her face and telling her how beautiful she was, how her body was made for lovin', how in a moment, right quick, they were going to fly to the moon.

His hoarse shout of completion echoed Julia's own cries as she clutched him tighter yet, and as her muscles clamped down on him he went rigid, and then with a deep sigh lowered himself atop her.

They lay like that for some heartbeats and Julia looked over one hard shoulder to the rough cabin roof.

"Rand—"

"Shhhh...." He put his finger across her lips, rolled over on his side, still inside her, his leg hooked over her hip to hold them together. She couldn't see his expression in the dark.

"No talking, Julia. I do not want to hear any regrets or recriminations or remorse."

She frowned, her fuzzy mind trying to take in not only what he'd said, but how he said it. But a moment later she felt him relax even more as he stroked his hand down her side, caressing her hip, and he drawled, "See, darlin'? I told you I could show you a good time."

He disengaged from her and stooping, picked her up in his arms and carried her into the next room.

Rand put her into bed, then climbed in after and pulled up the covers.

She thought about protesting, but instead yawned and rolled over on her side, snuggling up against him spoon fashion. It was too much effort to argue with him, so she mumbled something and fell asleep, his arm around her holding her close in the dark.

CHAPTER 10

The next days passed in a sensual blur of meals seasoned with laughter, days of sunshine, and evenings of passion. Julia found herself walking around with a smile on her face for no good reason. They never spoke about the secrets that lay between them, instead talking about inconsequential matters like the crops, and the weather, and whether the large plantations filling Middle Florida and crowding the small farmers were good for the territory. They stepped around the bales and parcels and bags piled in the front room, not discussing them either.

When the voices in her head would niggle at her to learn more about what Rand was up to, she pushed them into an imaginary room and shut the door on them. Into that room went the worry about what her family back at Ganymede's Cup, St. Augustine, and maybe even her parents in London might be thinking happened to her. She also shoved in there the hysterical voice wondering what she would do if she found herself pregnant with Rand Washburn's baby.

That imaginary room was getting crowded, but she knew troubles would come in their own time. In the meantime, it was a new world for her, a world of touch, and taste, exploration, and experimentation, and learning the intricacies of a lean male body, so different from her own and yet so familiar. Each scar, each sculpted muscle, the downy hair and the sheathed strength of her backwoods husband was a new delight to her each evening. And in the morning. And anytime the fancy took them.

"Somethin' smells delicious," Rand said, coming into the kitchen. The shutters were opened to the breezes and the flowers outside, and the scent of oranges and toasted pecans and sugar inside hung heavy, perfuming the rough wood walls.

"I am glad you are here. You're in time to lift this kettle for me over to that table," Julia said, pointing with her spoon. She stepped back and he grabbed the wooden handle, easily hoisting the iron pot onto the table for her.

Her face was flushed from the heat, and wisps of hair escaped from under the cloth she'd used to tie back her curls, sticking moistly to her skin. She paused for a moment, thinking.

"Keep stirring if you would, Rand, I will be there in a moment."

"Yes ma'am," he said, working the spoon through the creamy mass in the pot. "What is this, anyway?"

"I *think* it will be an American fruit pudding when I'm finished."

She returned back with some grated orange peel that she added to the pot and took back her spoon.

"Why an American puddin'?"

"Because what you Americans call pudding isn't what we call pudding. Thank you, I'll take it from here. I have to keep stirring it as it sets."

"That so?" He came up behind her and peered over her shoulder. "What happens if you stop stirrin'?"

"It will curdle. Now, go away and leave me alone, Rand. I have work to do."

He didn't move, and if anything inched a bit closer to her. She kept stirring the pot, but in addition to the smells of oranges and sugar, she smelled sun-warmed male, the scent that was uniquely his, a fresh change from the men she knew in England, who smelled of expensive French colognes and hair pomade.

"Did you know you put your whole body into it when you're cookin'? Like this here," he said, putting his hands on her hips. "You're just rollin' like a little manatee floatin' down the river."

"So now you think I look like a sea cow?"

"Dang, you're prettier than a sea cow! You're even prettier than Victoria, and she's a mighty fine lookin' mule."

"It is time for you to get your hands off me and leave, Washburn."

Instead of getting his hands off her hips and leaving, he moved them around to the front of her blouse, undoing the laces.

Julia kept stirring the pudding and tried to stomp on Rand's foot, but he was too fast for her.

"Now, now, you don't want your cream to curdle there. You keep stirrin'."

She did, moving the spoon around through the rich cream the color of sunrise, bits of orange and vanilla bean dancing together in the pot. It was quiet in the shack except for the scrape of the spoon, the deep breathing of the man close behind her, too close, crowding her against the table. His browned, knowing fingers finished at the laces, and her breasts were freed from their confinement. She took a deep breath to scold him again, but the air rushed out of her when his fingers came around to cover her, rolling the sensitive tips until they stood out like spring strawberries against her white flesh.

"Rand…"

"Shhhhh…keep stirrin', darlin', don't stop now."

He lightly squeezed her in rhythm to the circuit of the spoon, and she swelled in his grasp, stumbling where she stood. If he hadn't wrapped his arms around her, she would have fallen, but he held her with one hand around her waist, pulling her tight against him.

"Keep stirrin'," he whispered in her ear and she saw two fingers dip down into the kettle, scooping up some of the ambrosial custard, following behind the spoon she kept moving through the kettle in a desultory fashion.

He brought his fingers up to her mouth, cream dripping from the tips. With a moan she surrendered and licked the cream off, finishing by sucking his fingers into her mouth. He tasted salty and honeyed and stirred her insides into a froth of heat that left her breathless in the small room. She leaned back against him for support, feeling the rise and fall of his chest, the tension in his body centered on the erection pressing into the back of her skirts. She was melting, melting like an ice cream left in the sun, turning into a puddle of hot sugar beneath his rough hands.

"When I'm done here, I'm going to kill you!" she gasped out.

"This game is worth the candle," and she heard the smile in his voice as he dipped again into the cream and smeared his fingers across her bared neck, her earlobe, her shoulder where he lowered her shirt and the strap of her chemise, leaning down to lick the sweet treat off.

She dropped the spoon into the pot and he picked it up and put it back into her hand.

"Keep stirrin'," he whispered.

She did, bracing her other hand against the table as he nudged her forward, and she felt the breeze on the back of her legs when he lifted her skirts and tucked them into the waistband.

"Dear God, Rand, we're in the kit…ooooh," her husky voice trailed off as his fingers dipped into her, stirring her, and then were replaced by his shaft as he entered her as smoothly as a knife cutting through custard.

They stood there, frozen in the kitchen's heat until Rand said thickly, "You're not stirrin'." He took her limp hand in his, wrapping it around the spoon and moving himself in coordination with the spoon, slowly, in and out, going 'round and 'round, and all she could do was hang her head and watch the cooling pudding progress to the setting point, his large hand holding hers captive around the wooden handle, tightening on her fingers as his own needs drove him on.

The specks of fruit and spice blurred as the combination of scent and taste and passion took over her brain and moved her to her own setting point, one punctuated by her husband whispering in her ear all the places on her body he was going to cover in custard and lick off, and how she would do the same for him. That final image conjured up in her fevered brain drove her over the edge. She threw her head back against his shoulder and he braced himself, and pushed one more time, and she felt herself explode out to the ends of her hair and collapse inward like a soufflé.

The only sound was their mingled harsh breathing. Julia looked down at the pot.

"It's set."

"Me, too," Rand said, and blew out his breath. "Dang, I never knew cookin' could be so excitin'!"

He lowered her skirts and patted her on the rump.

"What do you suggest I call this dish, Rand? Maybe *crème d' amour*?"

"Naw, it don't need a fancy Frenchie name." He kissed her beneath her ear and wrapped his arms around her, holding her against him again, but quietly now, contentment radiating outward from him.

"That's it," Julia murmured. "I'll call it 'Sweet Contentment Custard.'"

But as the days passed, Julia noticed Rand becoming more tense, an urgency to his lovemaking that didn't fit his easygoing Cracker ways. He'd stare at the bales, and drink the smuggled brandy, and he'd watch her as she moved around the cabin. She never asked about the disposition of the bales and boxes.

Her imaginary room was full of gibbering voices, and bursting at the seams.

*   *   *

The waiting was driving Rand crazy. He was torn in two, one half of him focused on the job, the other sniffing after his wife. He'd never known anyone like her. She had the manners of a duchess in the parlor, and the enthusiasm of a highly paid courtesan in the bedroom.

And she loved the business of smuggling. He could see it in her eyes, when she'd go all thoughtful and look at the boxes and bales piled in the cabin, calculating in her head what each item was worth. He'd see her watching him sometimes, and he couldn't help but wonder if she was also thinking how much larger her share would be if she could get all this out of here and sold by herself, without having to split the money with him.

Rand was hitching Victoria to the cart when Julia emerged from the cabin. There was a spring to her step that hadn't been there days before, a glow about her. He paused in his work to watch her, knowing it was a rare sight, about to disappear like the mist burning off the creek.

"Good morning! I apologize for sleeping so late, but I'll have breakfast on in a moment. I, um, didn't get much sleep last night." She blushed. "Where are you taking Victoria?"

He didn't look at her as he tightened the mule's harness. "Into town."

"We're going to town! Oh, Rand, that is wonderful!"

"I'm not takin' you with me," he said flatly. He looked at her face and almost looked away again, but kept his eyes on her. Now she looked pale and deflated, the light gone, and he wanted to step forward and take her in his arms and tell her of course he'd take her to town, but he couldn't do that. Not yet.

"But...you are leaving me out here all alone?"

"You'll be fine, Julia, and I'll be back before dark. Give me a list of anythin' you need and I'll pick it up."

"Oh," she said, and swallowed. "That means I am still a prisoner out here, aren't I?" She hugged herself like she was cold, but it wasn't cold outside. "For some reason, I thought it was different now. Foolish me."

Rand cursed and stopped messing with the mule's harness.

"Different? Because we're sharin' the same bed? Yeah, that makes it different. It hammers home to me that you're my wife, and my responsibility, and part of that responsibility is keepin' you away from trouble! Have you told me the truth, Julia? The whole truth behind your little trip to Florida, and what you're doin' here?"

She raised her hand to her throat. "Why, Rand, of course I have told you the truth."

He watched her with narrowed eyes, then shook his head in exasperation. "Don't ever give up chess for cards. You'd lose your shirt."

Her eyes shifted away from his, and she looked at the ground. He didn't say anything else. There was nothing to say, because she was right. She was still his prisoner out here, at least until he was done with what he had to do, or found out the truth about his pretty English bride.

Julia turned to go back inside, her steps dragging through the dirt, but she paused and turned back to him. Her eyes were suspiciously bright.

"Could you…could you take a message to send to my uncle? He's going to worry about me because in my last note, I said I would be back at Ganymede's Cup. And now that is not going to happen."

"Tell him you're married to me, Julia. He may hear it from someone else given the traffic through there, and it's best he hear it from you."

If anything, the thought of telling her uncle she was married to Rand Washburn made her pale still more, but she nodded her head.

"I will let you read the letter before I seal it."

He flinched, but again there was nothing to say, because they both knew he'd read her letter whether she sealed it or not.

"Julia!"

She stopped, but she didn't turn back around. "Yes?"

"This will all be finished and…" He stopped, not knowing what else to say, but knowing he needed to say something. "When this is all over, it *will* be different."

"Those things I don't know, Washburn?"

She looked at him over her shoulder and he could see she was angry—calling him Washburn also clued him—but that was an improvement over her looking whipped.

"That's right, darlin', things you don't need to worry your pretty head about," he drawled, just to put some more starch into her. It worked.

"Someday there will be a reckoning, Mr. Washburn! And then you will beg me to forgive you, and I will laugh—*laugh*, I tell you!"

She turned back and stomped into the cabin. Rand watched her go. He knew two things were true—there wasn't going to be a whole lot of laughing on the day of reckoning, and it would be damn cold sleeping alone on his pallet tonight.

CHAPTER 11

Rand pulled his hat brim lower, shading his eyes from the sun shining in from the west as Victoria plodded her way home through the woods. The mule shook her head and brayed, and he paused in the dusty heat.

Something was burning.

Cold sweat popped out on his brow and he took the whip to the mule to hurry it along. When he broke through the brush into the clearing, he pulled back sharply. Tents were set up down by the creek, and an ant line of men trooped out of his cabin, carrying the stolen bales and parcels to oxcarts. Smoke rose over a pit dug into the sand, the source of the roasting odor.

James Crane had shown up, and he'd brought supper.

Rand pushed his hat back on his forehead, watching the couple on the porch. Crane sat in *his* rocking chair, one foot propped up on the porch rail as he watched the men work. Julia sat next to him, a small table between them with a jug of some cool beverage sweating in the late afternoon warmth.

Crane's broad face split into a grin at something Julia said, and he rose and waved.

"Glad you could make it back in time for supper, boy. We thought we'd have to start without you, or send out a search party."

Rand spat over the side of the seat and jumped off the cart, a flurry of trail dust coming off his clothes. He was hot, he was dirty, and he wanted to know why his friend and his woman were so cozy.

Julia stood also and brushed down her skirts. She was wearing the clothes Ma Ivey had given her, the shirt that was too small, the skirt that was too short, and she was barefoot, but she walked across the dirt yard with her head high and her back straight.

"Welcome home. As you see, your friend Mr. Crane arrived to gather the merchandise."

He looked at her and scratched his stubbled chin. "How'd you know he was the right man? Maybe he's some desperado come to steal our stuff."

"You are right, it *is* difficult to tell one desperado from another in Florida, isn't it? There's not much I could have done to stop them, however, and while I am willing to die defending myself—or you—I am not willing to die over smuggled wares."

"Can't fault the logic in that."

Julia looked back over her shoulder at the porch. Rand rubbed his hand against his pants leg, resisting the urge to haul his wife into his arms and see if he could kiss that frown out of her eyes. The frown that was there when she looked at him, 'cause when she was looking at James she was smiling, and he didn't like it one bit.

"There was something about Mr. Crane that made me feel confident he was who he said he was," the unspoken message being, "How did someone like *you* get such a trustworthy friend?"

Washburn grunted, and grabbing a paper-wrapped parcel

from the back of the cart, yelled out to one of the men crossing the yard. "Kelly! Put that down and come take care of this mule."

"These men are quite mannerly, and helpful," Julia said as they walked back toward the cabin. "James put them to work fixing supper and I haven't had to lift a finger."

"James?"

"Oh yes. Mr. Crane asked me to call him James when I explained I was your wife. He said you and he were such good friends, you would insist on it." Her nose wrinkled. "You might want to wash that dirt off before you come to table. And if you will excuse me, I have to see to something in the kitchen. Even though James was so thoughtful as to have his men fix supper, I whipped up a pumpkin cake and a batch of brandy snaps for a sweet at the end of the meal."

"They're not *his* men, they're *my* men. Crane takes his orders from me," Rand said through his teeth.

"Really?" Julia's brows lifted. "I never would have thought that. He has a way about him, don't you think? Rather a commanding presence. And such a well-read gentleman! We found we have a mutual fondness for the stories of Mr. Poe. It was a pleasure to talk with him."

She turned and passed Crane walking toward Rand, and she said something to him in passing that elicited a grin from the man. Rand stood there alone in the yard, clenching the package in his fists.

"Quite a beauty, that wife of yours."

Rand looked down at him and Crane took a step back, hands lifted in front of him, palms out.

"Whoa, boy, all we did was sit on the front porch and talk!"

"Stay there, *James,* 'cause I'm goin' to be out to deal with you right quick."

Rand stomped into the cabin and tossed his parcel on the bed, Julia's bed, grabbing some soap and toweling, and fresh clothes from his trunk. He paused as he was about to step out through the door. His wife was singing from the kitchen, mangling "Greensleeves."

Perfect. A song about another woman who couldn't treat a man right.

Crane was careful to keep his distance as they headed to the creek.

"I don't know what's going on here—" Crane started.

"That's right, you don't."

James watched him with a concerned expression on his face, and Rand felt some tension ease out. They sometimes favored the same women over the years, but James had never poached on his territory, and he'd never poached on James's. Rand didn't know why now he was getting all worked up over one curly-topped little smuggler, and that was part of the problem.

When they reached the creek, Rand stripped off his clothes and plunged into the cold water, shaking it off like an otter as he surfaced. Crane threw him the soap.

"I expected you earlier."

"I was delayed in Key West, following up on that information you gave me. You were right, Brewer's master is English, but I haven't been able to find out much else." He looked back toward the cabin. "I couldn't help noticing that your wife is English also. *Is* she truly your wife?"

"Aye, for my sins."

He plunged back into the water and came up as Crane tossed him the towel. Rand paused when he wiped his face, and inhaled. Julia had used the towel and it still held her fragrance. His friend was watching him when he lowered the towel from his eyes and Rand could feel the heat on his cheekbones. Crane shook his head.

"You always manage to scuttle yourself in grand style. This time you've set a new standard."

"You have a knack for stating the obvious, James. I'm aware my wife is English. I'm also aware she has been lying her head off from the day she showed up at the farm. Now *Mrs. Washburn* is throwing herself behind the smuggling operation, looking forward to amassing large amounts of illicit money." He smiled humorlessly. "At some point I know I'm going to have to settle this, but not until after we're finished."

"I'm not the only one who will want more information on the new Mrs. Washburn."

"Tell him I'm dealing with it."

Crane made a rude noise. "He won't have a lot of faith in that statement. Not based on your past performances. This is a complication we cannot afford. Do you want me to take care of it?"

"No!"

Rand looked hard at his friend. Crane's open, bland countenance masked a determination to do whatever it took to accomplish his tasks.

"She's my wife. It's my problem, and Julia is my responsibility. I'll take care of it." He twisted the towel in his hands. "I know what's at stake here. Nothing—and no one—is going to stop us."

The two walked toward the cabin, and Rand paused for a moment to watch the men work and the curl of smoke rising from the ground.

"When I drove up, I smelled the fire pit before I saw the homestead was safe…you can imagine what I thought."

Crane flinched. "It never occurred to me. Sorry."

It was a smell that made Rand's mouth water at the same time a slight tinge of nausea rose in his throat, because it was a smell he'd had in his nostrils too many times during the war. It was the same whether it was white homesteaders burned out, or Indians surprised in their *chickees.*

Burning flesh smelled like roast pork.

"We talked a bit, your wife and I, about how I met you during the war."

Rand looked at him sharply, but Crane fingered the chestnut side whiskers growing down his face. "Don't worry. I told her some generalities about how we served together. It did slip out that you could have gone farther had you not been insubordinate to your commanding officers, and Mrs. Washburn conceded you might have made a good sergeant."

Rand grinned at that. "The marine sergeants I knew from the war would tell her I shouldn't be given command of a ladies' tea."

"Who do you think she is?"

"I wish to heaven I knew. After you get rid of this haul, stop by Ganymede's Cup and see what you can find out. Julia is—or claims to be—Richard Cooper's orphan niece, and I'd like to know if at least that part of the story is true. Given Cooper's history with the pirate Christopher Daniels, he may be working on this job and if so, I want to know about it."

"You want me to go to The Greek Boy?" Crane looked around to see if anyone was listening.

"Don't worry, James, you're not pretty enough for the customers there. Besides, I hear the food's good."

Rand saw Crane glance at him out of the corner of his eye, but he said nothing and they reached the clearing where Julia directed the men in the supper preparations. She commanded them like she was to the manner born. Perhaps she was some orphan bastard, but if so, she could be the bastard of a member of the gentry who'd raised her up to take some position in society. Odd as that might seem at one level, if she'd been reared well and sent to the United States on a mission, she might be looking to this as her main chance to make a place for herself not in England, but in the Indies or in Canada, where attitudes were more relaxed about one's origins.

He couldn't fault her for that. Hell, there was a great deal he admired about her. She had, as Ma Ivey said, grace and grit and plenty of it. Crane left him to check the wagons, and Rand joined his wife, coming up close behind her.

"Somethin' sure smells good."

"Roast pig, gopher tortoise, venison, fish stew with hominy, and corn ears. They even chopped down some palms for swamp cabbage, and it is boiling up now."

"Nope, it wasn't supper I had in mind, darlin'."

She glanced at him over her shoulder. "How was your trip?" she asked coolly.

"I got done what needed doin'," he said, stepping back from her, but taking her arm in his as they walked through the yard.

The men tipped their hats or nodded respectfully as she passed, which was what Rand expected. His men were handpicked for their abilities, including the ability to keep their mouths shut and their eyes and ears open. They might discuss the new Mrs. Washburn amongst themselves, but the discussions wouldn't go any further than their campfires.

The men carried the table and benches out from the cabin for Washburn, Crane, and Julia. After that was done, Crane offered to fetch Julia a plate from the supper line.

"That would be very gracious of you, James, thank you." She smiled up at him in the firelight.

"See? Now ain't that what I talked about the other night? Ol' James there is going to be so busy observin' the amenities and fetchin' for you, he won't have a chance to get his own victuals afore they're gone."

Rand followed after his friend, but by the time he stopped answering questions from his men and had his own food, Crane was back at the table seated next to his wife and chatting about books or theater or fashions or some such ridiculous thing a grown man had no reason to be knowing about.

"Pass the pepper sauce," Rand said as he sat down across from them. He put a generous portion in his stew, then paused. "James, is Kelly gettin' ready to go after Shultz again?" He gestured with the pot in his hand. "You remember what happened between them the last time when Shultz carried on 'bout the Irish?"

Crane swiveled his head around and watched the men in

question for a few moments, but then turned back with a shrug.

"They look peaceable enough to me, Rand." He took a bite of his pork and chewed for a moment, then jumped up with an oath and grabbed the pitcher of ale on the table. He sloshed enough into his cup to fill it to the brim and drained it. James glared at him, then turned to Julia with a slight bow.

"I apologize for my language. If you'll excuse me, I need to get a fresh plate."

He grabbed his piece of tin and stomped off as Rand took another bite of roast pork.

"What happened?" Julia asked, confused lines between her brows.

"James don't like too much spice in his life. Me," he said, spooning more hot sauce on his food, "I like a little heat on my tongue just fine."

Crane returned with a fresh plate, taking a spot on the bench on the other side of Julia and further away from his friend. They finished their meal and, after praising Mrs. Washburn's brandy snaps, the men packed up from supper and brought out their noisemakers, as Crane termed it—Kelly on the spoons, Jacobs on the banjo, and Shultz with his fiddle. Jacobs led the way with "Shady Grove," and soon the men were paired off to dance, the "ladies" distinguished by bandannas tied around their upper arms. Crane, Washburn, and Julia joined them, sitting in the sandy yard and clapping and singing along.

Rand watched his wife from under lowered lids. He'd seen girls flirt, everywhere from raucous dances following the winter cane grindings, to fetes at other locations best left unthought about. He'd always been amused by the artificiality of it—the simpers, the smiles, the wide eyes, and eyelash batting.

But this wasn't artificial, this was the genuine article. Julia held court like a queen surrounded by knights, or a flower being buzzed over by the worker bees. She shone with the attention, the gestures, and laughter. Her smiles were not practiced and false, but part of who she was in some other world far from the Florida backwoods. She laughed at the antics of Jennings dancing the Short Dog, and clapped and joined in after a few verses of the nonsensical "Sweet as a Mocking Bird at Courting Time."

And James Crane, damn his blue eyes, was eating it up with a spoon.

"Do you dance, Mrs. Washburn? I think these fellows could manage to scrape out a jig or a reel."

"I'll dance with her," Rand said, standing so abruptly he knocked over the coffee cup at his hip. The dark liquid seeped into the dirt, but he didn't notice, holding out his hand to his wife.

Julia looked up in surprise, but took his hand and allowed him to pull her to her feet. Six of the men paired off to complete the set and as the musicians struck up a reel, Rand took her through the steps, similar enough to her English country dancing that she had it in short order. As she was passed off and switched with her partner, Rand watched her glow and felt a hollow feeling deep inside his chest. He wanted to shake the truth out of her. He wanted to kiss her senseless and protect her from her own larcenous nature.

He wanted to trust her, and tell her all that he'd kept hidden from her. It chewed him up that this sparkling woman he was bound to, so right for him in so many ways, could be the death of him. Too many people were depending on him, too much was at stake for him to put his own desires first.

Julia ended the dance back in his arms, color high in her cheeks from the exercise, firelight gleaming off her tousled hair. He brushed a wandering lock back from her temple, and her eyes grew darker yet as she looked up at him.

"A waltz! A wedding waltz!" one of the men called out, breaking the mood and bringing Rand back to where he was, and who was here with him.

"You have no card for me to sign, but may I nevertheless request the honor of this dance? Darlin'?" he added hastily.

"A dance card?" Julia looked up at him, a strange expression on her face.

"Yeah, I saw a lady with one a them at a dance in St. Augustine. Men would write their names on it and reserve a spot next to a particular dance. Kinda like that house James and I visited in Havana once, where they had a menu of what the ladies—never mind that, are you goin' to dance with me or not?"

"Of course," his wife said. "I love to waltz."

And she did. It showed in the lightness of her steps, the practiced ease with which she followed his lead. Which naturally led his mind to wonder where a tavern girl had learned to waltz like a duchess.

But only part of his mind. The part that wasn't taken up with how she fit in his arms, her trim waist beneath his hand, her head at exactly the right height for him to lean down and kiss, if he chose to do so. And it was hard not to. Her lips were moist and slightly parted, and her eyes were half closed as she gave herself over to the music and the moment. The ground was uneven, not polished parquet, yet he moved her adroitly over the rough yard, smelling the fragrance of almonds from her soap, and lemons from her hair, and beneath it all, pure Julia.

The music finished with a twang and clatter of spoons, and Rand paused, drinking in the sight of his wife, more lighthearted and happy than at any time since he'd opened the door to his shed. He raised her rough, ungloved hand to his lips, his eyes on hers.

"Thank you for the dance, Julia darlin'."

She would have stepped back, but he held her hand tight in his. By now it was full dark, and Rand looked up at the sky and said, "Looks like rain comin' on. You'd best bunk down in the front of the cabin, James, and let your men sleep on the porch and in the wagons."

Julia started to open her mouth and Washburn knew she would ask where *he* was sleeping if the men were in the front room, but she closed it and eyed him suspiciously, pulling her hand free.

"If you gentlemen will excuse me, I need to straighten up in the kitchen."

Rand smiled to himself, and dusting off his coffee cup, poured in some of the brandy lifted from the shipment. He'd counted on her not saying anything in front of the men about him sleeping on the pallet out front. With some careful maneuvering tonight he might find himself back where he belonged, in bed with his wife.

*   *   *

Julia dried her hands and rubbed a pea-sized dab of lard into them, wrinkling her nose. It worked, but left her feeling less than feminine. And she feared her feet would always be callused from running around barefoot in the Florida dirt. Oh, for the perfumed creams and lotions she used back home! Her mother, never one to fuss overmuch with her own appearance, was bemused on their shopping excursions as Julia flitted from shop to shop, trying out this scent, or that hair salve, or this lip pomade. Uncle Robin was more fun to take shopping than Mama!

The men were still talking outside when Julia entered the back room, and stopped. A lamp was lit, and there was a paper-wrapped parcel on the bed.

Rand's? she wondered, but if it was his, why did he leave it where she slept? Having thus stilled the little voice telling her not to snoop, Julia undid the string, and stared down at the contents, swallowing hard around the sudden obstruction in her throat.

A calico dress of dark blue, figured in flowers with a striped skirt, was folded on top. Beneath it was a white blouse in the Spanish style still favored by the Minorcan ladies of St. Augustine, a dark red skirt, a short embroidered wool jacket, and a wide-brimmed straw hat strewn with the most improbable daisies. There were tortoise shell combs for her hair, stockings, and wrapped in the center, a tin of Brooke's lavender hand salve and a tiny bottle of orange blossom perfume.

Rand had gone shopping, for her.

Julia broke the seal on the perfume and dabbed it behind her ears and on her wrists, breathing deeply of the spicy warm fragrance.

"It reminded me of you, 'cause you love the oranges so

much."

Julia turned on her heel. Her husband was standing in the doorway, and he came in now and closed it behind him, shutting off the noise of Crane and the men in the front.

"When this is over, and I am long gone from here, I will smell oranges and it will remind me of when I lived in Florida," Julia said, looking down at her hands. She looked back up at Rand Washburn, watching her from where he leaned against the door.

"They say if you get the sand in your shoes, you always come back to Florida." He pushed himself off the doorframe and went to check the shuttered window, adjusting it so the night air could enter. A moth fluttered in and Rand's hand shot out, capturing it, but he took it back to the window and released it into the night.

Julia busied herself with the clothes on the bed. "It was thoughtful of you to bring me these things, Rand. You did not have to do it."

"It weren't nothin'. I don't want people thinkin' I can't take care of my own wife."

She dwelt on her parents' expectations of the man she'd marry, the settlements and lengthy negotiations that would no doubt be involved, linking together two ancient families. She couldn't imagine herself married to a dry scion of the British aristocracy after this adventure. It wasn't just the bizarre marriage to Rand Washburn, it was the idea of looking across a breakfast table and engaging in polite conversation with someone who wouldn't name a mule after the queen, or make jokes about raccoons sneaking up on you when you weren't looking. Maybe she'd be an eccentric aunt, traveling the world, and bringing back exotic gifts for her nieces and nephews.

Gifts like Florida seashells.

"You looked like you was havin' a good time tonight."

Rand sat on the chest and pulled off his boots, and Julia chewed her lip.

"Um, did you bring your pallet in here?"

Rand loosened his braces, dropping the straps off his shoulders and started unbuttoning his shirt. The small lamp burning on the chest left his face half shadowed, but she thought there was a creasing at the corner of that well-shaped mouth.

"Nope."

Her eyes narrowed, because she had a long memory, and couldn't be bribed with a few fripperies. No matter how thoughtful the gesture, she remembered that the same hand that freed a trapped moth held her captive out in the woods.

"James and your men were quite entertaining this evening. I had a lovely time."

"Yeah, James looked real entertained by you, too."

His tone did nothing to make her feel more kindly disposed toward him.

"*James* said my eyes were like the sun, lighting up the autumn afternoon."

"'My mistress' eyes are nothing like the sun; coral is far more red than her lips' red...'"

The soft murmur carried across the room, and at first Julia thought she must have heard one of the men outside, maybe James in front.

It couldn't be Rand. Could it?

"You know Shakespeare?"

Rand stopped and looked at her, then grinned. "Dang, did he write that? I heard some travelin' players say that at a show in Savannah and thought it was right pretty. Not as useful as that poem about the snakes, but real pretty anyhow."

Julia sniffed. "I am impressed you can recite poetry, Washburn. Rather like a counting pig at the fair. One watches in amazement, wondering how an animal can do that."

"Now that hurts! I can say pretty things, too."

He crossed to where she stood beside the bed, and took her hand in his. His touch was warm, and she gave an involuntary shiver having nothing to do with the night air.

He stroked the ball of her hand with his thumb, soothing over the nicks and calluses raised by the chores of daily farm work. He took his other hand and lifted her chin, looking deep into her eyes.

"Y'know how when you whack the woodpile, and all them big ol' palmetto bugs come scamperin' out? Your eyes are just as brown and shiny as a palmetto bug runnin' in the sunlight, darlin'."

Julia made a strangled noise and pulled back on her hand, but Washburn was holding it tight, a smile dancing in his eyes despite the soulful tone of his words.

"It is clear that pretty words are not your forte, Washburn. Best you stick to smuggling salt. And you can fetch your pallet after you let go of my hand."

"Aw, now I'm gettin' warmed up. Let me think on it."

Washburn moved in closer, and still holding on to her hand, moved the other down her back until it rested on her backside. He began stroking her, a slow circular caress that seemed to facilitate his thinking if his furrowed brow was any indication.

However, it was putting paid to *her* thought processes.

"Your eyes are like pecans, Julia. Brandy brown, and like the nuts, you're hard on the outside, but buttery on the inside. It's a chore getting to that good stuff, but that's part of the fun, workin' your way past the shell to the rich meat. And when you crack a pecan and the nut comes out whole, have you ever noticed how it's like two lips, plump and tasty and just waitin' for the right someone's mouth to enjoy all the pleasure trapped within?"

A faint smile at that one. "Better, but not quite Byron."

"How 'bout this then?" He moved in even closer, and released her hand, running his finger along her eyebrow down to the outer corner of her eye, where he feathered it over the soft skin at her temple, a touch as light as a moth's wing passing in the night. The hand behind her back pulled her in until she was standing between his legs, and could feel how seriously he was taking this wordplay.

"Your eyes are the smoky bronze of coffee, rich and deep. It settles in your belly and warms you from the inside out. Hot, and able to get a man up in the mornin', and keep him up all day. Without coffee, the day is dull, flat, lifeless. But with that first taste of the stimulatin' brew, you know you can face anythin'. It makes your heart beat a little faster, and the colors all seem sharper, the air brighter."

Her mouth was dry as she swallowed. "Much better."

He angled his head toward her, his own lips a fraction from hers. "Jamaican rum," he breathed against her mouth.

She pulled back and looked at him, one eyebrow raised.

"Your eyes are like Jamaican rum, darlin', golden dark and potent. It goes down smooth but it has fire to it. A man has to be careful, too much can make him lose his head, drownin' in honeyed dreams."

"Don't lose your head," she whispered.

"Too late."

His mouth closed over hers and she tasted coffee and brandy, and the molasses-rich taste of her husband, and she knew, even if she lived another ninety years, she would never mistake anyone else's kiss for this man's kiss. It was hot and honeyed and smoky with passion, promising secret delights, tasting of stolen candy and forbidden treats. She almost wept with the knowing that someday she would have memories of this smuggler to warm her through the cold nights, only reminiscences of the sunlight and shadow that made up Rand Washburn.

But she had tonight. She had this moment to grasp in both hands as she grasped his shirt, holding on to him and embracing all he had to offer, the wickedness and the pleasure, the fire of an untamed man in a dangerous land. No matter what the morrow would bring, she would always remember how, for a brief time, she'd given all of herself. She would remember how she'd taken every delight offered, with no thought for consequences and recriminations.

Those could wait for Lady Julia Delerue. Tonight, she was Julia Washburn, smuggler's bride, in her cabin in the piney woods

And the smuggler's bride dared things the lady would never dream of.

She pushed back on his chest, breaking the kiss, and looked

up at him.

"You tell me I am out here at your sufferance, Rand Washburn, at the same time insisting on your comforts as a married man. Tonight, though, *I* will be in charge." She paused. "I think it is the least you owe me after those poor attempts at love poetry. You should be punished for that alone."

"Oh yeah? What did you have in mind?" he drawled. "Are you goin' to put me over your knee and give me a spankin'?"

Good heavens! Heat flashed through her body along with the image of a bare-bottomed Rand Washburn draped over her lap, her hand poised—

"No! I mean, I never even thought—you have a most strange imagination, Mr. Washburn!"

He gave her that bad boy smile, while one of his hands continued to roam over the thin skirts covering her bottom, and the other began working the laces in front of her shirt.

She slapped at his hand. "Stop that. Tonight you dance to my tune. You take off your clothes first."

"And you say I have an imagination!" But he didn't protest, and a glance downward showed his enthusiasm hadn't waned at all. If anything, her order to strip off his clothes had made his enthusiasm grow substantially.

Julia tried to keep her expression severe, but it was hard, though not as hard as the body being revealed before her, the shirt disappearing along with the trousers into a soft heap on the floor. He stood before her and she walked around him, slowly, admiring him from all angles in the soft lamplight. Outside she could hear the laughter and voices of the men as they bunked down for the evening, but in this room it was only the two of them in their own space, and nothing was going to intrude or interfere.

For his part, Rand appeared relaxed, loose limbed, his soft hair falling across his forehead, as if women admiring his nude form were an everyday occurrence. That thought made her frown and think on why it was important to keep the upper hand tonight. Julia vowed to test his resolve. He would break before she did.

She owed it to generations of Delerue women to uphold the family honor.

When he would have turned to embrace her she said, "Do not move. I have not given you permission to move, Washburn."

She put her hand on the vulnerable nape of his neck, underneath his sun-streaked curls, and felt a thrill of satisfaction as he froze at her touch, going still as a deer in the night when she rested her hand against the muscles and cords of his spine. She stepped up close behind him, as he had done with her in the past, bringing her clothed body up against him, while her arm snaked around to his front.

"Keep your hands at your sides, and your eyes straight ahead."

She put her feet between his and gently kicked at the inside of his ankles. He moved his legs out further at her touch, and she slid in even closer. She felt his hard buttocks against her, even through her skirts she could feel the muscles and sinews she loved to watch flow when he stalked across the yard like a tawny bobcat prowling its territory.

"Imagine you are seeing us in a mirror. You have a good imagination, Washburn, use it." Her face was turned to the side and pressed against his back and she surely heard his heart, beating fast as she spoke to him in the near dark.

"You can see in the mirror what my hand is doing as it roams over the front of your body. I imagine it looks quite white against your sun-darkened skin." Her hand moved as she spoke, running across his flat belly, the rigid muscles rippling beneath her fingers.

"This is not a good idea," Rand said through clenched teeth, but when he made to move forward Julia slid her hand down, clutching him in her fist, and he went stock-still.

"Do not move, Washburn. I have you right where I want you," she said against his back. She kissed him there, beneath his shoulder blade, then ran her tongue over the jutting bone, tasting salt as a fine sweat broke out over his skin.

"Damnation, Julia, let go of me!"

"Oh, your words say one thing, but your body says another," she sang softly as she began stroking him, moving her fist up and down his shaft. "And what it is saying right now, is that you need to stand there and let me do what I wish."

Maintaining her hold on him, much like Victoria on a lead, her mind thought wickedly, she moved around in front of him. His face was all stark planes and tension, the effort of holding himself still costing him. She reached up behind him with her left hand, sliding it beneath his hair to cup his head and pull it down to her, while her right hand released his shaft, only to move beneath and cup his sack, a move that made his eyelids shutter down.

"Careful, gal, you don't want to damage anythin' you may be needin' later," he said thickly.

"I will be as careful as I need to be. Now kiss me!"

He ignored her command to keep his hands by his side and grabbed her, pulling her up against him and grinding himself into her belly through the soft cotton of her skirts even as she fingered him, learning the shape and contours of his hidden parts. He had one hand fisted in her hair, the other clutching her, pulling her skirt up in back to reach her bare skin.

Julia released Rand's hair and his mouth, butterflying kisses down the thick column of his neck and across his chest, pausing to pay particular attention to the nipples standing out like copper pennies.

He froze again as she moved down his belly, still cradling him in one hand while she used the other to slide down his hip, past his leanly muscled legs, bracing herself against the floor. When she was on her knees, she smiled into the hair tickling her nose and rained kisses along the inside of his thighs, tracing a scar above his knee with her tongue, rewarded with a slight tremor racing over the surface of his skin. She knew what he wanted, even though she'd never done such a thing before, she could tell from the tension in his frame, from the way his breath caught when her questing mouth came close.

But tormenting him was so much fun, even if it was making her hot as well. Her skin sparked with sensitivity in the night air, the brush of fabric against her own thighs, the soft washed material straining against her swollen breasts.

"Bring your legs in a bit," she whispered and he obeyed. She slid her body up his legs, the rough hair abrading her nipples through her bodice. He made a sound deep in his throat as she reached her goal, the tip of his shaft gleaming in the light.

Moisture seeped out, her body answering with its own rush of liquid. She rubbed her thighs together, offering herself scant relief and leaned forward, her warm breath making him quiver.

"Hellfire!" he gasped when she brought her mouth around him, and he thrust forward instinctively, but she held him in her hands, controlling his movements even as she orchestrated her own, her head dipping and straining to take as much as she could, but there was still enough left to keep her hands busy. His hands were wrapped in her hair and her curls twined about the sinews and bone, the hard hands that held her captive, now held captive by her worship of his body.

There was an added element of arousal in being clothed while he was naked. Naked was vulnerable, yet Washburn looked anything but vulnerable. He looked like a god, or an ancient warrior come to life. But her clothing made her feel even more wicked. If Adam and Eve were innocent in their nakedness in the Garden, her clothing made her that much more aware of what was happening between them.

She moved her head on him, tasting him like a salted treat on her tongue, smelling his need, guided by his hands, and rewarded by the sounds he couldn't keep in, the tension he couldn't disguise. He was building toward his climax, and while that might be an interesting experience for another evening, tonight she desired a different conclusion, one orchestrated to show him the power she could wield.

"Move to the bed, Washburn," she said hoarsely, giving him a slight tug in the general direction so he'd get the idea. For a moment she thought he'd crack, the grim expression on his face sending a tremor down her spine, but then he took a deep breath and followed her lead onto the moss-scented mattress.

Julia rose and stood beside the bed and loosened her clothing 'til she was bare as her mate, who propped his head on his hand and watched the show with an appreciative gleam in his eye.

"On your back," she told him, and he raised his brows at this, but did as she asked.

"Do you know what I believe I miss most about England?" She threw her leg across his as she spoke matter-of-factly, settling herself at the top of his thighs, her hands braced on his chest as she looked into his night forest eyes. "I miss riding."

Those eyes narrowed, and too late she remembered that servant girls normally don't ride, but she wasn't about to try and backtrack with more lies. No, at this point a distraction was called for.

Julia leaned forward and kissed him, but when he reached to put his arms around her she leaned back and said, "But I don't need a horse, Washburn, because I have you."

So saying she shifted herself and took him inside her, slowly, because in this position he filled her almost more than she thought she could bear, but after some agonizingly stretching moments she was fully seated.

And then Julia began to ride.

She held on to him, his wide muscled shoulders offering support as she moved on him, taking him through his paces like a high-spirited stallion lathered with effort and heat, and she strained to meet his upward thrusts. Her slick body moved against his, and the ropes on the rough bedstead held, but the noise they made as they creaked was loud enough they likely could hear it down at the river.

She didn't care. Lady Julia might care, but Julia the smuggler's bride reveled in her newfound power, the power to make Rand Washburn lose control when he ground out, "I'm going to come," and took the rhythm from her. His movements as he braced himself and thrust upward shattered her own control. She threw her head back and silently screamed, sheer will keeping the cries inside her as her climax exploded out through her raw nerves. She soared even higher yet when Rand clamped his hands on her hips and gave a final thrust upward that raised them both. She gripped the bedstead to keep from tumbling to the floor.

The room was quiet again except for the sound of their harsh breathing. With a sigh, Rand rolled her over in the narrow bed, holding her up against him, their sweat cooling in the night. Julia wanted to say something, but she couldn't remember what it was, and she was very tired. Her last vision, as her eyelids fluttered shut, was of the moth returning through the window in time to immolate itself against the lamp flame.

CHAPTER 12

The puddles from the rainstorm reflected the morning sunlight as James Crane and the men prepared to leave the farmstead. Julia had been up since dawn cooking for the departing crew, who assisted her and thanked her as they passed the cane syrup and mayhaw jelly to sweeten their breakfast.

Rand watched his wife as she came from the kitchen with a pair of helpers and more food, moving gracefully among the men, pouring coffee and offering a remark or jest that made their rough faces light up or blush. Despite their physical attraction to one another, he feared there were too many lies between them for a real marriage. When this was over, if they both survived, he intended to see to it that she established herself somewhere safe. He owed her that much.

But that attraction was a powerful draw. She was funny, and bright, and gracious, and wild as a panther, and he was drawn to her like iron to the lodestone. If only he'd met her in a different time, a different place.

If only they were not the people they were.

James came up alongside him, swatting his hat at the gnats hanging in the cool air, and they watched the men loading up the carts.

"The rest of the crew will meet us out at the Bellamy Road and take the goods. Then I'll go to Ganymede's Cup and find out what I can about Mrs. Washburn."

"When I was in town, I heard the owner of Delerue-Sanders is on his way to Florida. This complicates our plans, so we'll need to act fast and make sure he doesn't interfere."

A noise behind him had both men whirling around, James with his hand on the pistol shoved in the pocket of his coat. Julia stood there, coffeepot in hand, looking white as the grits she'd cooked that morning.

"I thought you would like some more coffee," she said in a shaky voice.

Rand's eyes narrowed. He didn't know how long she'd been standing there, but this was the second time she'd heard him talking about Delerue-Sanders, and it seemed to upset her.

Maybe her connection was to *them* and she was lying about not knowing the owners. The idea of her being a nobleman's bastard suddenly took on new shape. Delerue-Sanders's owner was some English lord, and if they were smuggling their own goods—and counterfeit American currency—it made sense that he might plant a contact here in Florida. Someone whose loyalty would be to Delerue-Sanders. Someone who could mess up Rand's own plans for Delerue-Sanders something fierce.

Julia swallowed at the look on Rand's face, and backed away toward the house.

"But I forgot, you like it sweet, Rand. I'll, uh, take this back to the house if you want some."

And with a swirl of skirts she hurried back to the cabin. The two men watched Mrs. Washburn, and James shook his head.

"Remember, Rand, cool and temperate perseverance."

"I am always cool and temperate, James. I haven't killed you yet."

"You married in haste—"

"And I have not yet had the leisure to repent." Rand turned back to him and smiled, but it was more a baring of his teeth than anything else.

"You come and get me when it's time. If what you find is urgent, you know how to reach me."

"Remember when we were skylarking in Key West and you saw that Cuban juggler? The one who tossed flaming batons through the air? Remember how you bet me you could juggle those flaming batons?"

Rand didn't say anything. It had taken months for his hair to grow back.

"That's what you're doing right now, boy. Juggling fire. And I wish you a lot of luck."

James put his hat back on, gave his friend an ironic salute, and gathered the men up for the trip back through the woods.

*   *   *

As the men and wagons cut off on the road to Picolata, James took his horse off on a side road, a sand track that meandered through the palmettos. He reached his destination toward sundown, a low, unpainted and weathered building, its windows and shutters shaded by oak trees dripping Spanish moss. Horses, mules, and wagons were hitched out front, or being led to the stables. An ancient sign hung over the door, so faded its drawing of a person in a short skirt had worn to a wash of colors, but everyone on the river knew Ganymede's Cup, or The Greek Boy, by reputation, if not by firsthand experience.

James watered his horse and tied it to the post under the

shade trees, pausing as he entered the smoky tavern through the front. There was a bar, and an older man sat behind it on a stool, a pair of crutches propped alongside him. James guessed this might be Cooper, the owner, and headed to the bar first.

"Rum," he said, slapping down a coin, and the silent barkeep served him, motioning toward the menu scrawled on a slate at the end of the bar when James asked about supper.

When his order arrived, James was not only pleased, he was astounded. He'd eaten at establishments from Havana to Boston, but he'd seldom had a meal as well prepared as what he ate in the riverside inn, and he remarked on it to the silent Cooper.

Cooper just grunted, but a high, light voice chimed in, "It would not kill you, Richard, to say thank you when someone gives us a compliment. If I depended on *you* to share these comments with me, I would waste away, just waste away, from lack of praise!"

Cooper's harsh face softened, but he still didn't speak, and James looked toward the other man, who he guessed was Cooper's partner and the cook, though chef was a better title given the man's talents, and he said so.

"Thank you." The cook, who introduced himself as "Robin, just Robin," glowed with the praise, his round face red, and his thinning curls flying away from the heat and humidity of the kitchen.

"I don't believe I've seen you around here before."

"James Crane. I've been in Florida since the war, but now I'm thinking of heading out to Texas. But you know how it is." He smiled. "A man needs a stake to make a new life, and fighting the Seminole didn't pay well, not unless you're looking for land to settle on. So in the meantime, I'm picking up a little here and there, hauling goods, that sort of thing."

He looked around the tavern. "Got any gals working here who might be available to conduct a little business, if you know what I mean? I've been out on the trail a long time," he said with a leer.

Robin sniffed and pulled back. "This is a respectable tavern, sir! We don't do that kind of business."

"Now that's a shame," James said, lifting his mug of rum. "My friend Rand got married a while back, and I was sure he said his wife used to work here."

The mug never made it to James's mouth.

The cook had a razor-honed knife up against the pulse of his neck and Cooper had his hand around the wrist holding the mug. James didn't resist when Cooper pulled his hand back down to the bar, and set the mug down.

"I was only funnin' about wanting a gal for the night. I didn't mean anything by it!" James croaked.

A few of the patrons heard the commotion at the bar, but turned back to their own drinks and dinners when they saw Robin and Cooper had things under control. One of the specialties of the house at Ganymede's Cup was not interfering in other people's affairs.

"You are a friend of Rand Washburn? You will take us to him." The jovial innkeeper was gone, replaced by someone who James could well imagine had sailed with pirates.

"I can't." he gasped, rising up on his toes as the knife dented his skin further. A fraction more and he'd be spraying his life's blood on the sawdust-covered floor.

"Ease up," Cooper said to Robin. "Talk, Crane."

"I meet Washburn in St. Augustine. I've never been out to his place, but I hear tell he's so deep in the woods, the Indians couldn't find him if he didn't want to be found."

"What about his wife?" Robin pulled the knife back, but had it still within striking distance.

"Talk on the river is Washburn married a pretty little gal from this tavern, and when I met with him he seemed real happy with it. Said her name was Judy, or Julie, or something like that."

"Bring him," Cooper said with a nod toward a back room. Robin kept a grip on him and a knife at his back. James thought he could break away from the older man, but he still needed to gather more information, so he allowed himself to be pushed into a back office, unexpectedly decorated with pots of flowers, a bowl of potpourri, and colorful rag rugs and pillows.

"Washburn mentioned that his wife—"

"Julia," Cooper said.

"—Julia—was kin to you."

Cooper looked at Robin, then back at Crane. "Julia's my niece."

James relaxed a fraction. That part of Mrs. Washburn's story appeared to be true.

"Well then, maybe I can help bring Washburn into the family, if you know what I mean." He gave them a disarming smile. "I know Rand's always looking for business—"

"What kind of business?" Robin interrupted.

"Washburn's a trader. Handles goods for people, gets them redistributed to where they can do the most good. This tavern seems to be real busy, and there's a lot of traffic out on the river.

204

Maybe you've got some trading going on here that you could bring him in on? Him being part of the family and all."

"A smuggler," Cooper said.

"Whose goods is he handling?" Robin asked.

The way they'd veered from concern over Cooper's niece to interest over the smuggling seemed to bear out Rand's concerns. He threw the line further out to see what he'd catch.

"Right now he's handling some cargo that came in off of Delerue-Sanders's ships. But he's got some more lined up and may need a place to stash it until things cool down." James looked around the tavern office. "Maybe you've got some room here to warehouse some goods for a while? I could broker the deal with Washburn for you."

The two owners looked at each other again, silent communication honed by years of companionship.

"Maybe we do," Robin said. "But before we work with Mr. Washburn, he needs to come here, and he needs to bring Julia with him so we know she's well. Then we'll talk business. The next time you see him, you give him a message: Julia is not alone and friendless. Her family is concerned for her welfare and wants to know she's safe, in a face-to-face meeting."

James rubbed the nick on his neck, glad at one level that Mrs. Washburn did have someone out here for her. He knew nothing would keep Rand from doing what he had to do to finish this, but he liked Julia. It could go badly for her if she was alone when Rand lowered the boom.

"I'll pass the word along."

"How will we contact you to meet with Washburn?" Robin asked.

"You don't contact me," James said flatly. "I'll be in touch with you."

The two men exchanged one of those communicative looks again, then Robin looked back at Crane and nodded.

"Very well. But remember what I said, Crane—you make sure Washburn knows that Julia has friends. Powerful friends, and I don't mean just us. Any harm comes to her, he's going to wish he'd gone to Texas, too, and kept on moving west, because no matter where he goes, they'll find him."

James nodded his understanding, then turned to leave. He glanced back over his shoulder one more time before he exited the office. The two old pirates were watching him, and the look in their eyes hurried him through the door.

*   *   *

A table at Ganymede's Cup after hours held cups of coffee, and Robin's decadent rum cake, its fumes filling the air. But the famous cake was untouched as the two partners talked. "Should have followed him," Cooper said.

Robin leaned over and patted his hand. "It's all right. We both know how hard it is to find someone hiding in the backwoods who doesn't want to be found."

Robin studied the letters spread out before him. "I can hope Julia's telling the truth when she says she's well. I believe that to be the case," he said, tapping the letter. "Her handwriting is firm, not shaky or hesitant, and she's trying to pass along information."

Even though they'd gone over the letters numerous times, Robin picked one up and read aloud.

"'Dear Uncle Richard,

'I have the most incredible news to share with you! I am married, to Rand Washburn, a local farmer. It was quite sudden, and there was no time to get word back to you. As you know, I have been a guest on Washburn's farm. When he proposed marriage, his words were so persuasive I had no choice but to accept.'

"Obviously, she's been forced into marriage with this Cracker Washburn, but I think she was trying to tell us in this next part what Crane said, that Washburn is a well-known smuggler. 'You and he have some common interests.' But what do you make of this? 'I believe my sainted mother looked down on my marriage from heaven.' Why would she say the countess is dead?"

Cooper thought about it for a time and took a drink of his coffee before answering.

"Orphan named Cooper has no hope of ransom. She's not Lady Julia, the heiress."

"That's my girl," Robin said with approval. "She's using her head. And again, the fact that Washburn didn't outright kill her, but married her when there was no dowry or settlements for him, gives me hope that we may be able to extricate Julia from this mess unscathed."

The last words hung heavy in the silence. Neither of them believed a well brought up young lady could escape even relatively unscathed, and still be considered marriageable back in England. Or even in the social set in which she moved in America.

"I only want her back safe and sound before her parents arrive," Robin said, concern making his eyes large in his face. "My poor baby! I can't bear to think of what awful indignities she must be suffering at the hands of that scoundrel!"

*   *   *

"Oh yeah, baby, right there, you almost have it."

"This would be much easier, Rand, if you would stop licking me."

"Takes my mind off my sufferin'," he said, giving another swipe at one honey-sweet arm. "You have a really tasty elbow. And I don't say that to just anyone."

The day had started out simple enough, until Rand found the gallberry honey tucked in a cypress tree buzzing with golden bees. As Julia watched from a safe distance, he built a smudge fire to stupify the bees who manufactured the dark honey from the bushes dotting the palmetto scrub.

Even with the fire and his layers of clothing, some of the bees managed to sneak in to bite him. Rand was paying for the sweet treat now as they sat on the breezeway at the back of the cabin while Julia plucked the black stingers from his skin.

He'd insisted she undress down to the skin, too, so he could check her over, a process that seemed to take a long time and was done most thoroughly. When he said *he* had a stinger, she gave him that look down her nose that made him just have to kiss all the uppity stiffness right out of her.

So it was midafternoon when they heard the shout, "Anybody home?" from out front.

"Ma Ivey!" Julia gasped out, scrambling for her clothes as Rand cursed. He'd been all set to slip her some uppity stiffness of his own, and he did not appreciate the interruption. Goddamn it, what was the point of being the laziest farmer on the river if you couldn't take time in the middle of the day to diddle your own wife?

But that wife was gone, dashing around to the front of the cabin in a flash of calico skirts. Rand sighed, and pulled on his trousers and shirt.

It had been over a week since James Crane and the men had taken off, an unreal week for the two of them isolated out in the woods, going through their daily routine and neither talking about the future. One part of the future had been dealt with though. Julia's courses came, and Rand heard her weep out back at the outhouse. He stood on the veranda helplessly, not knowing what to do.

He didn't know why she wept, though a part of him wished that she had been increasing. It would create problems, but solve others. There would be no question of Julia leaving him if she carried his child. He'd do whatever it took to guarantee her protection, and keep her with him. He kept his thoughts to himself, and said nothing about her red and swollen eyes.

When he reached the front yard, Julia was escorting Ma Ivey up to the cabin while Benjamin watered their mules. Julia clutched a bundle of cloth to her chest, and the smile she gave the old woman was full of warmth. Rand stopped in his tracks and watched her, a yearning in his chest that had nothing to do with playing hide the stinger, but more to do with imagining that warm smile turned toward him.

"Hey, Rand, we brung ya a letter!"

Benjamin's voice broke Rand's reverie, and he looked away from the women to Benjamin, who was slapping dust and sand off his pants as he crossed the yard.

"I got it here somewhere. One of your men brung it by and

paid me a whole two bits to deliver it. Then Brewer stopped me at a cockfight, and said to give ya a message, too. But Brewer didn't give me nothin'." Benjamin frowned in confusion.

Rand grinned at Benjamin to put him at his ease, because he knew the slower man would worry it over in his mind like a dog with a bone until he got the message out.

"No problem, Ben. I got 'nother two bits for you, if you can remember Brewer's message exactly as he said it."

"Let me think," Benjamin said. He worked the tobacco in his cheek as he ruminated, then his face lit up, and he spat to the side, helpfully hitting a gourd plant.

"I remember it! Brewer says you're to meet him at the cane grindin'."

"Are you sure he said he'd be at the grindin'?"

"Yessir," Benjamin said with confidence. "And Ma ripped a piece outta me somethin' fierce for gamblin' at the cockfights. Wooeee, my ears are still ringin'!"

"Here's the other message," he fished the note out of his pocket.

Rand broke the seal and read Crane's message about what had transpired at Ganymede's Cup.

"Is it bad news, Rand?" Benjamin asked anxiously.

"Yes. But not surprisin' news," he said, looking toward the cabin. The women's laughter floated out in the autumn air, and he crushed the note in his hand.

*   *   *

"...so when I heared ya got married to Rand, I wanted to bring a weddin' gift."

Julia stroked the quilt laid across her lap. It was painstakingly

210

stitched, the Star of Bethlehem pattern laid in bright scraps of cloth. She didn't ask, but wondered if the quilt had been made for a daughter who hadn't survived to marry.

"It is lovely, Ma Ivey. I will treasure it, and thank you." She looked down at the old lady in her rocker and smiled. "And I also want to thank you again for the possums."

"Hmph," Ma Ivey said, "t'weren't nothin'. Now that the weather's coolin' for the winter they'll be some good eatin', fat and juicy on a cold night."

The women turned at the sound of footsteps on the veranda. Rand stood there, shadowed by the light coming in through the door.

"Look, Rand, Ma Ivey brought us a wedding gift. And she said there's to be a cane grinding tomorrow at their farm."

"This gal's never been to a cane grindin', Rand," Ma said, pausing to spit tobacco into the jar at her feet. "We're gonna need your help with the cane, and Julia here can come, too. There's goin' to be a powerful lot of victuals being cooked and eaten', and we need all the hands we can get."

He watched them and the silence stretched, until he said, "Yes, Ma. I'll be out to help."

Julia cocked her head and looked at him, but his face was a blank.

"Well, I can bake some things tomorrow morning and bring them with me, and I thank you for the milk, Ma Ivey. It will be a pleasure to make buttermilk biscuits tonight, and a nice cake tomorrow. Oh, and we have something for you, too!"

She ran out to the kitchen and grabbed one of the crocks of honey, comb and all, and brought it to the house.

"Rand found a bee tree and we have not strained the honey yet, but here is some you can take with you."

"Long sweetnin'!" The widow's face lit up. "Now ain't that special!" She pushed herself up out of the chair and toddled toward the door.

"I'd dearly love to stay and chat some more, but we need to stop at 'nother farm and let them know about the grindin' before we head on back. Rand, I'll see you and the missus tomorrow."

She pulled her shawl close about her as she stood in the doorway. "Winter's comin' on, for certain. Looks like I dropped off that weddin' quilt just in time."

She cackled and nudged Julia in the ribs, and Julia smiled back. In England, she might never have noticed a common old woman, other than the family's tenants. Their worlds wouldn't cross, unless a carriage broke down in front of the woman's farm.

She leaned down and put her arm around Ma's shoulders, giving her a hug. "We'll see you tomorrow then. You have a safe journey."

They watched from the veranda as the mules pulled the cart down the track, then Rand looked at her for a long moment and said, "I'm going out huntin'. I may not be back 'til late."

His face had the shuttered look it wore when he was that other Washburn, the one with dangerous secrets. Julia wanted to ask him if something was wrong. But she didn't ask him. She was afraid the answer might throw open all those shut doors behind which her fears lurked.

So she only looked at him and said, "Hurry back."

For a moment she thought he'd kiss her good-bye, but he

turned and gathered his rifle and gear and left the cabin without a backward glance.

Julia stood on the veranda and watched him disappear down the trail, then with a sigh, turned away from the sunlight back to the house.

CHAPTER 13

"Possum hangin' in the tree,
"Raccoon on the ground;
"Raccoon say, you stingy rat,
"Shake them 'simmons down!"

Julia paused in her singing and frowned down at the spoon stirring through the cake batter.

"Possum hanging in the tree?" *Where had that come from?* "Goodness, I'm becoming countrified!"

She chuckled, looking out the kitchen window at the activity in the yard. Rand was doing the morning chores in preparation for their trip to the Iveys' farm. For a moment she watched him as she stirred, indulging herself in a fantasy that theirs was a normal marriage, two people on the Florida frontier, making a new life together.

But it was as much a fantasy as singing raccoons.

*   *   *

The hot smell of the boiling cane syrup reached their noses even before the noise and laughter from the Ivey homestead floated up the trail. When Rand and Julia arrived at the clearing, Victoria brayed to her cousins and flicked her ears forward in greeting, and was soon unhitched to join the mules, horses, and a brace of oxen at the homestead.

A cane grinding was a communal affair, too much work for

one family, and a good excuse for an autumn get-together. All day long the hot syrup was boiled and stirred, the long-handled ladles skimming the top and keeping the sugar from spilling over. Inside an open shed shaded by palmetto thatch, the younger, mostly unmarried men and women took turns, while the more settled ones watched over toddlers and babies, or helped with the skinning of game and the cooking for the coming feast.

For a feast it was, a feast for all the senses. Heat radiated out from under the oversized kettles, and there was the mouthwatering tang of meat slow cooking over hardwood coals in ground pits. There were more kettles of swamp cabbage and corn boiling up for later in the day. The eyes were treated to a sky so blue it nearly hurt to look at it too long, but the colorful calicoes and more subtle shades of homespun drew the eye back to earth.

An old man with few teeth but still nimble fingers was fiddling on the front porch, and following Ma Ivey with his eyes every time she'd troop back and forth from her cabin, supervising the women like a hen bossing the chicken yard. Her son Benjamin stirred syrup alongside a young woman.

"Howdy, Miz Washburn," Ben called out, waving an arm. "Come over here and meet Rosie."

Julia put her basket of cakes over her arm and walked to where heat from the boiling syrup and the fires shimmered out of the shed, but the couple kept stirring and skimming, even as their clothes darkened with sweat.

"Miz Washburn, this is my friend, Rosie Bryant. Rosie, this here's Miz Washburn. She's the gal what we borrowed from The

Greek Boy, but she's married to Rand now, so it's all right."

Rosie raised her bonneted head and looked at Julia, and then ducked back down again, but not before Julia saw that Miss Bryant had large eyes the color of the morning glory flowers twining 'round the fence, and a harelip.

"Rosie says she'll save me a dance later, Miz Washburn. You're goin' to like the dancin', but don't tell the preacher 'bout it when he comes 'round, or he'll hammer us with a sermon good and proper."

"I promise not to tell," Julia said. "It is nice to meet you, Miss Bryant. Will you show me how to stir the syrup later? This is my first cane grinding, so it is all new to me."

"See, Rosie's shy," Benjamin said in what he thought was a confidential whisper. "She don't like people lookin' at her 'cause a her mouth, but it don't bother me none. I think she looks like a pretty little kitty."

Rosie Bryant nodded once at Julia, and Benjamin beamed at her. Rosie ducked her head again, but not so quickly Julia didn't see her looking at slow Ben like he'd hung the moon.

Goodness, Julia thought, *the minister may have more to do than preach a sermon next time he rides through!*

She excused herself from the heat of the cane fires and walked to the tables where the women were laying out an array of pumpkin and pecan pies, shortbread oozing with sweet jam, all of it covered with light cloths to keep the insects off. Crocks of preserves and pickled tomatoes, cucumbers, and relishes shone in the sun. Her persimmon cakes were added to the pile. While once Julia might have wondered who could consume so much food at one sitting, she'd seen the Crackers sit down to their victuals and knew the food would be little more than a memory by the time the day was done.

Barefoot children chased a brindle hound bitch through the yard, stopping long enough to beg for slices of buttered cornbread before heading down to the creek for some of the last swimming they'd do before the air and the water were chilled by winter.

Julia took a moment to go over and watch the cane mill, where a placid ox hitched to a lever walked 'round and 'round the contraption. The cane mill was two vertical iron rollers set in a heavy wood frame, and Franklin Ivey and the other feeders slowly passed the towering red cane stalks between the grinding rollers as the ox worked the treadmill. As the juice was squeezed out of the stalks of cane, it ran into a trough attached to the mill frame, while the cane pulp fell from the other side.

The uncooked cane juice in the barrels was pale green, and as it cooked and was stirred it thickened and ripened to a deep amber, becoming the syrup prized for sweetening everything from coffee to pecan pie to biscuits.

"It's a lot of work to get a little sweetness in your life."

Julia looked over her shoulder and favored her husband with an arch smile. "But worth the effort, don't you think?" She looked back at the primitive mill. "It's different, and yet not so different here at the cane grinding—the food, the music, all the people working together. I imagine there is a pattern to harvest festivals everywhere, whether it is Devonshire or Florida."

She didn't add that the harvest festivals at Rosemoor were separated by class. Her family funded the event and mingled with the local people on the estate, but the formal Harvest Ball inside Rosemoor's glittering ballroom was where they spent their evening.

Julia remembered sneaking out one night during the Harvest Ball, when she was still in the schoolroom and too young to attend the adult festivities. She'd gone down to the meadow where the villagers and farm workers celebrated. From the cover of a hayrick she'd watched the lively dancing, the ale and cider flowing free from the barrels sent by Lord Smithton and his lady. There was the occasional fistfight, and couples pairing off and sneaking away. She was to remember the openness and gaiety of that night when she attended her first Harvest Ball at Rosemoor. As wonderful as the ball had been, it all seemed muted compared to the farmers' celebration. The jewels and military uniforms and satin gowns were worn by people who didn't laugh out loud, or dance too exuberantly, or do more than nibble at their food.

They'd never sweated over a kettle of cane syrup or made crude jokes about the stalks of cane, or laughed together as they set up tables groaning under the weight of food.

Rand looked more relaxed than he had in days. Getting away from the homestead seemed to be good for both of them.

"Wait here, and I'll bring you a treat."

He sauntered over to the syrup kettles, exchanged a few words with Benjamin, and tipped his hat to Miss Rosie. Then he reached for a stalk of cane and cut off a short section, scraping it around the edge of the pot. He blew on it as he walked back to his wife.

"Here you are, darlin', a little sample of the cane."

Julia took the stalk from his hand and after touching it to make sure it was cooled, brought it up to her mouth and stuck it between her lips like a candy stick.

"Mmmm," she said as she sucked at it to get the sweet crystals off. "This is delicious!"

Rand was watching her mouth, her lips wrapped around the stick, and he swallowed, once.

"I'd best go see if they need some help with the roastin' meat," he muttered. He looked over his shoulder one last time, and almost fell into a barbecue pit as he watched his wife daintily stick her tongue out and give the sugar stick a long lick.

Julia turned away with a smile and went to help the farm wives. Ma Ivey spotted her, and put her to work stirring a thick soup of fish and hominy flavored with peppers and tomatoes. She listened as the women discussed the chores of preserving the vegetables and fruits for the winter. No one had to starve in Florida if he was willing to do a lick of work, Ma Ivey declared, as the good Lord sent food and plenty of it. Why, if anything, you were more likely to go hungry in the summer than the winter, when the heat spoiled the meat and wilted the greens in the garden, but even then there was always corn and fish available.

But autumn and winter was the time to feast, when the possums were fat and the pigs were butchered into the bacon, ham, and lard so prized by southern cooks.

"This here's Julia Washburn," Ma Ivey said in the way of introductions. "She's from England and talks funny, and don't know our ways real well, so y'all help make her feel welcome."

The other women eyed Julia with open curiosity and some dark looks from one or two who'd had their own eyes on Rand Washburn.

"I hear you worked at that Ganymede's Cup tavern," one of the younger women said with a sniff, arranging some biscuits on a platter.

"That is correct," Julia said with a polite smile. "And you are?"

"I'm Becky Hawthorne. I was mighty surprised when I heard tell that Mr. Washburn married a saloon gal," Becky said sweetly. "Why, you could have knocked me over with a feather! I was sure he was a bachelor for life."

Unlike the other girls, she wore a cotton sateen dress, not a skirt and blouse, and it was obvious she had on a corset beneath. Clearly Miss Hawthorne came from a family with some wealth and wanted to make sure people knew it, even at a cane grinding.

Julia's smile sharpened. Miss Hawthorne might fancy herself the belle of East Florida, but Julia'd had four Seasons in London, not to mention an education at an exclusive academy for the daughters of the British aristocracy. There was nothing she didn't know about declawing cats.

"No doubt Rand was content to wait until the right woman came along."

A couple of the other women snickered, and Ma Ivey shot a stream of tobacco juice onto the jasmine growing at the base of the house, alarming a dog sleeping under the porch.

"Whew! This young'un's givin' me what-for today," a pregnant matron complained as she straightened and rubbed the base of her back. "I'm glad it's coolin' off some, because I've had 'bout as much of summer I can handle, carryin' this one around."

"I ate so much watermelon when I was carryin' my Jeremiah,

I wouldn't have been surprised if he had popped out spittin' seeds," said one lady with a grin. "That was the only good thing about bearin' a July baby—gettin' as much melon as I wanted. That summer I must have eaten a wagonful!"

"I just wish my hair didn't fall out so when I'm carryin'," a red-cheeked woman wearing a blue flowered bonnet fretted.

"What you need is some onion juice, gal," an old lady chimed in. "You put the juice in your hair and go sit in the sun a spell, and it will grow back in all thick and curly."

"Yes, but will her husband want to be next to her if she is smelling of onions?" Julia asked.

"I'll do it!" Jeremiah's mama said. "If Samuel don't cuddle with me, I'll get a break from all these young'uns I been poppin' out!"

That sally brought more laughter from the women, and she added, "Maybe Miz Washburn here's goin' to be wishin' she'd married up with Rand sooner, otherwise she might be havin' one of those summer babes."

Ma Ivey misinterpreted the look on Julia's face as the women discussed her getting pregnant with Rand's child, for she leaned over and patted Julia on the arm.

"Don't you worry none, missy. The good Lord will send you a baby of your own by an' by, and in the meantime, you got those cold winter nights ahead of you to snuggle in and work on it. From the looks of you both, Ah'd wager even onion juice couldn't keep you apart."

The older women cackled at this, while the younger ones blushed, and Julia kept her thoughts to herself and watched her husband. Rand was well received by the other men, and was comfortable with them, but there was something setting him apart. It may have been his stance, or his clean looks, or having all his teeth and nose, but for all his piney woods talk, he carried himself like a lord.

Clean him up, take him to a premier tailor, and he'd fit in to any drawing room in London. At least until he opened his mouth.

But it was a daydream worth lingering over, the idea that perhaps Rand could return to England with her. They might settle at one of Lord Smithton's more distant estates—Northern Scotland looked attractive at the moment—and Rand could handle the estate management.

Or they could use her money to buy their place. Keen as Rand was at taking other people's property, she didn't think he'd quibble over using his wife's funds to settle down somewhere else, as long as he understood his life of crime was over. She was willing to spend the rest of her life as wife to a gentleman farmer. She was *not* willing to spend it married to a smuggler, especially if he was targeting her family's ships.

Julia sighed. It was far from the life she'd envisioned for herself when she was younger, and it would mean her virtual banishment from her social world. But a life with Rand, flaws and all, looked more attractive to her right now than the life she was raised for, if it was a life without him.

As the shadows lengthened, the men began gathering around the tables like wasps drawn to sweet fruit, cozying up to their women and trying to talk them out of some of the food before the feast officially began. Ma Ivey ruled her dirt yard like an empress and wasn't above slapping a reaching hand with a wooden spoon when they drew too close. Finally though, the last of the cane was put through the mill and the syrup cooked down, and as the night sky filled with stars the feast began to a chorus of tree frogs and crickets serenading the workers. They lined up before the platters of roast pig and venison, quails, turkey, and doves. Even a possum or two joined the potatoes in the smoldering coals. There was fish stew and slow-cooked turtle, gator tail and fresh bass, and plenty of home-brewed ale and scuppernong wine to wash it down.

The ever present corn was there, too, as meal, mush, bread, pone, grits, and "roasenears," cooked in the hot coals. Julia grinned to herself. There would be plenty of cobs for the privies after tonight's feast.

The children and old folks were served first, then the men, then the women took for themselves, the fires from the pits and fat pine torches lighting up the yard. By the time Julia had her plate filled—and Rand had his second serving—the men were rosining their fiddle bows and bringing out the banjos and whistles.

Rand made room for Julia to sit beside him, and held up an object in his hand.

"Look, the wishbone!"

"And that means…what?"

"It means you and me got to make a wish."

He showed her how to grasp the bone, and warned her it would take some strength to make it snap since it hadn't dried out yet.

"So give it a good tug and make a wish."

"What should I wish for, Rand?"

He looked at her, his face half lit from the fire, and for a moment she thought he was someone else, someone she didn't know. Then he smiled and said, "Wish for your heart's desire, darlin'. That's what I'm goin' to wish for."

They tugged the bone, and it broke with a crack that sounded too loud in the night air.

Julia held the larger piece. "I wished we could always be as happy as we are right now."

Rand looked down at the broken fragment in his hand, his face hidden in the dark. "They say if you tell your wish, it won't come true."

The musicians were playing a lively little tune and Rand tossed the bone on the table, then held his hand out to his wife. "Let's go join the others."

They may not have been willing to call it dancing lest the preacher hear about it, but whatever was happening in the hard-packed yard certainly involved swinging partners and music, and a lot of laughter and movement.

There were jigs and reels, Highland flings and clogging. By the time they were into "The Piney Woods Ballad," most of the women had taken off their pinching shoes, and brown bare feet skimmed across the dirt. The ones past their dancing days kept an eye on the babies and younger children. Even then callused and arthritic toes could be seen keeping the beat as wrinkled eyes gleamed with memories of past cane grindings, when the dancing and drinking would last far into the night, and a troop of babies would be born on the farms before the next year's harvest.

Julia danced set after set, with her husband and with the other men, including one toothless, white-bearded farmer who told her if she ever tired of livin' with Rand Washburn she was welcome to come to his place, 'cause she was about the sweetest thing who'd ever wore calico.

Julia thanked him prettily, but noticed Rand was not dancing this set. He was scanning the woods, the darkened area where Franklin Ivey and some of the other men were passing around a jug of corn squeezings. When she looked back at the group, she almost lost her step in the dance. Daniel Brewer was there now, slapping Franklin on the back, and taking a long drink from the corn jug.

Rand headed over in the direction of the men. As Julia watched him, she silently willed the musicians to play faster so she could finish the dance.

*   *   *

"If this works out, Dan'l, I know what I'm going to do with my share," Franklin said. "I'm goin' to buy me a nigger, so I don't have to work this farm from sunup to sundown. Mebbe I'll buy me a likely wench while I'm at it, and put her to work, too."

The other men sniggered, and Brewer said, "Shit, Franklin, you bring some nigger gal out to the farm and your mama's going to whip you from here to Sunday."

"Old Rand there's sure sittin' pretty," Franklin said, gesturing toward Julia dancing in the firelight. "Here I thought we was bringin' him some old slut to clean house, and he ends up with a gal as ripe and juicy as a peach." He shook his head and took another drink. "I hoped he'd be so beholden to me that he'd take me on with his crew."

"You start dealin' with Rand Washburn, you're going to come out short of everythin' but experience," Benjamin said.

225

"I'd listen to him if I was you, Franklin."

Rand stepped into the light, and Franklin passed him the jug. Rand tipped it on his shoulder and took a long swallow, eyeing Brewer, who took the jug from him as he finished. Rand looked around. All the men were flushed from the strong drink except for Benjamin, who'd only had some ale earlier. He was watching the women clearing up the dishes, a soft expression on his face as Rosie Bryant moved gracefully among them.

"You still pinin' after harelip Rosie?" Franklin sniggered. "Parts of her ain't bad at all. You could always put a bag over her head and do her that way."

Benjamin's mind was slow, but the rest of him wasn't. A moment later Franklin was looking up at his brother from the ground.

"There ain't nothin' in your head but wind, Franklin!" He said angrily as Franklin rolled over and spat out blood. "Don't you ever say nothin' like that about Miss Rosie again! I'm goin' to marry that gal!"

Franklin got to his feet, and Rand gripped Benjamin's arm to hold him back.

"That's enough, both of you. Now go on, get back to the dancin'. I need to talk to Brewer."

After the others left, Rand looked at Brewer, who was watching him.

"I hear Delerue-Sanders' owner is comin' to town. Is this goin' to interfere with our plans?"

"Nope," Brewer said, spitting into the dirt. "They already docked at Fernandina, but that's not the ship we want. Another one's due but it's going to make a stop first. If you meet us at the

226

landin' tomorrow night, you'll find a haul so rich you'll be able to buy enough niggers to plant cotton from here to Pensacola and live high."

Rand's glance sharpened. "What kind of cargo is that rich? You bringin' in slaves?"

Brewer looked around, but they were alone.

"No, not slaves. It's in chests your crew can handle without problems. I can't tell you what it is, but my man has a need to bring some special cargo here to Florida. He needs to move fast and quiet, and I told him you can do the job. He'll be there tomorrow. He said this one's big enough that he wants to check you out hisself."

"Who is he?"

"Now, that you don't need to know 'til you come tomorrow night, Washburn. Can you get your men together by then?"

"Oh yeah," Rand said. "My men will be there. Don't you worry none, Brewer—it's goin' to run smooth as pond water."

The men shook on it, and separated back into the darkness.

*   *   *

Julia crouched down in the palmettos, afraid to breathe for fear she'd give herself away to the conspirators. She needed to get word to Uncle Richard, but would never find her own way to the tavern in time. But she knew someone who could.

When she worked her way back to the festivities, Rand was there eating a piece of pie. He gave her a sharp glance.

"I was worried about you, darlin'. You was gone a long time."

Julia smiled at him wanly. She didn't have to worry about faking looking sickly, for that's how she was feeling after

227

overhearing the conversation in the dark.

"Those pickled tomatoes disagreed with me, and I had to make a visit out back. But I think I'm over it."

He looked at her with genuine concern. "Are you sure? We can leave now if you're poorly."

"No, just something I will know not to eat next time. Really, I am well."

"Would you care to dance with me then?"

"I'm not sure I am that well, Rand. Why don't you ask Miss Bryant for this dance?"

Rand smiled at her and said, "That's a right thoughtful idea," and he tilted her head up for a quick kiss on the lips. "I'll be back in a few minutes. You go sit down if you need to."

"Maybe I will," she said, willing away the tears that threatened to fill her eyes. When Rand stepped out into the yard with Rosie Bryant, Julia sidled next to Benjamin, who was clapping along with the music.

"May I speak to you for a moment, Benjamin?"

CHAPTER 14

"Pssst—Rand!"

Rand stopped crouching over the trap he'd set down at the creek and turned around, his hand on his rifle.

Benjamin Ivey stood behind him, wreathed in the morning mists rising off the forest floor. Rand was chagrined Ben got the drop on him, but while Ben's mind didn't always work fast with words or ideas, there was nothing lacking in his woodcraft.

"Good morning, Ben. Did you come out here for breakfast? 'Cause after I'm done here, I'm headed out. Julia's at the cabin though, and she'd be right glad to see you."

Benjamin shook his head, and took off his hat, turning it 'round and 'round in his hands. He looked about as unhappy as Rand had ever seen him.

"I got a problem, Rand. It's your problem, too, I think. We need to talk here, aways from the house."

Rand stood. "Is this about Julia?"

Ben nodded, looking more miserable than ever. He jammed his hat back on, reached into his pocket, and pulled out a grimy note.

"Miz Julia talked with me last night, and asked me to take a note for her to that Greek Boy tavern today. She said it was real important, life and death." He wiped his hand across his mouth and looked up into Rand's eyes. "She also said you wasn't to know about this. But I think Miz Julia's in trouble. And you're supposed to take care of her, ain'tcha? Ain't that what husbands do? I know if I married Rosie, I'd want to know if someone was botherin' her."

"You're correct, Ben. Husbands take care of their wives," Rand said heavily. "Give it to me."

He took the note scrawled out on grease-marked brown paper, and read it while the mockingbirds twitted overhead.

———

Washburn planning raid on DS. Warn DS owners they are in danger! I will do what I can here. —J

———

"Miz Julia gave me this to run the errand. I said I'd do it for nothin', but she insisted. But I can't keep this, Rand."

He held out his grimy hand and dropped something into Rand's palm. It was a gold ring, with a ruby inset. The ring he'd given his wife at their hasty wedding ceremony.

"It's worth a lot, ain't it?"

"I thought it was, once." Rand looked down at the ring he held in his hand. He'd been planning in his head how he'd replace it for Julia, with one daintier and finer, when this was all over. His hand closed convulsively around the gold and the cold stone.

"I know exactly what this ring is worth. You did the right thing, Benjamin, and I'm grateful to you."

"You'll take care of Miz Julia then?"

"Oh yeah," he murmured, looking in the direction of the cabin. "I'm going to take care of her." He took a deep breath, and shoved the ring in his pocket.

After Ben left, Rand looked at his empty traps. There were some creatures that couldn't be held, no matter how secure the rope. He untied the mule and continued down the trail to his meeting with James Crane.

And if he had to occasionally wipe the wet from his eyes, there were only the mockingbirds to see it.

*   *   *

Julia spent the day cooking and cleaning up a storm, in a frenzy of nervous energy waiting on Rand's return. He told her when he left in the predawn dark that he'd be gone all day, checking traps. She knew better after the conversation she'd overheard last night. She used her excuse of the stomach upset to keep her distance from him, fearing he'd read in her face her knowledge of his activities.

As Rand had said, she wasn't much of a card player.

If he wasn't home by dark, she'd know he'd gone straight to the landing, but she had to wait and be sure. If he came back and found her missing, he'd set out after her.

Finally, after the shadows lengthened to near black and the lamps were lit, Julia heard Victoria's bray. She took up a lamp and looked in the mirror, smoothing her hair back and adjusting the neck of her blouse, taking a moment to dab on some of the orange blossom perfume.

She stood in the entrance to the breezeway off the kitchen and waited, hands clasped in front of her, heart pounding so loud she was sure Rand could hear it out in the yard. He came around the corner to the kitchen and washed up, not speaking, not looking at her.

"Did you have luck hunting today?"

231

Rand finished rinsing his hands, and dried them on some sacking before looking at her.

"I found what I was lookin' for." He kept his eyes on her, traveling down her neatened hair to her bare feet.

"You look like you're feelin' more the thing."

"Oh, I'm doing much better," Julia said, then stopped in confusion. Perhaps if she'd told him she was still ill, he wouldn't go out tonight? No, it was unlikely a sick wife would keep him away from the promise of so much gold.

She smiled at him, and tried again. "I am feeling better. And I fixed supper. There's hash from the turkey, and corn fritters, biscuits and pecan pie. Your favorite."

"Well now," Rand said softly, not moving from where he stood in the shadows, "that was right nice of you to fix my favorite pie."

Julia took a fold of her skirt and twisted it in her fist, releasing it as soon as she realized what she was doing. "I thought, maybe, since I was feeling better, you might want to play chess tonight, and um, go to bed early. Looks like it is going to be a chill night."

He walked through the breezeway to where she stood, and put a hand on her hair, wrapping one wayward curl around his finger. Julia relaxed her stiff shoulders. If he was looking at her that way, his eyes all soft and tender, then everything was going to be all right.

His next words disabused her of this fantasy.

"I surely wish I could. Stayin' in with you tonight sounds just dandy. But there's more huntin' I need to do, 'specially since I came home empty-handed without anythin' for your cook pot."

He smiled again, winsome and open. "What kind of husband would I be, if I didn't take care of my own wife?"

She chattered through supper, talking about the cane grinding, and Ben and Rosie, and anything except the need for Rand to go back out. He was mostly silent. At one point, when she glanced over her shoulder at him as she carried the plates into the kitchen, she saw him watching her, an unreadable expression on his face.

Julia leaned over the sink, her supper threatening to come back up on her. With shaking hands she splashed water from the jug over her burning cheeks, and when she dried it with the sacking on the table, she inhaled deeply. It smelled of her husband. The man who now threatened all she held dear.

"I'm leavin'."

She straightened slowly and turned around. Rand stood there, his rifle in his hand, gear slung over his shoulder. He gazed at her, unblinking.

"Julia." He stopped and looked at her, then set his gear down and walked over to where she leaned against the sink. He gazed down into her eyes, his own dark, and she read such pain there that it was a natural thing for her to reach up, and put her arms around his neck, and pull him down for a kiss, a kiss that held all the things she couldn't say to him. All that she might never be able to say to this smuggler who'd stolen her heart.

His arms tightened around her, almost to the point of pain, as he poured his feelings out in that kiss.

"You'll wait up for me?"

She looked up at him and nodded, then lowered her eyes to his neck where his pulse beat, fast now in the wake of their farewells.

He gathered his gear and headed out the back, one final glance over his shoulder at her before he stepped out into the darkness. She watched until she could no longer see him moving through the palmettos.

Then with a small sob, she turned and closed the door behind her, shutting out the night.

*   *   *

Julia slipped from the cabin, standing motionless on the veranda. She waited there, in the blackness, letting her eyes adjust to the moonlight before moving out toward the palmettos, silently into the cool winter night.

"Goin' somewhere?"

The drawl came out of the darkness, freezing her blood.

She spun on her heel and dashed for the cabin, slamming the door behind her, but a hard shoulder crashed into it, and the force of the blow threw her halfway across the room. She moved back until the unyielding logs of the cabin wall were against her back, as Rand Washburn gently closed the door behind him.

There was no light but for the faint glow from the coals she'd banked, and without looking at her where she huddled against the logs, he went over and stirred up the fire, tossing on another log to light the room. The fire blazed up, lighting his face when he turned to look at her, illuminating the smile that curled his expressive mouth up at the corners.

It was the smile one saw on the face of the monster just before he devoured little girls in their nightmares.

"I think it's time you told me the truth," he said in even tones, "and you can start with why you came to my farm."

She gasped and pushed herself further against the wall, a motion that Rand seemed to note with satisfaction as he rose to his feet. Julia realized she was playing into his hand.

"Your friends the Iveys kidnapped me from Ganymede's Cup! And what I was doing at the Cup is none of your business!"

"Now that's where you're wrong, *Mrs. Washburn*," he said in a low voice, stepping in closer. "It is very much my business."

She was fast, and almost made it to the back door, but he was there a second ahead of her. She struggled fruitlessly to open the door, but he shoved himself against her, pinning her against the hard wood, his arm wrapping around her, trapping her two hands in his.

"Let me go!"

"I don't think so," he said in her ear. She pushed back against him, but he was like granite at her back, keeping her exactly where he wanted her. He put a hand on her shoulder and yanked her around, still leaning his body into hers so that she could not move, still holding her hands in his. He moved his head closer, and she could feel his hot breath against her ear. He kissed her there, where her pulse beat hard in her neck, then he put his free hand over that pulse point, tightening it just enough to make her stand very straight, and very still.

"You're my wife, remember? You belong to me. Squar' Reynolds said so. You ain't never going back to your England. I can do what I want to you, Mrs. Washburn. Pick you up, throw you on the table, and toss your skirts over your head. Use you like a two-bit tavern whore, or treat you proper, dependin' on how you behave. And on how badly you want to live."

A shudder she couldn't suppress raced over her frame and he

felt it. When he pulled his head back to look into her eyes, he was still wearing that gallows smile, speaking to her in that soft, even drawl that terrified her more than his voice raised in anger.

"I'm gettin' pretty darned tired of your lies and stories, darlin'. If I get tired enough, I can take you so far back into the woods, even the crows won't find your bones."

"You wouldn't do that!"

"Would I not? Who's gonna miss one smart-talkin' English gal?"

Julia licked lips gone dry as paper, and saw his darkened eyes flick down to that small movement. All thoughts of self-preservation made her want to push as far away from him as she could go. Instead, she thrust herself forward. She felt him, at her belly, through his clothing and hers. He was excited by the danger, and his anger, and her fear.

"You would miss me."

He stared at her for an endless time, his face unreadable. "Damn you, Julia," he said hoarsely.

His head blocked out the dull light as his mouth lowered to hers, and she braced herself to absorb some of that anger radiating off him, but he surprised her. His kiss was tender, soft, like the smiles he'd given her earlier. His tongue coaxed her mouth open, and he slipped past her defenses.

She felt him move his hand down the front of her gown, over the swell of her breast where he paused, feeling the heart beat there, and she pushed herself further into his grasp. But he only made a low moaning noise in his throat and she was distracted by the roaring of the blood in her own ears, the desire for this man who was so bad for her pounding through her veins.

When he lifted his lips from hers, she felt his regret, so much regret that he moved back in for one final taste, before pulling back again, his hands still on hers.

The hands he'd tied together with his handkerchief while they were kissing.

Julia looked down in horror at her bound wrists and then back up at him, all laughter and softness gone from that face.

"I'm sorry, but this is the way it has to be."

Rand manacled his hand around her upper arm and pulled her, stunned and unresisting, into the bedroom. He took a length of tarred rope from the bottom of his chest, and tied her bound wrists to the bedpost with a knot that would have done a sailor proud.

She finally found her voice. "Rand, don't do this! We can leave, tonight, go away! I have money. I am really an heiress. I can buy you your comforts! We could leave for Australia or South America...or...or Italy, I don't care! Just don't go out there tonight to meet with Brewer. I'm begging you!" Her voice broke. "Trust me, Rand!"

He stopped fussing with the rope and grinned at her mirthlessly. "Trust you? Now that's the one thing I can't do, not if I want to see another sunrise. But that story about havin' money is real sweet. You got a good imagination."

He kissed her again, hard, and as he left her he stopped in the doorway and turned. "I'll be back for you, Julia, never doubt it. A man takes care of his wife."

And then he was gone, out through the cabin and into the night.

CHAPTER 15

Julia tore at the bindings. Sweat poured off her body and slickened her fingers, trembling with the effort of picking at the knot, one bloodied tip testifying to the nail lost in the process that seemed more fruitless by the minute. The fire in the other room had died back to embers, and it was dark but for a shaft of moonlight moving across the floor, showing her how much time passed while she was bound and helpless.

"Anybody home?"

Julia stopped breathing, not daring to believe.

"Ben? Ben Ivey? Come in, and hurry!"

A few moments later she heard the heavy tread of Ben's boots on the rough floor.

"Jumpin' catfish! Miz Washburn, what happened? Wait, I'll get a light."

She could hear him in the other room, stirring the coals and then the advancing glow of the lamp as he returned.

He set the lamp on the chest and bent over her bound hands, and with a wicked-looking knife used the Gordian knot method to free her.

"Ma got wind of Frank's plan to meet up with Rand tonight, and slipped some licorice syrup into his coffee, and he's been in the little house since, howlin' and cursin' up a streak. But he ain't goin' nowheres tonight. Ma said she may have raised two idiot sons, but she didn't raise them to go to prison."

"Why are you here then?"

"Rand told me to come out here and check on you in the mornin', just in case…"

"Just in case he didn't make it back," Julia finished for him bleakly.

"When Ma heard that, she walloped me upside the head, and told me to get on over here tonight and bring you back to our farm, where you'd be safe. I never thought Rand would do this to you though!"

By now Julia was free of the ropes and rubbed her wrists where they were numb and chafed from her efforts to free herself. She smiled at Ben, then surprised him by leaning up to put a kiss on his bearded cheek.

"Ben Ivey, I think Miss Rosie Bryant would be a fortunate woman if she had you for a husband."

"Aw, Miz Washburn…"

He ducked his head, embarrassed, but Julia had already turned away and reached for something under the bed.

"Ben, did you come out on your mule, or in your cart?"

"I saddled the mule, Miz Washburn, but it don't matter, 'cause I can hitch him up to your cart."

Julia stood, holding in her hands the pistol she'd stashed during supper. Foolish of Rand to leave his chest unlocked that way. She pointed the gun at Ben, whose eyes grew large as he gulped. "Jumpin' catfish! Miz Washburn, put that away! You might shoot someone!"

"I'm sorry, Benjamin, but I have no choice. You will stay here tonight while I take the mule to the landing. Please don't try anything. You stay here, and this will be a story you can tell Rosie and your grandchildren."

"Aw, Miz Washburn!"

"No arguments."

Julia began backing out of the room, but a glint of gold on the chest caught her eye. It was the ring, her wedding ring, Rand's ring, sitting atop the note she'd sent with Ben to Ganymede's Cup.

Her eyes narrowed at Benjamin Ivey, but he looked even more miserable…and scared…and the night was getting old. She snatched the ring off the dresser. "Stay here, Benjamin. You do not want to make me angrier than I am right now, I assure you!"

"Yes, ma'am." Ben sighed unhappily, and sat on the edge of the bed, hands in the air.

With a last glare at him Julia backed out of the room, slammed the door, and kept her eyes on it as she left the cabin.

Ben's mule was saddled and waiting out front. Julia untied him and after a few false starts managed to mount, turning the animal in the direction Rand had traveled earlier on Victoria. She'd have to move fast if she was going to save the life of the stubborn criminal she'd grown to love, and keep him from killing her parents. Or them killing him.

"Time to burn the wind, boy," she said to the mule, giving it a smack on the rump to get the point across. The mule started out, the gait surprisingly smooth to a woman raised to ride horseback, and it was surefooted along the darkened path.

The ride through the pine and scrub seemed to take forever, and at one point a hunting cat screamed, near enough to spook the mule, who went stock-still and shivered like a dog, then refused to move. After a few attempts to get moving again, Julia leaned down and said in his long ear, "If you don't start moving, right now, I'm going to dismount and leave you here for that cat's supper."

Whether it was the conviction in her voice, or the smell of other mules and water down by the river, the animal picked up its hooves and began ambling down the path again until Julia halted it as the trees on the bluff above the river came into view. She dismounted, tying the mule so it wouldn't bray her presence to the smugglers. She loaded the pepperbox with Washburn's ammunition and powder, cursing its weight and its short range. Right now a rifle to pick off a varmint or two would be ideal, but beggars can't be choosers, and the solid heft of the pistol gave her more confidence than walking in on them empty handed. Best to be prepared for the other creatures of the night who fancied themselves predators.

The frogs down at the river were clamoring so loudly she was sure they'd hide any of her sounds, and off in the distance she heard a bull gator roar as the night mists rose. It was a night for wildlife. She inched her way through the brush along the ridge, careful now of the leaf mold and hidden deadfalls of the woods.

*   *   *

"I'm here, my men are here, and we're ready to do business. Where're the goods?"

"Hold your water, Washburn, I hear the boat now."

Brewer spat and pointed out to the river, where a torch bobbed and drew closer. A sloop was anchored on the water, and a boat was being rowed to shore while men worked by lantern light on deck, hauling and securing cargo.

241

A man sat in the bow of the boat, wiping his face with a handkerchief while others rowed. He jumped out onto the sand, and made his way to where Brewer and Washburn waited. Even at a distance Rand could see his florid face was shiny with sweat, though he appeared to be directing rather than doing any actual work. Of course, it would be hard to do any work in such a fancy waistcoat and tight breeches.

"You are Washburn?" he said in accents similar to Rand's wife.

"Yeah. Who're you?"

The Englishman slapped at his cheek, where a mosquito was making inroads. "I am the man delivering to you a special cargo, and you will be handsomely rewarded for conveying it to the locations I direct you to."

"Is that right? 'Xactly what is it we're conveyin' here?"

Men were unloading locked strongboxes onto the sand, and it looked like more were being rowed out from the ship, the operation efficient and silent.

"You are being hired to haul goods, Washburn, not to ask questions. You do not need to know the nature of those goods."

"Ooowee, you sure have a way of talkin' on you, fella," he drawled. "But I got to tell you, I get twitchy all over not knowin' what it is I'm haulin'. I mean, what if it's powder or somethin' that might explode in my face?"

The sounds of guns being cocked by Washburn's men brought answering movement from the Englishman's crew, but even as Brewer reached for his sidepiece Rand said, "Don't do it, Brewer. My men got you covered. I just want to get me some answers, that's all."

And with that, negating his earlier comments about the powder, Rand cocked his revolver and shot the lock off the strongbox nearest his feet, kicking the lid back as the smoke rose in the still air.

He reached into the box with his free hand and pulled out bundles of American currency, brand new, fresh off the presses.

"Put the money and the gun down, Rand, and stand away from the box."

Julia stepped into the firelight, the sole focus of all eyes that a moment ago had been captivated by the money.

"Shit," Rand said, as the money fluttered from his nerveless fingers down to the ground. And then he started to laugh, and shook his head.

"You just don't stay put, do you, darlin'?"

She may have been surrounded by desperadoes armed to the teeth, but Julia's eyes never wavered from her goal as she approached, her gun steadied by her two hands.

"Stop that. We're leaving now. These other men are going to have to take care of business tonight."

"Julia, you don't understa—"

"Do not try my patience, Rand Washburn!" she snapped. "I want my husband, but I'm willing to take him with a bullet in him!"

"Julia?"

Julia whirled around, her eyes off her husband, and her mouth dropped open when she saw the other man.

"Reggie Whitehead?"

"My God, it is you!" Whitehead blinked, then raised his voice and yelled, "It's a trap, men, make for the boats!"

There was an explosion of guns, and powder smoke in the air a moment before a heavy body slammed Julia to the ground.

She tried to throw her husband off of her back, but he pushed her back down, getting her a face full of dirt.

"Get off me, Washburn, so I can shoot, too!"

"Who you goin' to shoot, them or me?" he laughed in her ear.

"I'll shoot them! I'm watching your back, you thieving bastard!"

He whacked her on the butt, hard.

"Don't you go insultin' my mama," He kept her pinned beneath the safety of his body while the lead flew around them. "You want to tell me how you're knowin' that Whitehead fella?"

Whatever she was going to say to him at that point was forestalled by an explosion that lit the night sky, a rocket going off overhead freezing everyone in its glare.

A voice amplified by a speaking horn called out, "This is the United States Revenue Marine! Throw down your weapons, and come out with your hands in the air!"

"Kelly!" Rand yelled. "Get over here!"

Rand rolled over, still shielding Julia, then jumped to his feet, holding his hand on her head to keep her low to the ground when she tried to stand.

"You stay down there, outta harm's way."

The young Irishman from Rand's crew came running over, blood streaking down his arm from a riverman's knife.

"It's just a scratch," Kelly assured him, and Rand thrust Julia unceremoniously into his arms.

"Haul this stowaway back into the woods, and keep her there until I come for you!"

"But—"

"That's an order, Kelly!"

"Yessir," the young man said, looking put out over missing the fight.

Rand turned around and at Julia's scream, "Duck!" crouched low, a bowie knife whistling over his head. Brewer reared back for another swipe, but a pistol ball whizzed by Rand's head at the same time he heard Brewer grunt and fall backward.

Rand grinned over his shoulder at Julia, whose smoking pepperbox hung by her side while Kelly goggled at her, his good hand clutching her left arm.

"Thanks for not shooting *me*, darlin'."

"I hit what I aim for, Washburn. And I have three shots left."

"Give me that!" Kelly snarled, grabbing the pistol from her hand, shoving it into his belt.

Rand turned to go, heading straight toward the morass of men in blue coats fighting with the smugglers down at the river's edge.

"Wait!" Julia called, and broke away from Kelly, who cursed and started after her, but Rand held up his hands, catching her as she flew into his arms.

"Until later," Julia whispered, pulling his head down to kiss her.

Rand pulled her to him and her mouth was hot and sweet, then he pushed her away with a final laugh. "She's all yours, Kelly, least 'til I come back. Then we're goin' to have ourselves a nice, long chat, darlin'." And he ran off into the night, after Whitehead.

*   *   *

"Come along, Mrs. Washburn, I have to get you out of here." He pulled her by the hand toward the woods even as she looked over her shoulder, trying to keep track of the tall form with golden hair heading into the night. She and Kelly were at the edge of the clearing, and Julia heard Ben's mule braying from the top of the ridge. Maybe she could ride back around and catch up with Rand downriver.

"Halt! You with the woman! Stop and put your hands in the air!"

Kelly muttered something inaudible under his breath, and turning to Julia said, "*Please* don't cause trouble, Mrs. Washburn!"

The armed men coming out of the woods wore sailors' clothing and carried torches, except for the man in front, who wore a blue uniform and a grim expression, a bloodied cutlass in his fist.

"Both of you, hands in the air," he said. As he came closer he started to speak, but Kelly forestalled him.

"Hold on there, lieutenant, I have some information about this woman you might want to have."

He walked over to the officer, his hands still in the air, and leaned over to whisper something to him.

The lieutenant's head whipped around and he stared at Julia. She was getting fed up with this entire evening and put her hands down, crossing them over her chest and glaring at the sailors when they shifted their weapons nervously.

The officer walked over, looked her up and down, and pursed his lips in bemusement.

"*You're* Mrs. Washburn? Ma'am, it is my duty to take you

into the custody of the United States Revenue Marine."

Fists clenched, Julia rounded on Kelly, who took a cautious step back.

"Judas! False friend! Turncoat! You should have told him nothing! How could you turn on Rand that way?"

Kelly looked at her in exasperation, rubbing at his sore arm. "The best thing you can do for your husband right now is to stay out of trouble! If there is one thing I am grateful for this evening, it is that you are another man's problem and not mine."

"Uh, Lieutenant Smollett, sir? Does she need to be tied up?" one of the sailors asked.

Julia bared her teeth at him, and he stepped back with his fellows.

Third Lieutenant Isaac Smollett wiped his hand down his face, giving Julia a fleeting suspicion he was hiding a grin, but when he looked up his face was composed.

"This is Lieutenant Hawkins's operation and his orders are that Mrs. Washburn be kept safe—and secure—until he can question her."

"But sir, Lieutenant Hawkins—"

"Belay that, mister. There is to be *no* talk with, or in front of this lady. None!"

"Aye, sir."

"And I am giving *you* charge of her, Tompkins, along with Weaver. You are to make Mrs. Washburn comfortable and wait here for me. And, gentlemen, if I come back and she's gone, you are going to wish the gators get to you before I do!"

Tompkins, who was quite young, looked at Julia as if she'd suddenly sprouted snakes for hair, and swallowed. Weaver, who looked like he'd sailed 'round the Horn more than a few times, just shook his bald head, and said, "Aye, sir."

Smollett turned back to Julia, and had the audacity to smile at her. She did not return the gesture.

"Mrs. Washburn, will you give me your word you won't try to escape from Mr. Tompkins's custody? If not, I *will* be forced to restrain you."

Julia's eyes narrowed as she watched the lieutenant's open face and considered his words. Out on the river, she saw the flash of the revenue schooner's pivot gun, but the smuggler's sloop wasn't returning fire. Whatever Washburn's plans for the evening had been, they were now going up in smoke. She might help him best by allowing herself to be taken in, where she could put her real name and influence to work on his behalf.

Surely there must be an American official who could be bought off for a sufficient amount of money, if she promised to take Washburn away from Florida. Far away. Maybe her father could arrange it. She smiled grimly. She expected to bring settlements to her marriage, but she never expected she'd use her money to buy her husband's freedom.

"Yes, lieutenant. I will give you my word, and wait here."

*   *   *

Rand heard the shouting behind him as he ran through the woods after Whitehead, the revenue troops coming after them both. He pushed aside a hanging mass of Spanish moss and ducked under an oak branch. Whitehead was headed downriver, but he wouldn't get far, not in the dark, not without knowledge of the woods. But Rand knew cornered prey was the most dangerous kind, and he wanted to catch the Englishman alive. He

248

wanted both of them alive when this was done. He grinned to himself as he thought of Julia threatening to shoot him and drag him away. That woman of his had bigger ones than most of the men he knew.

"Whitehead! You better stop running!" Rand shouted. "There are gators in the river, and if you get into the water they'll get you!"

For answer a gun exploded and a shot whizzed past Rand's ear.

"Shit!" Rand muttered. Who would have thought that dandy would be armed?

He pulled the Colt out of his belt and moved more cautiously, not that he had to worry too much about giving himself away, long as he didn't yell like a damn fool any more. Whitehead was making enough noise to cover both their movements, but he was also making it easier for the Revenue Marine to come after them, and Rand wanted to get him first.

He could smell the water and saw the break in the trees at the riverside. Rand stood behind a cypress as a raccoon scampered away from the noise and confusion in the dark.

"That's enough, Whitehead," he called out. "You'd best surrender, 'cause the Revenue Marine is two steps behind me!"

More shots rang out, going wide of where Rand stood. He stuck his head around the tree and the smoke from the Whitehead's gun was enough to give Rand something to sight on, and get off a shot of his own before he ducked back. The muzzle flash compromised his night vision and he waited a moment before looking back around, in time to see a silhouette at the river edge—and a darker silhouette moving swiftly through the water.

"Get away from the river, there's a gator coming after you!"

"You can't fool me that way, Wash—"

A piercing shriek split the night, followed by a large splash.

"Hellfire!" Rand said as he ran from behind the tree in time to see two shapes thrashing at the river bank. The alligator would drag Whitehead into the water, where it would flip to drown its prey before pulling it below to its nest to eat at leisure.

He moved close enough to see the alligator had Whitehead's lower leg clamped in its jaws and was pulling, and only Whitehead's death grip on a cypress root was keeping him out of the water.

Rand nearly shot Whitehead himself in frustration, but sprinted forward, smelling the rank odor of the carnivore, and the fear stench of its prey. He'd seen this done once—successfully— but it was the Englishman's only hope. Rand clenched his fist and swatted the end of the gator's snout. The surprised lizard opened its jaws to deal with this new threat, but Rand had already jumped back over Whitehead's prone form and grabbed him by the back of the collar, hauling him over the wet ground to higher land.

The gator growled a protest at the loss of its meal, but the night was cold, and there was old meat rotting in its den, so it slipped back into the water, its scaly tail pounding the surface before it submerged.

Whitehead was going into shock. Rand whipped off his belt and tightened it around Whitehead's bleeding lower leg for a tourniquet before removing his own jacket and wrapping it around the shaking man. If he was lucky, Whitehead would only lose his foot. An alligator's bite left about as dirty a wound as a body could sustain, and amputation was the remedy of choice to keep the poisons from spreading.

The Englishman's eyes rolled back in his head as he slipped into unconsciousness, and Rand cursed again. He'd get no answers from the man tonight, if ever. The breeze off the river plastered his sweat-soaked shirt to his back, and he pounded his fist on the hard ground in frustration. Then he raised his hands into the air as he heard the crash of the Revenue Marine troops stumbling out of the woods behind him.

CHAPTER 16

Smollett sent Tompkins off, and he returned with an empty crate with D-S markings on the side and a blanket. He upended the crate beneath a magnolia for Julia to use as a seat and offered her the blanket, which she accepted. She was somewhat surprised to find herself shaking, no doubt a reaction to the night's events, but the night wasn't over. She wrapped the blanket more tightly, and settled herself on the crate to wait and see what would happen as the lieutenant and the other men returned to the fray.

Rand was alive, she could feel it in her bones. The shouting had died down from the river as the Revenue Marine wrapped up its operation, taking the smugglers into custody and securing the goods.

She leaned back against the tree as the two sailors talked to themselves, occasionally glancing over at her. Her brow furrowed as she thought about Reggie Whitehead's involvement in tonight's debacle.

It made much more sense now that Washburn might think Delerue-Sanders was involved. After all, Whitehead was the new factor for Delerue-Sanders and it would not be unreasonable for either Washburn *or* the Revenue Marine to believe the owners knew their man in Florida was involved in smuggling.

Perhaps she and Washburn would be placed in the same cell

and he could finally explain it all to her.

Julia looked over at her guards. "Are you taking me to Fort Marion?"

Tompkins jumped at her voice, then looked at her. "No, ma'am. Why would you want to go to Fort Marion?"

"I don't," she said dryly, "but I thought that is where prisoners are held."

Fort Marion, once known as the Castillo de San Marcos to the Spaniards who'd built St. Augustine, dominated the skyline of the town her family called home when in Florida.

Rand had told her of Indian prisoners held captive there during the war, including the famous war chief Osceola, captured through treachery, and the daring escape of Coacoochee, who managed to climb up the fifteen-foot cell wall to a narrow slit cut through the six-foot thick coquina wall of the ancient fort. Iron bars blocked the opening, and twenty feet below the wall was the moat. Coacoochee broke one of the iron bars out and with the other Indian prisoners, including two women, wiggled through the fortress wall to their freedom through that narrow portal, a feat the soldiers and sailors still spoke of in awe.

Julia grinned to herself. She might be as slender as an underfed Indian warrior and able to shimmy out, but it was unlikely Rand would be able to fit those shoulders of his out a narrow opening.

"Mrs. Washburn?"

The sailors came to attention as the officer stepped into the clearing, but it was Lieutenant Smollett again, not Hawkins.

"Lieutenant Hawkins sent me to inform you that Washburn is

in custody and is unharmed."

Julia's shoulders sagged in relief. She'd felt her husband was safe, but it made a world of difference to have it confirmed.

She stood, and thought for a moment before speaking. "Lieutenant Smollett, I am not being disloyal to my dear husband in telling you this, but I say it because I would like to see him remain unharmed." She took a deep breath. "Rand Washburn is a low-down, devious, thieving, piney woods scoundrel, and I would not trust him any further than I would a pond alligator. If I were your Lieutenant Hawkins, I would put chains on the man, a guard around the clock, and not believe anything Washburn says. Let me assure you, sir, that man would lie about the color of his own eyes if he thought it would help him get his way!"

Smollett grinned hugely. "Ma'am, that is about as accurate a description of Rand Washburn as I have ever heard, and I will surely pass your words on to Lieutenant Hawkins."

Tompkins and Weaver were staring at her, but Julia raised her nose in the air. "What is to become of me, lieutenant? And when may I see my husband?"

"You cannot speak with Washburn until Lieutenant Hawkins has spoken with you. Those are my orders, ma'am. Tonight Mr. Weaver and Mr. Tompkins will escort you back to your home, where they will stay with you until Lieutenant Hawkins comes to fetch you."

He grew serious and added, "While you are in the custody of the Revenue Marine, ma'am, you are also under its protection. No harm will come to you from my men, and they will protect you from any outside dangers."

Julia inclined her head with all the graciousness of a duchess, and thanked the lieutenant. Staying at the farmstead was far preferable to being dragged to St. Augustine in chains.

She may have given her word not to escape, but that didn't mean she wouldn't try to get word to her parents.

*   *   *

Weaver and Tompkins took her to fetch Ben's mule from the ridge. Then, with their own gear in hand, they escorted her as she rode home in the predawn mists, reaching the homestead in time to hear the rooster announce the start of another day. Ben Ivey was feeding the chickens, and he dropped the bowl and ran over to her and her jailers.

"Jumpin' catfish, Miz Washburn! I was worried about you!" He looked around the men from the Revenue Marine. "Where's Rand?"

"He had to stay behind, Benjamin, but these men are going to stay out here at the farm to help me until he gets back," Julia said. "And here is your mule, Ben. Thank you for the loan of him."

"Aw, you don't have to thank me, Miz Washburn. 'Specially since you held a gun on me to take him."

Julia smiled wanly and started to dismount, and Benjamin was there a step ahead of her escort, helping her down.

She wavered on her feet, sure that in a moment or two she'd collapse where she stood.

"Good night, or rather, good morning, Benjamin. Give my regards to your mother. And tell Franklin I hope he feels better soon." She turned to her captors and pulled herself up, drawing on her last reserves of energy. "Gentlemen, if you will excuse

255

me, I will see you later today. If you wish to make yourselves useful, the woodpile could use replenishing and there are eggs to be gathered."

"Yes, ma'am," they chorused, and Tompkins touched his cap. She turned her back on them and with queenly grace entered her house, went back to her room, and after pausing long enough to remove her shoes, collapsed across her bed.

*   *   *

Julia awoke that afternoon refreshed. After washing and changing her blouse, she came out to find Tompkins and Weaver repairing some fencing that Washburn had never bothered to fix.

She pulled her shawl closer around her for the air was cooling as the sun went down, and Tompkins waved a greeting.

"You got a nice piece of property here, ma'am," he said, wiping his forehead, "but it sure needs some work."

"Are you a farmer, too, Mr. Tompkins?"

"Grew up on a farm, ma'am, in New York. That's why I ran away to sea."

At Weaver's shout, Tompkins picked up the end of split rail and hoisted it up in place. Julia watched for a few minutes, then said, "If you gentlemen are working on my farm, the least I can do is fix you some supper. Give me about an hour, and I'll see what I can do."

Two hours later, two satisfied sailors were leaning back and heaping praise on the cook.

"Mrs. Washburn, that was the best sweet potato pie I ever ate," Tompkins said, as Weaver eyed the last slice before shaking his head and pushing his plate away.

Julia smiled and rose to her feet, the men jumping up a

moment later, and with their help cleared the remains of the ham, corn, and greens off the table. After helping her with the dishes, the duo excused themselves to bunk out on the front veranda, giving her the privacy of the house.

But the house was dark and empty, even with the fire crackling in the fireplace. Julia pulled her shawl about her shoulders and heard an owl mournfully hooting in the woods, its call echoing through her own mind.

The chessboard was still set up from their last game and she studied the moves. Rand was black, and his king was being threatened by her queen's rook and her queen's knight, with the queen strategically in place.

How would a reckless player like Rand Washburn get out of the trap?

Julia shifted in her seat and felt a hard lump pressing through her skirts. With an exclamation, she reached into the pocket and pulled out a man's ring, inset with a ruby. She turned it over in her fingers, the firelight giving the gold a warm sheen. It was a wonder the ring hadn't fallen out during the events of the night before.

She rose from the table and went to the back room with a lamp, retrieving a slender strip of hair ribbon that she looped through the ring, tying it into a secure knot before pulling the ribbon over her head, so the ring nestled between her breasts.

It comforted her, the weight of the gold. It was a symbol of a wedding that led to not-quite-a-marriage, but something more, something as one-of-a-kind as her low-down smuggling, maybe-not-a-husband.

But if Rand Washburn wasn't her husband, he was still her

man, and she'd do whatever she could to bring him out of this safely.

*   *   *

Tompkins and Weaver wouldn't talk with her about anything that mattered, like Washburn, or the Revenue Marine, or whether she was going to jail for smuggling, but they were nonetheless good company. After a hearty breakfast that again earned paeans of praise for her cooking, Julia gathered up some fishing gear and Tompkins, and went down to the creek to see if they could fetch back something for supper.

"What I hate most about catfish is not the cooking of them, but the cleaning."

They were walking back through the sun-dappled trees, and as Julia passed a particular magnolia memories of her picnics at the creek with Washburn brought a small smile to her lips.

"You don't have to worry 'bout cleaning them fish," Tompkins was saying. "Weaver's an old hand at that and will have them filleted for you real fast. Are you going to fry them up in cornmeal?"

"With hush puppies on the side," Julia promised the young man, who was looking rather like a hopeful and hungry puppy himself at the moment. But when they came through the trees to the farmstead she stopped, for an unfamiliar bay gelding with elegant lines and a military saddle was tied to the fence, and Weaver was walking rapidly across the dirt yard to them, his face like a thundercloud.

"Boy, you'd best get your gear together fast, or you're going to be holystoning decks all the way to Boston! Lieutenant Hawkins is here, and he was right unhappy when I told him you

258

and Mrs. Washburn went fishing."

Julia felt chills run down her spine and she looked toward the darkened doorway of the cabin. Inside was the man who held her fate in his hands. Perhaps, even now, he was watching them. And here she stood, covered in sand and holding a string of catfish.

But she straightened her spine, and raised her chin. She was Lady Julia Anne Sanders Delerue, descendent of generations of women who'd done everything from raining arrows down on castle raiders to fighting pirates alongside their husbands. And she was Rand Washburn's woman. She was not about to let an American sailor intimidate her.

"Mr. Weaver," she said sharply.

His head snapped around, and he nearly came to attention.

"Yes, ma'am?"

"You and Mr. Tompkins will take charge of these fish and put up the equipment. *I* will deal with Lieutenant Hawkins."

She marched off toward the cabin, head high, and the two men watched her go.

"My money's on her," Tompkins said. "Two bits says she makes him strike his colors."

Weaver spat in the dirt.

"I'm not taking that one, boy. Only a fool would bet against that woman."

*   *   *

Julia paused in the doorway. The table was pulled in front of the window for light, and official looking papers were strewn across it. A single chair stood in front, placed where miscreants would be seated directly across from the man behind the table, a man in a dark blue uniform who stood erect with his hands clasped behind his back, staring out the window. Lieutenant Hawkins blocked the light, so her first impression was of height, and width, and hair cropped short across his neck with military precision.

She must have made a sound, for he turned then, and unhurriedly came further into the room, into the light coming through the window.

The blood drained from her head in a rush. For the first time in her life, Julia felt faint, and she grasped the back of the chair for support. The naval officer looked at her with cool eyes, his face expressionless, and he motioned toward the chair.

"Sit down, Julia," her husband said. "It is time we had that nice, long chat."

CHAPTER 17

Rand watched her, his eyes inscrutable, his hands once again clasped behind his back. He was dressed in a dark blue uniform which she at first thought was United States naval dress, until she realized there were subtle differences. The badge on his sword belt was a shield with scales over a key, surmounted by a fouled anchor. A cloth cap with two bands of gold braid sat on the desk, and it bore the same anchor and scales ornament in gold.

She knew that scales and anchor symbol. After all, her family was in the shipping business. And she'd seen the uniform recently. Very recently.

Julia collapsed into the chair, her legs giving out on her.

"My God," she said in horror. "Who *are* you?"

He seated himself behind the table, hands steepled in front of him, then gave her a small bow of his head.

"I am Second Lieutenant Randall Washburn Hawkins of the United States Revenue Marine."

Every consonant was in place. He was shaved so close his jaw gleamed, and his hair was trimmed tight and brushed exactly into order. His uniform boasted expert tailoring, the black braid on his standing collar perfectly framing his square chin, and the brass buttons marching down the front of the coat and decorating the sleeves shone in the sunlight. He looked as expressionless and cold as an engraving, "American Naval Hero."

If he was cold, she was simmering, and getting close to a full boil. Cracker Rand Washburn had been replaced by a starched and uniformed officer, while she had rope burns on her wrists, a throbbing torn fingernail, smelled like a fishwife, and had chafed thighs from that damned mule ride.

Julia stood and walked over to the shelf where there was some excellent smuggled French brandy, put it up to her lips and downed a shot straight from the bottle, then brought it with her and sprawled into her chair. She did not offer to share.

"Did you ride all the way out here in the piney woods to charge me with smuggling, *lieutenant?*"

"Put down the brandy. As difficult as it is dealing with you sober, it is better than dealing with you drunk." He looked at her in patent disapproval. "Smuggling? I wish that were the only charge you faced! Do you know what the penalties are for *counterfeiting*, Julia? I have been sitting here, trying to figure out how I am going to keep my wife from going to a federal prison for ten years. At hard labor. Oh, and there is a fine of five thousand dollars as well."

He didn't wait for her reply before continuing. "But that is only the penalty for counterfeiting. You are no ordinary smuggler, or ordinary counterfeiter, Julia Cooper. You are an agent of British parties seeking to disrupt and overthrow the United States government!"

Julia stared at him, then burst out laughing. "Rand Washburn—or whatever you are calling yourself today—you have been out in the sun too long without your hat. That is the most ridiculous story I have ever heard. Why in heaven's name would I work to overthrow the United States government?"

"Not for patriotism," he said grimly. "You did it for the oldest reason in the book. Money. You consorted with known pirates, your Uncle Richard Cooper and that Robin person at Ganymede's Cup. I know things about your past you would just as soon keep hidden," he said with a certain smugness. "Aren't you going to ask about your friend Whitehead?"

Frankly, she'd forgotten all about him, given everything else that had happened. "How is he?"

"Not good. He was attacked by an alligator and has not yet regained consciousness. I must say, Julia, I am disappointed by the company you keep. You have shown more fortitude during this criminal enterprise than that English wastrel did."

"Poor Reggie," she murmured. She was sad for him, but she wasn't about to rise to the bait and say she had no connection to Whitehead beyond a social acquaintance. And his being hired by Delerue-Sanders. She winced. *That* didn't look good at all.

"And so, Julia, it all began to fall into place for me. Your relationship to Cooper, your English background, Whitehead— once all the clues were there it was easy to put them together.

"Do you remember our conversation about England's anger over the United States' role in the Canadian rebellion? And the fragility of the southern ports? We have long suspected that counterfeit specie is being brought into the United States from the British West Indies through Florida. Do you have any idea how easy it would be to destabilize Florida's fragile economy? The territory is still reeling from the war and the bank collapses in Tallahassee."

Julia stared at him, her attention arrested by something he'd said, and the faint accent coloring his speech.

"Washburn…banks…" Her brow wrinkled as she thought of why there was a connection, and then her eyes opened wide. "*That* is how you know so much about the nature of money. You are no smuggler! For all I know, you are not even a real officer! You are a damned banker!"

His brow arched in surprise. "I always knew you were a bright one, Julia. But to clarify something for you, I *am* an officer in the Revenue Marine. It is my mother's family that owns the Washburn Bank in Boston. How do you know about us?"

"Everybody involved in shipping in England knows the Washburn banking system helped the northern United States weather the bank suspensions. Boston and nearby ports were still importing and exporting when other Atlantic and Gulf markets were cutting back…"

She stopped and shut her mouth.

"Go on," he said politely. "Don't stop there. I am waiting with bated breath for the part where you explain to me how an English tavern girl is so conversant with American banking practices."

When she said nothing, he sighed, and rising, adjusted the fit of his blue coat and walked around to stand beside the fireplace, hands clasped behind him again. His presence filled the cabin and made the room—and her—look shabbier than ever. Now that he was in uniform, she marveled to herself that she hadn't noticed before that he had a sailor's gait, a gracefulness from years on pitching decks and holding on to soaked rigging during storms.

"Allow me to fill in the gaps in your rather eclectic education. Back in '37, the United States' banking system almost collapsed, and we are still recovering. The Washburn Bank was one of the few that managed to hold on after the initial suspension, largely because it set up a system with other banks to clear their notes. Because of its financial stability it was still lending money when other banks were suspending payment again."

He looked at her steadily. A small breeze blew in, daring to flutter the precision of his combed head, and she heard the faint sounds of voices and horses from outside.

"New England is strong," he continued, "but the south? With its concerns about British troop invasions, and slave uprisings, its unguarded coastline and a cotton economy always one crop away from disaster? It would take little effort, even now, for the entire United States economy to collapse, leaving us vulnerable to our enemies. Rumors of massive amounts of false money flooding this territory would send ripples through the entire country and its other territories, just at the time it is beginning to recover.

"I can help you, Julia. I *want* to help you, but you are going to have to tell me everything you know about this affair. I am especially interested in your connection to Delerue-Sanders."

"De-Delerue-Sanders?" she stammered, raising her hand to her throat. "What would I know about Delerue-Sanders?"

"Do not play coy, Julia, it doesn't become you!" His eyes glittered as he stalked toward her. "Delerue-Sanders. The English company that ships to Florida and the West Indies. The company that employs Reginald Whitehead as factor. The company whose ships brought the counterfeit money to our shores. The company *you* have ties to. If you expect me to be able to do anything for you, you will tell me everything you know about Delerue-Sanders. You will tell me about Delerue's officers and owners. You will tell me about its cargoes and shipping schedules. If you help me, I will do my best to save you. But if you do not help me, then God help you, for I fear I can do nothing."

This is what he wanted in exchange for his help? That she betray her family? She rose out of the chair, fists clenched.

"Help you? Help *you*? Not if I were on fire and you had a pitcher of water! Not if I were starving and you held a loaf of bread in your hand! Not if my life dep—"

"Enough," he gritted out, "I get the general idea. And not to put too fine a point on it, but your life may very well depend on your assisting me here, today. At least a life on the right side of the prison door!"

"I think not, Lieutenant Hawkins! It is *you* who has much to answer for and I demand you take me to St. Augustine so the entire truth is brought to light! *Your* cohorts kidnapped me and *you* kept me against my will at your farm. Instead of acting like a revenue officer and a gentleman, you lied, you threatened me, you offered me a choice of death or marriage, you exposed me to snakes and bugs and killer sea cows, you wormed your way into my bed—"

He raised one brow and raked her with an insolent look, from the top of her tangled head down to her bare toes.

"Wormed my way into your bed? Are you deluding yourself that it was some other woman screaming in ecstasy in that bed?"

She'd never understood the expression "seeing red" until that moment, but *his* reflexes had been honed fighting the Seminole and smugglers. Before she could reach his throat, Randall had his shoulder under her waist, and with an inelegant "Oof!" Julia was hoisted into the air to pound on his back.

"You deceitful dog! I'm going to kill you!" she screamed.

"JULIA! Ow! Stop that, or you're going to—"

"Now, this looks interesting…"

Julia heard that soft voice over her own shouting, the one voice that had ever been capable of bringing her tantrums to a screeching halt. She propped a hand on Hawkins's shoulder and looked behind her.

"Papa?"

Lieutenant Hawkins kept his grip on her as she slid down his body to her feet, but his eyes were trained on the middle-aged man who stepped into the cabin.

"Are you Smithton?"

"I am he," the gentleman said mildly. His head was crowned by ebony hair, silvered at the temples and matching the locks of the spitting fury Randall held by one arm.

He looked down at her, and his face lit triumphantly.

"Hah! I was right all along! You, Julia Cooper, are the bastard daughter of Lord Smithton, the owner of Delerue-Sanders!"

If she were a couple inches taller, Randall Hawkins might be sporting a broken nose. The punch she threw was just as her brother Charles had taught her, thumb outside, and from the shoulder.

"Don't you go insultin' my mama!" Julia snarled, at the same time Justin Delerue, Lord Smithton said, "Oh dear, I am afraid that is not *quite* correct."

He motioned with his hand, and was joined by a Junoesque woman who stared daggers at the wounded Hawkins.

A woman with familiar sherry-brown eyes.

"The young woman you are manhandling, lieutenant, is Lady Julia Delerue," Lord Smithton went on in the same mild tones. "And I assure you, sir, she is the daughter—the legitimate daughter—of Lady Smithton and myself."

"Hellfire and damnation," he said muzzily, holding both hands over his streaming nose.

"Quite."

Hawkins looked over the countess' shoulder and came to attention, or attempted to, while holding his nose with one hand.

"Excuse me, Countess," said a stocky man sporting a revenue captain's fouled anchors on his shoulders. Christine Delerue stepped aside and the grizzled officer looked at his errant lieutenant, then shook his head. Without bothering to tell Hawkins to stand at ease, he turned back to his guests.

"Lord Smithton, Lady Smithton, Lady Julia—please take my gig back to Picolata. I'll deal with this."

"Thank you, captain," Smithton said. "Will you and the lieutenant be returning to St. Augustine?"

"Eventually," the officer said, not looking at the hapless Hawkins. "We will talk more then."

Julia smoothed down her crumpled skirts.

"I am ready to leave now, Papa."

"Julia—" Hawkins said, forgetting his discipline and taking a step toward her, bloodstained hand outstretched.

She ignored him. Without turning back to take a single item

from the cabin, or for a last look at Lieutenant Hawkins, Julia marched out the front door alongside her mother.

It was Smithton who paused in the doorway and looked back at the young man, and for a brief instant there may have been a gleam of sympathy in his eye. Then he followed the women out, closing the door behind him.

CHAPTER 18

Randall stood woodenly at attention across from his commanding officer, ignoring his throbbing nose and the icy sweat trickling down his back. He was standing in the same spot where Julia had been seated while he interrogated her, while his commander was shipping a quarterdeck face as he sat in *Randall's* chair, fingers steepled in front of him.

All his life he'd yearned to command a cutter. When his father died and his mother moved the family from Savannah to her hometown, it was seeing Captain Sturgis's famed topsail schooner *Hamilton* in its Boston berth that built in Randall a lifelong love for the cutter service. As the scion of a banking family, he knew how important a strong economy and the collection of tariffs was to America. The war had tarnished some of that, but the Revenue Marine was still where he expected to do his life's work.

Until now.

"Sir, I am prepared to immediately resign my commission."

"Resign your commission? Don't be ridiculous, lieutenant. I am not going to accept your resignation," Captain Josiah Collins said. "If you are a civilian, I cannot have the pleasure of keelhauling you."

This was said in such soft, even tones that Randall almost took a step back. Almost. The Old Man was at his most dangerous when he grew quiet, and you strained to hear every word.

"I have seen a lot of men sabotage their own careers, Hawkins, but you've raised it to new levels of damage. Except for that unfortunate incident with the boatload of maroons, your behavior has always been exemplary, your name a watchword among the younger officers for appropriate demeanor.

"Until now. It wasn't enough during the war that letters were flying back and forth between Washington and Florida, *that* was a national scandal. Now you've managed to get yourself embroiled in an *international* incident."

Randall kept his eyes straight ahead and said nothing. He knew this was far from over.

"I have spent the morning with Lord and Lady Smithton. It was not the most pleasant morning of my life, but they are being reasonable about the return of their daughter."

"Julia Coo—Julia Hawkins is my wife, sir. She is my responsibility."

"You realize that if she *is* your wife, she's still Lady Julia, but Lady Julia Hawkins? That is going to look real nice on your correspondence: 'Lieutenant Randall Hawkins and Lady Julia Hawkins.' Of course, if you resign it will be plain old 'Mr. Hawkins and Lady Hawkins.' I wonder if you have to address your own wife as 'your ladyship?'"

He was having too much fun, if fun was the right word. It clearly tickled his republican sensibilities to think of Randall Washburn Hawkins, grandson of heroes of the American Revolution and son of a naval officer during the second war with Britain, married to Lady Julia Delerue.

Captain Collins sighed and waved his hand. "At ease."

Randall went to parade rest, hands clasped behind his back. Collins pulled a box out of his pocket, and he slid it across the table.

"Take them. They're yours."

He looked at the small box, after all that had happened not daring to believe what might be inside. But then he reached forward and opened it. The shiny double bars of a first lieutenant in the United States Revenue Marine winked up at him.

Once, these bars had meant everything. Redemption for his wartime peccadilloes, advancing toward command of his own cutter—but that was before he'd opened his shed and found a misplaced Englishwoman—and now the taste of triumph was mixed with ashes in his mouth.

"Despite everything, Hawkins, you did manage to break the counterfeiting operation. The Treasury Department is grateful, and for once is recognizing someone's achievements. Commandant Fraser made particular note of your performance during this operation."

Commandant Alexander Fraser hadn't held the post for long, but he was determined to show critics of the Treasury Department that a strong Revenue Marine was needed to patrol the coast. Fraser's planned reforms were ambitious, including a merit system instead of the old patronage for promotion and assignment of officers, and creation of an engineering officers' rank for the new iron steamers and the Steamship Inspection Service. Even the uniform Rand wore was designed to build zeal and loyalty to the service.

"We're going to have warrant officers now, lieutenant, the

ratings won't be at the whim of every captain. And we need you to be part of this new service. So no, I won't accept your resignation, even though the last thing we need right now is an international incident! But if you find yourself on the wrong side of the fence before the reforms go into place, especially with your Washburn political connections, you could find yourself like that poor sod Captain Dobbins."

Randall winced, but didn't say anything. He didn't have to, for everyone in the Revenue Marine knew the price of political involvement.

Captain Daniel Dobbins was an able and experienced commander who'd supervised the construction of the *Erie*, and in 1837 commanded her when the secretary of the Treasury sent the sixty-five ton cutter to Buffalo to enforce U.S. neutrality laws during the Canadian rebellion. But despite his service, the Whig president William Henry Harrison had replaced him with Gilbert Knapp, another revenue cutter captain.

At this point, Captain Dobbins could only hope the Democrats would get into office during the next election and reinstate him to his command. Knapp was no doubt banking on the Whigs.

"Now, as to the other business, we are satisfied that Lord Smithton did not know his ships were being used to transport the money, and in fact, has been highly cooperative with us. You will head to Key West to finish the investigation."

"Sir, I would like to request some leave to take care of personal business."

"Denied," Collins said crisply. "Your personal business will wait. In the meantime, it is unlikely anyone will make the connection between Julia Cooper and Lady Julia Delerue. The earl wants to keep it that way."

Randall looked at his commander and said again, "Julia Delerue Hawkins is my wife, sir."

The look Captain Collins returned was not unsympathetic, but he said, "Not according to Lord Smithton. You both used false names, or in your case, part of your name, and it will take some time to straighten this out. Now, can you follow your orders, lieutenant, or will I have to find someplace else to stash you?"

"I will follow my orders and do my duty, sir."

"That's all we ask, lieutenant Hawkins."

*   *   *

Weaver and Tompkins fixed lunch for the officers and the other men. The catfish was fried to charcoal lumps, and the hush puppies could have been used for fishing weights. When Tompkins waxed rhapsodic about the wonderful meal they'd had the night before with Mrs. Washburn in the galley, Randall pushed himself away from the table.

He walked down to the creek, loosening his jacket. He'd forgotten what it felt like to be buttoned up so tight you couldn't turn your head. A jay scolded him from a cypress branch as he tossed sticks into the water, disturbing an otter sunning down-creek who showed her displeasure by rolling over and gliding away. He fingered the new bars at his shoulder, wishing he had someone here to share it with. A particular someone, and he smiled at the thought. Maybe if he rescued Julia from a vicious otter, or a sea cow, throwing himself into the creek to protect her bonnets, he'd redeem himself in her eyes.

But then the smile faded. He missed her already. And not just her cooking. He missed her sassy attitude and the wiggle in her walk. He felt nothing but self-disgust for his delusional fantasies of how he'd been going to rescue her from a life of crime, and she'd be so grateful to him...

He didn't want to think about how she'd show her gratitude. He was uncomfortable enough.

All his life he'd been so focused on the prize in front of him, the cutter captain's fouled anchors, that he'd never thought ahead to what would happen beyond that.

He had a duty to the Revenue Marine, and his country, but he also had obligations to his wife. And no matter what happened, no matter what anyone said, Julia *was* his wife. He'd given her his word as Rand Washburn, and while he wanted to put the backwoods charade behind him, it was still his word to give. He wouldn't abandon her.

Randall shoved his hands in his pockets and watched the twigs swirling on their lonely journey out to sea.

CHAPTER 19

"I wish the town wouldn't keep changing on me," Lady Smithton fretted as they rode through the rough streets of St. Augustine. "I would like to come home and find things as they were, not so, so *Americanized.*"

"Things change, my dear, it is the nature of life," the earl said, looking at his daughter.

Julia listlessly watched the scenery go past the carriage window. She'd been silent on the trip back to town and would catch her mother watching her, but she did not press for details. She did say Suzanne Marlowe had told everyone who asked about her that Julia had gone up north to visit friends, so there were no rumors about her disappearance. But that was the last comment her ladyship made on the events of the past weeks. Instead she spoke of other matters, the health and welfare of Julia's brothers—the younger boys manned ships making the Baltic and China runs, while the eldest managed the day-to-day business of Delerue-Sanders in London. Lord and Lady Smithton were in Florida on what was to have been a long overdue holiday, now that they could leave matters at home in the hands of their heir.

When they reached Christine's childhood home, Julia allowed herself to be fussed over and cosseted by her Aunt Suzanne, but then excused herself to go to her room, clutching the rail as she dragged herself up the steps. Word was sent ahead upon their arrival and Aunt Suzanne's own maid was waiting to help Julia out of her clothes and into a hot, fragrant bath. Tilly looked horrified by Lady Julia's clothing, and from the stiffening of the maid's posture, she knew Tilly was equally shocked by Lady Julia's lack of corset and the browned condition of her skin.

"I want that clothing cleaned and returned to me, Tilly," Julia said. "I know you are thinking to give it to the rag man, but…"

Her voice trailed off. She couldn't say why the clothes Rand bought her were special, but they were.

"Just bring them back to me."

"Yes, miss," Tilly murmured, and helped Julia into the bath. "Would you like me to wash your hair for you, Miss Julia?"

"No! I mean, no, thank you. Please leave now."

Rand had washed her hair, the night before the cane grinding. She could still feel his strong fingers running through the strands, untangling the curls and massaging her scalp until she purred like a panther cub.

Afterward, they had sat in front of the fire as he brushed out her hair, each of them saying what animals and shapes they saw lurking in the flames. It had been a crisp fall night, and when she'd joined him that evening beneath Ma Ivey's wedding quilt, he'd made love to her with a tenderness he'd never shown before, as if she were precious and breakable, and very dear to him.

He'd made love to her as if it were the last time.

The door had barely closed behind Tilly before Julia leaned forward in her bath, her face in her hands, the saltwater mingling with the scented bath oils.

*   *   *

Randall stood on the doorstep of Sanders House on an early winter morning bringing fresh breezes off the river. Through habit he glanced at the clouds above with a weather eye, thinking ahead to the packet leaving for the Keys. When he'd arrived at his quarters, a note from Smithton was waiting, requesting a meeting with Lieutenant Hawkins at his earliest convenience. Captain Collins hadn't approved his leave, but there was no reason Randall couldn't pay a call or two before his scheduled departure.

The knock on the door was answered by a portly butler with a peg leg and gold earring flashing in the morning light.

The older man's eyes widened in appreciation as he gave him the once-over, from his cap down to his boots, and when Randall offered his name he said with an arch smile, "Oh, so *you* are Lieutenant Hawkins!"

He opened the door wider, and Randall brushed past, getting a whiff of lavender.

"Let me hazard a guess," he said dryly, "You were hired away from Ganymede's Cup."

"Oh my, no. Unlike Robin, I am such a terrible cook no ship would have me in its galley. I am Sylvestre, the butler. Follow me, Lieutenant."

Randall stopped him with a hand on his arm.

"Is Lady Julia in?"

The old pirate shook his head. "She went with the countess to Jacksonville. You'd best come with me, matey. If you have questions, Lord Smithton will answer them."

278

Randall tucked his hat under his arm, smoothed back his hair, and followed the servant as he stumped his way into an upstairs study and announced him.

"Thank you, Sylvestre, that will be all," said the earl.

Rand took a deep breath, and the butler winked at him. "He don't bite," Sylvestre said in a hoarse whisper.

The earl might not bite, but Randall felt like a schoolboy about to get a caning. Even facing Captain Collins had not caused so much trepidation. *That* only entailed the possibility of losing his career.

The room was a book-lined study with windows thrown wide to catch the breezes off the river. Smithton was seated behind a desk, sanding a letter, and to his credit did not make Randall wait on him but gestured toward a deep leather chair in front of the desk.

Smithton watched him as Randall tried very hard not to squirm. He'd commanded enough men to know the value of extended silences. In a minute he'd be babbling like a fool just to fill that void. He wondered if he'd ever master that trick with the eyes, the one of looking slightly bored, yet completely aware of everything.

Perhaps it was a trait of the aristocracy.

"I trust the innocence of Delerue-Sanders in this unfortunate incident has been established to your satisfaction, lieutenant?"

Randall cleared his throat. Any fantasy he'd had of the earl coming out from behind his desk and embracing him like a son—or son-in-law—flew out the window.

"Yes, sir. Captain Collins told me of your cooperation with the Treasury Department. You should not encounter any difficulties with the Revenue Marine over your ships."

He stopped at that point. The less he had to relive the painful conversation with Captain Collins, the better.

"It is a relief to know I am on good relations with the American authorities," the earl said. "If that is the case, we can discuss what is really important to me—the welfare of my daughter."

Randall sat a fraction straighter. "Julia Hawkins is my wife, sir. Her welfare is now my concern."

"Commendable, lieutenant, that protective attitude of yours is quite commendable. Tell me, did you feel as protective toward my daughter when you kept her against her will at your farm? Were you *protecting* her when she begged you to return her to her uncle and you refused?"

The mild look in the earl's eyes vanished and Randall saw the steel core inside the man who'd brought an end to the career of a notorious pirate. A dangerous man, who'd received an account of events at the farm from a far from unbiased source.

"Now that you have discovered her true identity, and no doubt are aware of her substantial fortune, you are committed to keeping Julia by your side," Smithton continued.

A muscle twitched in Randall's jaw. "Julia's fortune means nothing to me. You can take all of her money, all of her fancy gowns, all the jewels she wore in London, and sink them to the bottom of the St. Johns River and I will take her in her shift. If your concern is my ability to care for my wife, I assure you, sir, that will not be an issue. I can well maintain Julia in the style to which she is accustomed, fulfill my obligations as her husband, and provide for all her needs."

Smithton's brows rose. "Aren't you going to add, lieutenant, to reassure me, that you have already inherited a substantial estate from your late father, and as a stockholder in the Washburn Bank you are quite, ah, comfortable?"

Randall knew he shouldn't be surprised. If he were in the earl's shoes, he'd leave no stone unturned investigating the man claiming his daughter's hand. But the thoroughness of Smithton's information with scant notice was impressive.

"If you like, sir, we can each engage attorneys who will hash out the details of any settlements under discussion. That is not why I am here today. I came for my wife."

"Do you intend to take her back to that decrepit farm of yours? Or do you have apartments here in town?"

"I am normally not based in St. Augustine," Randall said. "I plan to take her up to my home in Boston."

"Really? You have discussed this with Julia?"

"No, but—"

"Your plan is to take my daughter away from her home in England, and everything that is familiar to her, and deposit her like a leftover sea trunk in Massachusetts? You might as well have left her out on your farm, lieutenant."

"Julia seemed content there," he said, the words out before he could call them back.

"Not that she had any choice in the matter about staying or leaving," the earl said softly.

Randall stood. "What is the point of this conversation? If you wish to harangue me for mistakes I made while trying to fulfill my duty, have at it. But I came here today hoping to work out..." He stumbled, now at a loss for words. "I want to see Julia, sir. I want my wife back."

Justin Delerue leaned back in his chair, and looked up at the younger man. "Sit down, Lieutenant Hawkins."

Randall sat.

"For the first time during this rather strained conversation, you have told me what I wish to know, lieutenant. You said, 'I want my wife back.' You mentioned your duty. You did not say, 'I want Julia to be happy' and you did not say 'I want to do what is best for Julia.'"

Smithton leaned forward over the desk. His soft tone did not change, but every word was encased in ice. "I will not force my daughter to stay in an unacceptable situation because of a backwoods farce of a marriage that is easily set aside, or because of your notions of duty, lieutenant. Believe me, I am not concerned about the proprieties at this moment. We are strong enough to deal with it, and Julia's entire family is behind her, whatever she decides. Whether she stays with you, goes back to London, or establishes her own home somewhere else is *Julia's choice*. Her contentment and happiness are my paramount concerns.

"While it is after the fact, you have my permission to pay your addresses to my daughter. And only that. *If* she decides upon further reflection that she wishes to be married to you, then she—and you—have my blessing and you will have a proper and legal marriage sanctified by church and state. Until that point, Julia will reside here, under my protection. Now, is there any part of this you do not understand, Lieutenant Hawkins?"

Randall stood. If the earl's words were ice, his were the heat of anger kept a hair's breadth from exploding. "My marriage to your daughter is neither a backwoods farce, nor a situation you can make disappear by pretending it never happened. It is a reality. Julia is *my wife*, and my responsibility, not yours, sir, and all the wishing and pretending it never happened will not change that. I *will* talk with Julia when she returns. Good day to you, sir."

Randall turned on his heel and left, *not* slamming the study door behind him, but Sylvestre barely had time to stump over to the front door before Randall was out on the street, tearing his collar buttons open.

Out of the corner of his eye he saw someone fall into step beside him.

"Boy, you look like the back end of bad luck."

"Bless you, James. I can always count on you to pour soothing balm on my wounds," Randall said through clenched teeth.

Second Lieutenant James Crane, USRM, hurried to keep up with Randall's longer stride through the narrow streets of St. Augustine, maneuvering around the horses and carts in the constricted space.

"Do you want to tell me what happened?"

"I feel like a raccoon skinned and nailed to the cabin wall. Between Collins and Smithton I'm scraped as raw as a new recruit, and I still haven't seen Julia! Everyone is insisting we are not married, but she's the one I have to convince. Instead, I am ordered to head down to Key West."

"At least the swelling around your nose has nearly faded. When you do see her, you'll look more like yourself."

"The only way she is going to think I look like myself is if

Rand Washburn shows up instead of Lieutenant Randall Hawkins."

He paused so suddenly James shot a few steps ahead and nearly collided with a fruit vendor, but then Randall shook his head.

"No, what I need to do is *court* her. My own wife! The earl has graciously given me his permission to pay my respects to *Lady* Julia Delerue while she visits the Florida peasants."

Randall grimaced as he recalled his concerns over introducing his smuggler wife to his Mayflower-descended family in Boston. They were people who, as his father had been wont to drawl, considered themselves slightly below God and far above everyone born south of Cape Cod.

They hadn't met the earl.

"Sounds to me like you need to cool down some." James looked up at the sun. "It's almost noon, Randall. Why don't we get some luncheon and plot strategy for your courtship of the fair lady? Then we can go back to quarters and if you like, I'll box with you and you can beat the stuffing out of me. That always makes you feel better."

Randall stopped and looked over at his companion for a heartbeat or two, then slapped him on his uniformed shoulder.

"You are a true friend, James Crane. I can always count on you, can't I, to save me from myself?"

"Someone has to do it, Randall."

*   *   *

The trip to Jacksonville produced enough boxes and parcels to fill the hold of the *Manticore,* or at least that's what the earl said as the loot was ferried past his study door.

But when he joined his wife in their bedroom a short time later, he found her trying on not her new clothing, but an old pair of boy's trousers and a knit sailor's shirt.

The shirt was snug on her in a manner that brought a gleam to his eyes, but the trouser buttons were not fastening over his wife's rounded hips. She was looking at herself in the glass with a dismayed expression.

"Justin, tell me the truth. Am I fat?"

"Absolutely not," he said firmly. Justin Delerue was no man's fool. But he also knew Christine was smart enough not to be put off by a facile response, and he was brave and gallant, so he strolled over to give her a complete glance.

"I believe, my dear, that you are quite beautiful and look just right. Every inch the countess."

"But I want to look like a *pirate*!" she wailed. "Look at me!" She waved at the reflection of a woman trying to fit into clothes she'd worn four pregnancies ago. "No one's going to be afraid of me if I look like a countess!"

Justin stepped up behind her, and peered over the top of his spectacles at their joint reflection in the glass.

"My dear captain, I can say with complete honesty that you still terrify me."

"Really, Justin?" She brightened and gave him the wide smile that brought out all of the charming lines at the corners of her eyes. "That's so sweet!"

"It is absolutely true." He waggled his eyebrows at her in the mirror. "Would you like to play pirates? You can tie me to the bed and have your wicked way with me."

Lady Christine Sanders Delerue, once known as Captain

Christopher Daniels and the scourge of Delerue Shipping, lowered her lashes and arched back against him. He put his hand on her belly and pulled her tight while the smile on his reflection in the mirror deepened into something more appropriate to incidents piratical than an interlude with one's spouse.

Unless one's spouse *was* a former pirate.

Later, as they were dressing for supper, Christine asked about the interview with Lieutenant Hawkins.

"No doubt that is the person you wish to terrify? I would like to think I took care of that today, but to give the young man his due, he has an iron will and this trip continues to prove interesting. After speaking with him, I remain optimistic that if Julia does not kill him, this may work out."

"I just wish he were not a revenue officer!"

"I am told it happens even in the best of families, my dear. Shall we join Julia and Suzanne?"

They were dining *en famille* this evening, with the kind of spirited table talk that would send the more conservative members of Florida or British society reaching for their vinaigrettes or harrumphing portentously over the port. Even Sylvestre chimed in as he lurched around the table refilling wine glasses—figuring as a former shipmate of the captain's, he was entitled to share his thoughts with the group.

"We're going to have to hire a new factor," the earl said.

"Julia and I stopped by to visit Reggie today." Christine sighed. "It is a tragedy that he lost part of his leg, but he is cooperating with the Americans and I expect they will allow him to return to England when he is sufficiently healed."

"I spent the better part of the morning writing letters to

London and Washington City," her husband said. "Reggie's cooperation and Captain Collins's evidence is enough to stop Whitehead and his group from fomenting more problems. I believe the United States would vastly prefer to deal with problems in its own backyard, like Texas, than engage in more squabbling with Great Britain."

The countess wiped her lips delicately. "Florida is inching closer to statehood as the legislature's petitions are promoted in the nation's capitol, and I'm sure the territorial leaders would also like to avoid any political unpleasantness right now. That could work to our advantage if we need to present a petition to the Territorial Assembly," she said with a glance at her daughter. "When statehood happens, Florida will have a stronger voice in the country, but I am not optimistic St. Augustine will regain its former glory. The bank collapses and the freezes did serious damage to the local orange groves. We may need to think about relocating our United States business offices, though I wish to hold on to the house." She looked around at the dining room where she'd spent so many evenings as a child. "My father would be disappointed at much that has happened here, especially the shameful way the free coloreds are being treated. But he would be pleased to see how Sanders Shipping has grown in its partnership with Delerue."

"It is amazing how well that partnership turned out," Justin said, favoring his wife with a soft smile and a wineglass raised in salute.

Julia was used to this intellectual give and take, and had missed it. But she toyed with her meal and wondered who was taking care of Victoria while Randall was away from the farm, and if the lettuces she'd planted were being feasted on by worms and deer.

And she wondered who Randall dined with this evening. Was he glad to be back with his shipmates, secure in his position as Lieutenant Randall Hawkins, hero of the hour? Or was he missing her as much as she was missing him?

"Julia?"

Her attention came back from where she'd been rolling her peas into a row to her father's face. "I'm sorry, Papa, I did not hear the question."

He had that look of concern again. "I asked if you had any thoughts on Captain Collins's suggestion. Lieutenant Crane is interested in selling out, and Collins thought he might be a suitable new factor for Delerue-Sanders."

Julia thought about it for a few minutes while the sweets and coffee were brought in. She'd been too restless to sleep in this morning and made brandy snaps, and seeing them reminded her of the evening James and the men stayed at the farm.

"To give him his due, Papa, I found no fault with Lieutenant Crane's behavior during my stay at Rand Wash—at the farm. He seemed a trustworthy and capable officer, and after observing the demeanor of the men under his command, I would have to agree with Captain Collins. If he believes James to be suitable, I have no objection."

She grinned as she thought about it. "Having a former revenue officer as our factor may be to the good, Papa. He will know all the tricks of the smugglers *and* the habits of the Customs Department."

They turned their attention to dessert, and as they rose from the table Justin asked Julia to join him in his study.

He did not seat himself behind his desk, but instead perched on the edge, and watched her for a moment, a different silence from that used on Lieutenant Hawkins. Nonetheless, Julia's hands were clasped in her lap as she looked up at her father.

"Julia." He hesitated, and she braced herself for a long overdue lecture on her hoydenish ways.

"Julia. I am so thankful you are safe. If I live to be one hundred, I will never be able to express to you how much it meant to me to find you alive and unharmed in that cabin."

This was so far from what Julia expected that before she realized what was happening, tears were flowing down her cheeks. Her father pulled her into his sheltering embrace as she clutched his lapels and sobbed into his jacket.

"Oh, Papa, I was so afraid," she sniffled after soaking his shirtfront. "I was so afraid that you and Mama would be ashamed of me!"

"Here, blow," the earl said, pressing his handkerchief into her hand. "Ashamed of you? My darling girl, your welfare is my sole concern! And far from being ashamed of you, your mother and I admire your resourcefulness. Few young women would have dealt so well with your situation."

He led her over to a leather couch, and sat there listening as Julia shared with him what she could of the events out in the piney backwoods.

When she was done, Justin sighed, removed his glasses, and rubbed at the bridge of his nose before placing them back on and blinking at her.

"Some of the correspondence that arrived today was in

289

response to my queries about the legality of your marriage. According to the attorneys I consulted, there may be a question of the validity of your marriage vows, as you both gave less than full names. However, the courts are usually more interested in maintaining a marriage than dissolving one. Had you married each other with the intent to defraud, that might make it easier to get the marriage annulled. You could claim that Lieutenant Hawkins knew your identity, and was trying to defraud the Delerue heiress to get access to your inheritance."

"No!" Julia said sharply. "I won't have his name blackened that way. I believe he was unaware of my true identity when he married me, as I was unaware of his."

"If that's the case, there is another way. Florida Territory's laws are more liberal than England's regarding divorce. If you return to England and don't live with Lieutenant Hawkins for three years, he can sue for divorce in the Assembly on the grounds of desertion, provided he maintains his home here. I imagine money spread around to the right people in Tallahassee would speed the process," he said, echoing Rand's comments following their wedding night.

"Lieutenant Hawkins visited me while you were in Jacksonville. Did you know he has been promoted to first lieutenant?"

Julia sniffed. "Odd that the American government should reward one of its officers for kidnapping a British subject."

"I rather think it was more in recognition of the man's efforts to halt smugglers," Justin said dryly. "Regardless, he was adamant in his insistence that you are his wife and the marriage is legal. You two need to discuss this further, and I expect he will call on you tomorrow.

"I am willing to do anything to help you, my dear, but I want not only what is best for you, but also what will make you happy. Do you *want* to stay married to Randall Hawkins?"

Fresh tears trickled down Julia's face. "He is a domineering, self-satisfied, obnoxious prig and I despise him!"

"Of course," her father said, his face carefully expressionless.

Julia blew her nose and looked down at the wadded cloth in her hands. "But the worst of it is, he lied to me, Papa. Every day that we were together, from the morning 'til the night, it was all lies. How can I trust him? I know no marriage is perfect, but you and Mama never lied to each other like that, did you?"

"No matter what difficulties we had to deal with, I have to say your mother and I were truthful with one another—even when the truth was hurtful. But, Julia, you are wise enough to look at all the circumstances involved here and ask yourself, what is the real character of Randall Hawkins?"

"That is what I am not sure of, Papa."

"I know." The earl leaned forward and kissed his daughter on the forehead. "You have a few days before your mother and I leave for Savannah." He hesitated, then went on. "Your Aunt Suzanne wishes to return to England. If you are sure that you cannot stay married to Hawkins, you can travel with her and go home, too."

Home, Julia thought. But the image that rose to mind was not the magnificence of Rosemoor, but the sunlight sparkling off a Florida creek, and the shade of the oaks dappling a rough cabin in the woods.

CHAPTER 20

It would not have been entirely correct to say the Delerue household was aflutter the next day, when a note arrived asking if it would be convenient for Lieutenant Randall W. Hawkins, USRM, to call upon Lady Julia Delerue. Nevertheless, Cook was busy in the kitchen whipping up pecan pralines for tea, while Sylvestre inspected the house servants to make sure all was shipshape and Bristol fashion for the lieutenant's visit.

"The Revenue Marine will find nothing to comment on during my watch," he growled at a manservant sweeping the front walk.

The only ones who appeared calm in this hurricane were Lord Smithton and his countess as they worked together in the office, the earl at his desk, the countess aloft in the library loft that had been her favorite childhood reading spot.

Christine poked her head over the loft rail. "Julia, you are wearing a hole in my Aubusson. If you must pace, do it outside."

Julia tugged at the neck of her daffodil muslin. "I am not pacing," she said mendaciously. "I am *bored*. Surely there is something we could be doing besides sitting around here waiting on callers."

"Some of us are working, Julia," her father said. "If you cannot sit quietly, go annoy Sylvestre, not us."

"And why did he write on the note 'Lady Julia Delerue?'" she continued as if picking up the thread of a solitary conversation. "I thought he was insisting I was still his wife?"

"No doubt the lieutenant is doing his best to keep rumors and gossip to a minimum until this is resolved," Justin said without looking up from his ledgers. "Commendable behavior on his part. Speaking of the lieutenant, according to this I am still missing a case of brandy from the recovered goods."

Julia's cheekbones heated as she recalled some of the occasions when that brandy had been put to good use.

"It is at the farm, Papa, or at least part of a case is. It was excellent, by the way. A good selection."

"Our customers will be pleased to hear it," the earl murmured. "A personal testimonial from Lady Julia. Perhaps we should have engravings done for advertisements."

A rap at the door was followed by Sylvestre's grizzled head poking in.

"'E's here. I put 'im in the parlor." He gave Julia the once-over and said, "You look right smart, Miss Julia. As finely rigged as I've ever seen."

"Thank you, Sylvestre. I will be there shortly."

As soon as the butler left, the countess shimmied down the loft ladder and smoothing down her skirts, joined her daughter.

"Justin?"

"You go, my dear. I believe the lieutenant and I have said all we need to say to one another for now."

Christine patted her daughter's shoulder and the two women entered the parlor. Randall Hawkins jumped to his feet as the ladies entered, and Julia's eyes narrowed on him.

How dare he try to impress her with good manners at this

stage!

He was dressed in the same dark wool uniform as before, the sole difference being his shoulder straps carried two bars instead of the single bar he'd worn at their last meeting.

"Ma'am," Randall said, giving Julia's mother a bow. "It is good to see you again, even if we were not introduced at our first meeting."

"Do not concern yourself, lieutenant," the countess said. "Events *were* rather stressful on that occasion. And congratulations on your promotion."

"Thank you, ma'am," the lieutenant said, waiting until the women were properly seated before resuming his own seat.

The ticking parlor clock sounded as loud as rifle fire as the three sat, Christine Delerue watching the other occupants with all the interest of a spectator at a highly anticipated play.

"It is hot out. For winter, that is," Julia blurted, as her mother looked at her as if she'd lost what little sense remained to her.

"Yes, yes, it is quite warm, even for Florida," Hawkins said, then fell silent again, fiddling with the gloves in his lap.

"That's it," the countess said, rising to her feet as Randall jumped to his, a heartbeat ahead. Julia wanted to take the vase of camellias on the side table and dump them over his head, water and all.

"If the best you two can do to entertain me is discuss the weather, I am leaving."

Without a backward glance the countess exited the room, closing the door behind her.

Randall looked at Julia, who shrugged.

"My mother has never suffered fools gladly."

"I cannot argue with her assessment of the two of us."

He sat and looked down at his hands, then up at her through his lashes. "You look well, Julia. Quite lovely in fact."

"Thank you. You look fine also, lieutenant. I could never mistake you for the Cracker who lived out in the pinewoods. You are to be congratulated on an astoundingly successful ruse."

She stood and again, he leapt to his feet a moment before her. It was tempting to get up and down just to see if he would bounce like a marionette, but she resisted temptation.

"Now that we have discussed the weather, bored my mother into leaving, and complimented one another, I do not imagine there is anything else to say. Good day to you, sir."

At that moment Sylvestre came in, directing a servant carrying a heavy tray.

"Do not bother, the lieutenant is leaving."

"No, the lieutenant is *not* leaving. Put the tray down," Rand snapped out in a voice suitable for the quarterdeck.

"Aye, sir," Sylvestre said, and the footman placed the tray with tea and pralines on the side table, then the two hurried out, again closing the door behind them.

Julia looked at that closed door in astonishment. She'd never expected her own crew to mutiny on her this way.

When she looked back around, he was standing in his best military stance, hands clasped behind his back. He looked formal, and formidable, and unapproachable. He looked like who he was—Lieutenant Randall W. Hawkins.

At that moment she hated him with a passion so white-hot it stole her breath. She sat at the tea table and poured them each a cup, mostly to give her hands something to do to keep them from trembling.

"How do you take your tea, lieutenant?"

"Stop fussing with the tea tray, Julia. I did not come here today to take tea and exchange pleasantries about the weather."

"Oh? Why are you here then?"

Julia leaned back and sipped at her own tea. Manners be damned, he could get his own cup if he wanted some. Serve him right for all those times in the cabin she'd waited on Rand Washburn.

"We left things unfinished the other day, and there is still a great deal to be said. You know quite well that our marriage is of questionable legality, and repeating our vows formally will solidify what we already have." His face softened, in spite of his pompous speech. "I want to make it right, Julia. A real marriage between Julia Delerue and Randall Hawkins, in a church, not two people under the gun lying to each other. Will you do me the honor of being my wife, again?"

She set down her teacup, clasping her hands in her lap. "I am appreciative of the great kindness and honor you do me by asking me to be your wife, Lieutenant Hawkins, but I must respectfully decline your offer of marriage."

This was said in the same inflectionless voice she'd used when she'd accepted Rand Washburn's forced proposal.

Randall stiffened. "Stop playing games, Julia! I am here because we need to shore up the legalities of our marriage and discuss our future, and we need to take care of it before I leave for Key West."

"Our future? Our marriage? Ah, but you see, that is the best part of this farce. Lady Julia Delerue does not have a husband

296

named Lieutenant Randall Hawkins of the United States Revenue Marine. *Julia Cooper* married a man named *Rand Washburn* under dire circumstances. The paper that exists bears that out. The witnesses who know about it can only testify to that. As far as I am concerned, there was no marriage. There is no marriage. There is not a future to discuss."

She stood, and centuries of breeding showed in her stance.

"Congratulate yourself, lieutenant. You have been saved from an unpleasant mésalliance with a tavern wench *and* you have still managed to fulfill your obligation to Lady Julia Delerue."

He stared at her, his own face as hard and cold as she had ever seen. He turned on his heel, but stopped at the door, his hand on the knob, and looked back at her where she stood in the middle of the parlor.

"Do not attempt to flee before I return from Key West, *Lady Julia*," he said from the doorway. His voice was soft, but she still resisted the temptation to take a step back. "This is far from over between us."

He bowed, and left, and in the silent room the ticking of the parlor clock sounded like a heartbeat.

CHAPTER 21

Julia was the first one in the dining room at breakfast. It was to be expected, since she hadn't slept all night.

From the looks of the bags under her mother's eyes as she poured herself coffee, it had been a rough night for Lady Smithton as well.

"I must return to England," Julia said, looking down into her coffee cup.

Christine sighed and sat, not bothering to take a plate from the sideboard. Neither one of the women had much appetite at the moment.

"I thought I could do some good here, Mama, helping the family. All I have done is manage to get myself into trouble again. I would be better off staying home. Or traveling somewhere where my scandals will not come back to harm you and Papa."

"Julia, look at me."

Julia looked up, to find her mother gently smiling at her only daughter.

"Your father and I, and your brothers as well, love you and will always love you. We have weathered far worse than your scandals, as you call them."

"Oh, Mama, I wanted to be more like you. Bold and adventurous, not afraid of anything!"

Christine set her cup down with a click and stared at her daughter. "My dear child, there is so much I am afraid of! Every mother has constant fears for her children's safety, and their happiness. But you were the daughter I dreamed of. You sparkled and shone. I would watch you at parties with all your friends, filling your dance card and laughing, and I was so proud of you and so happy for you. I did not want you to be like me when I was young, sitting on the sidelines watching the other girls have fun."

Julia shook her head. "And here I did not want to be known as a social leader. I wanted to have an adventure like *yours*, Mama, fighting pirates like Captain Daniels."

"Hmmmm," the countess said. "Those adventures, as you put it, almost ended my marriage to your father. But here's a thought for you to ponder, Julia. If your father and I could work past *our* differences—and no, I am not going to tell you how we did—is it so unbelievable that you and Lieutenant Hawkins could work past your problems and make a go of this marriage?"

"Papa asked me the same thing. What I can't get beyond is, Ran—Randall Hawkins lied to me. And in a way, he is still lying to me. And to himself."

"Then let me ask you a different question. How do you feel, Julia? These past weeks out on the farm, despite all that has happened and what you term a scandal, how do you feel? How do you feel about yourself?"

She thought about it as she stirred cream into her coffee. It was a legitimate question for her mother to ask.

"Strong. I am stronger, and frankly, I am proud of what I was able to accomplish out at that cabin in the piney woods. It is what women like Ma Ivey do all their lives, every day, but I did not know *I* could do it. I think about my friends, many of whom would swoon at the sight of a live possum, much less a skinned one…" She shook her head. "It is never going to be the same for me anymore, is it, Mama?"

"No, and that is what growing up, and life, are all about, darling. But I suspect Hawkins will never be the same either. Regardless, if you do not want the lieutenant, there are plenty of young men in England who would marry you," Christine said, studying her nails. "Nice, quiet boys who won't upset you, or give you a moment's worry."

Julia looked at her mother. "You are a devious woman."

"Yes, well, I believe it is one of the things your father likes best about me." The countess stood and stretched to her full, impressive height. "If you decide you want the lieutenant after all, Julia, your father and I will give you our blessing. But while it is fun to watch them crawl when they have been stupid, don't make Lieutenant Hawkins crawl too much. Men have their pride also."

Justin strolled in carrying the newspaper, but stopped when he saw their faces. "What are you ladies discussing?"

"Recipes," Julia said brightly.

"Shopping," Christine smiled, which made her husband look even warier.

Justin took off his eyeglasses and rubbed between his brows. "I do not want to know the details. And if there are bodies to be disposed of, I do not want to know about that, either."

"Hmph," his wife said. "Uncle Julius always said your *real* friends are the ones that help you hide the bodies."

She kissed her husband on the cheek and breezed out of the room, humming to herself.

*   *   *

The residents of St. Augustine loved a party. Hosting Lord and Lady Smithton and their daughter, Lady Julia, was all the excuse needed for a gala ball at one of the lavish hotels built to house northerners, and visitors from across the ocean fleeing harsh winters for a softer climate. It was a uniquely Floridian event, with plaintive Spanish guitars strumming out the rhythms of Andalusia and Minorca, and American fiddlers playing lively jigs. The older population in particular enjoyed the Iberian dances, their gliding, intricate movements designed to showcase the grace of the dancers.

Lady Smithton delighted in the opportunity to indulge in the dances of her youth, but she knew the soft murmurings of the language spoken in the city decades before Lieutenant Hawkins's forebears ever caught sight of Plymouth Rock wouldn't be heard in a generation. The Americans were here to stay, stamping their mark on the town, from the rechristened Castillo to the open Parade at the center of town, once known to all natives as the Plaza.

She remarked as much to her daughter as Julia scanned the room full of men in evening clothes and uniforms of all descriptions, the bright braid of the U.S. Navy officers eclipsing the more subdued dress of their Revenue Marine counterparts.

"Their uniforms reflect what they are," she overheard a spotty-faced navy midshipman say to his companion. "Bureaucrats and penny counters for the Treasury."

Julia wanted to snap at the youngster that *real* fighting men

301

didn't need fancy dress to look martial, but she was forestalled by a familiar voice at her side.

"I declare, I thought I had been introduced to all the beautiful women in St. Augustine when I met you, Lady Smithton, but here's one slipped right past my bow. Would you be so kind as to introduce me?"

"Certainly," Christine said with a smile. "Julia, may I present Lieutenant James Crane of the Revenue Marine? Lieutenant Crane, my daughter, Julia…Delerue."

"Charmed, Lady Julia," James said, bending over her gloved hand with a wink. "I had the pleasure of meeting your parents earlier this week, and having heard so much about you, I longed for an introduction."

Julia favored Lieutenant Crane with a small smile. "Yes, lieutenant, my father told me he met with you. He said you were thinking of leaving the service?"

"Indeed," James said, releasing her hand. "I have had my fill of chasing scoundrels and desperadoes through the backwoods, and am ready for some peace and quiet. But tonight is too fair a night—eclipsed solely by the company in this room—to be discussing business. May I request the honor of a dance?"

Julia held out her dance card and as James bent over it she murmured for his ears alone, "Not quite like the menu of services in a Havana bawdy house," prompting a coughing fit that brought tears to the young man's eyes and a concerned look from the countess.

"Perhaps a bit of fresh air would help," James gasped out, offering his arm to Julia, who accepted it with grace. She had many questions for Mr. Crane.

"I didn't know Randall mentioned that Havana excursion," he said when they were out of earshot.

"Oh, yes, Randall was good at telling me the *unimportant* things," Julia said, languidly moving her fan through the evening air as they walked in the hotel's gardens. The smell of night blooming jasmine mingled with orange blossoms, scenting the light breeze. "Has he returned from Key West?"

"No. He won't return until he's finished his tasks. Randall is a dutiful officer, and has been since I've known him."

"How did you two meet?"

"During the war. We were both assigned to the revenue cutter *Washington*. The older officers nicknamed Randall 'Sir Galahad' because he was so upright, and saw everything as black and white, right and wrong. Fighting the Seminole took care of that."

"He was the young officer from Boston who tried to help the slaves, wasn't he?"

James stopped walking and looked at her.

"You are wrong about one thing, Julia. If Randall told you about that night, he told you about what was important to him. As far as I know, he has never discussed what happened. I know about it only because of what followed."

They'd reached a stone bench and she sat, while James clasped his hands behind his back, a pose so reminiscent of his brother-in-arms that Julia's breath caught on the memory.

"Did you hear that he made first lieutenant?"

"Yes, I saw him."

And she was glad, a special corner of her heart celebrating his accomplishment.

"Haven't you wondered why an officer of Randall's integrity

and skill didn't make his lieutenant's bars before now?"

He looked over her shoulder, as if seeing far into the distance, a stare she'd seen on veterans of English conflicts returned home.

"Back in '40, after that disaster on the Withlacoochee, Randall was sent to New Orleans with a group of captured Seminoles to prepare them for their removal to Fort Gibson in Indian Territory. Waiting there was a Mr. Spencer. He was the agent of a Georgia slave owner who claimed some of his slaves were mixed in with the Indians."

"Were they?"

James shrugged. "I wasn't there. All I know is, Randall complained to General Taylor that there were people in New Orleans wanting to press fraudulent claims for the return of escaped slaves."

When a healthy young male slave was selling in the St. Augustine markets for close to one thousand dollars, and an infant could be bought for one hundred and fifty dollars, Julia thought it was no wonder claims—fraudulent or legitimate— were being vigorously pursued by the owners.

"What happened?"

"His complaint was part of the problem, because you had different services under different commands. General Zach Taylor was army and in charge of the war, but the Revenue Marine was a whole different operation, as you'll hear. While Mr. Spencer was waiting on a meeting with Randall, *someone* chartered a boat and snuck the Seminoles and maroons out of New Orleans and up to Fort Gibson." He grinned. "I heard those Indians were so painted you couldn't tell if they were black, red, or purple. Once they arrived at Fort Gibson they were absorbed by the Seminole that had gone ahead, and now they're all in Indian Territory and not our problem any more."

"But that wasn't the end of Randall's troubles, was it?"

"No. Spencer wrote a letter to his employer, who complained to friends in Congress that Randall had shown a 'great disregard if not outright violation of orders.' What that midshipman said earlier has some truth," James said bitterly. "We are the Treasury's pet navy, at least so far as appointments and promotions go. Get on the wrong side of those with power and you can bid farewell to your career."

"Or attempt to salvage it with some daring and dangerous mission that puts you in good graces again."

"That's exactly right, Julia. And that's one reason why I am looking to get out. I hear the Revenue Marine is changing its methods, but I've seen too many good men fall victim to pettifogging politicians who don't understand what is at stake on our nation's borders."

The strains of a reel drifted in from the ballroom and he smiled at her, and held out his hand.

"But enough of the military lesson. I believe that's our dance, Lady Julia. Shall we return inside?"

*   *   *

The ball was in full swing and brightly colored gowns twirled through the candlelit air like wind-tossed flowers, while sweating musicians sawed furiously at their fiddles and hammered the piano.

Randall Hawkins stood at the top of the staircase, watching his wife dance a vigorous polka in the arms of a midshipman who looked like he'd never done anything more seaworthy than give an order to weigh anchor.

"Damned rosewater sailors," he muttered, but accepted a drink pressed into his hands by James Crane.

"I'm glad you could join us, but for heaven's sake, school your expression," James hissed in his ear. "You look like you're going to do something violent."

"If that navy bastard doesn't stop looking down her dress, I *am* going to do something violent!"

"Remember, lieutenant… 'A revenue service officer's deportment should be marked by prudence, moderation and good temper.'"

"Quit quoting Alexander Hamilton to me, James, or I will give you a piece of my good temper right up your—"

"I just want to keep you from trying anything suicidal. I seem to remember a cutter officer back in '41 who walked into a tavern full of navy men in Key West, telling them they were nothing but 'goat-buggering marines.'"

Randall grinned at the memory.

"It wasn't the goat buggering that bothered them, they were sailors after all, but when you called them marines…"

"I didn't realize how fast you could run until that day, James." He took a deep swallow of the wine as his eyes followed one figure on the dance floor.

Julia shone in a satin gown of deepest carnation, her shoulders and bosom rising above the froth of Brussels lace at what could not be called a neckline, low cut as it was. There were no jewels on that long neck to distract the eye from the lush expanse of flesh. Instead, her hair had been parted and pulled back in ringlets over her ears and trimmed with satin flowers that mimicked the blush in her cheeks and deepened the color of her eyes and lips.

The hue of the gown highlighted her radiant skin, kissed by the Florida sun until it was the color of palest gold silk. She looked like a rose mallow blooming in the swamps, putting to shame the hothouse roses that faded in the heat.

She also looked like the very available and unmarried Lady Julia Delerue, not Mrs. Washburn, and Randall clenched his fists as he fought the urge to bull his way through the couples on the dance floor, and throw a shawl around all that skin being ogled by the boy at her side.

He also wanted to throw her over his shoulder and carry her far away, all the way back into the deep woods.

But that was not an option for Lieutenant Hawkins.

Julia glanced up and saw him watching her, and for a moment her expression was arrested before she looked back at her partner.

"There! She's doing it! That thing with her eyes, where she looks bored, yet aware of everything at the same time. How do they do that?"

"You've finally lost your mind, haven't you, Randall? How was Key West?"

"Pestilent and bug ridden, as usual, with the cry of 'wreck ashore!' bringing out an assortment of scoundrels and misplaced pirates, all of whom will assure you they are upright businessmen, pleased to see representatives of the United States government. The good news is, once they realized I was after other miscreants most of them were willing to steer me in the right direction, so long as it pointed away from them."

The dance was ending, and Randall shoved his glass into James's hand and then set course to intercept his wife before more men could drool over her.

Her fan came to a stop when he stood before her, and he saw the slight tightening of her fingers on the sticks.

"*Lady* Julia? I believe this is our dance."

He did not phrase it as a question.

"Hey there, sailor!" a florid-faced merchant protested. "My name is the next one on Miss Julia's card!"

Randall raised one brow, yanked the dance card—and its attached wrist—up and unceremoniously scratched out the merchant's name before writing in his own.

"Not anymore."

The man started to protest again, but thought better of it as he looked up, way up, into Randall's cold eyes.

"Another time, Mr. Winston," Julia said before turning to scowl at her new partner. But whatever peal she was planning on ringing over him was forestalled by his pulling her onto the floor to the murmurs of the surrounding ladies and gentlemen.

Randall didn't care. He was tired of pretending this *lady* who smelled of perfume and expensive hair pomade wasn't the same woman who'd worked up a sweat in his kitchen.

And in his bed.

He was tired of always toeing the line, lest some slip push his career back into drydock. This would be settled between them, tonight, one way or another.

The band struck up a waltz as they headed onto the floor.

"Oh no, not this dance," she protested.

"Yes, this dance," he snapped back, hauling her up against him, too close for good manners, but not nearly close enough for him.

But he was gentle as he moved into the rhythm of the waltz. Their hands were gloved, but he could feel her through his fingertips, just as he knew her form, even laced and corseted as it was this evening. She was his Julia, his wild smuggler's bride, no matter how she covered herself up or pretended, or what life she thought was hers back in England.

*   *   *

"Don't you find Florida an unpleasant land, Mis—I mean, Lady Julia? So far it seems to be populated by snakes and insects. Nothing ever happens here." The midshipman sighed. "Not like on the western frontier or the China sea."

A Revenue Marine officer looked down on the crowd, his gaze seeking out one dancer, and Julia felt that stare from across the room like a hit from a nine-pounder.

He was standing with James Crane, and as with the other Revenue Marine officers, Randall's dress uniform was more subdued than that worn by the navy men, but he hardly needed gold braid to stand out. When he left James's side, more than one pair of feminine eyes followed him as he crossed the ballroom, his dark blue coat set off by black braid and a black silk cravat. There was a flash of gold from the epaulette on his right shoulder, and from his service sword with its spread eagle beneath the Roman hilt. The sword with its gold bullion and silk sword knot was the most elaborate accoutrement of the revenue uniform, but it said what it needed to say: The Revenue Marine was a service that battled during peacetime, guarding the young

309

nation's borders and protecting the economy that drove it toward the first ranks of the world's powers. It was a more powerful statement than gold trim and lace, and she thought he looked like a dark raptor among the uniformed popinjays.

Julia tried to concentrate on her partner and the dance, but she knew what and who would be waiting for her at the end. As she was escorted back to her seat and the youngster excused himself to step out with his next partner, Julia turned her bright smile on Mr. Winston, but wasn't surprised when Randall took matters into his own hands moments later.

As he led her onto the dance floor she toyed with the idea of causing a scene in the middle of the ball, but thought better of it. Randall looked grim enough to haul her away and use that all too lethal-looking sword at his side to repel boarders.

Better to get this over with, she told herself, but she could feel him, even through the layers of his uniform, his presence stirring her as none of her other partners had.

And she was honest enough to admit it wasn't just her dancing partners he eclipsed. Randall Hawkins put every man of her acquaintance in the shade.

But as he pulled her close, too close for the proprieties, she smelled his costly cologne and she knew she was in the arms of Lieutenant Hawkins, not Rand Washburn. Rand never wore cologne. Out in the piney woods, he smelled of the fresh air, and himself, and the almond soap he used for shaving.

But it was a nice cologne, she admitted, moving in a fraction closer. A hint of sandalwood and spice. Rand Washburn had his rough charms, but she'd also have to be on guard against Lieutenant Hawkins's stern appeal.

"Frolicking with the lower classes, Lady Julia?" he whispered in her ear.

That made it easier to keep her emotional distance, even if their bodies were too close for comfort.

"You must have laughed when I said I would stay married to you, that morning on the river. Imagine, Lady Julia Delerue married to some Cracker."

"My goodness," Julia said with a smile sharp enough to rend cloth. "The form is the proper and dutiful revenue officer from Boston, but the attitude is someone completely different. What role are you playing today, *lieutenant*?"

"I am not playing a role, *Lady Julia*. I had a long time on the trip to the Keys and back to think about how you played me for a fool. How it must have amused you to pretend affection for Rand Washburn," he said bitterly.

"I admit, Rand Washburn was amusing on occasion. Unlike you, Lieutenant Hawkins." Unfair, she knew, but she wasn't feeling charitable at the moment.

He stopped dead on the floor, unmindful of the dancers who swirled about them.

"Come with me," he said, grabbing her hand and pulling her behind him.

She hurried to keep up and make it at least appear like she was going with him freely. Out of the corner of her eye she saw her father frown and start forward, but her mother forestalled him with a hand on his arm. Julia lost sight of them as Randall dragged her out and down a breezeway.

He pulled her into a room and locked it behind them, then leaned against the door, watching her. It was a reading room with a lounging sofa and overstuffed leather chairs, the single lamp on the table not lighting the dark corners. Her eyes came back to the man whose presence filled the room, and she almost looked away again, his half lidded eyes reminding her of what happens to girls who tease panthers.

"Time for another little chat," he said, advancing toward her. She backed up, and saw that smile flash across his face, the smile raising the hairs at the back of her neck.

Her knees came up against the edge of the sofa but he moved in closer, until the wool of his uniform pants rustled against her satin skirts.

"My name is Randall. Not 'Lieutenant.' You can say it, Julia."

But she kept her thinned lips mutinously shut and glared at him, a move that didn't seem to cow him in the least.

Instead, he moved in closer, close enough that even in the dim light she could see the sharp planes of his face, as desire and anger worked together in him, and her own pulse beat faster in her neck.

Her instinct was to flee from the danger his anger offered.

Her instinct was to throw herself headlong into that danger.

"Just like this," he said in a low, husky voice, putting his forefinger and thumb alongside the corners of her tight mouth and squeezing gently. "Rrrrrrr...."

Her lips pursed, and she resisted the impulse to lick the leather-clad thumb at the corner of her mouth, but she couldn't suppress the throaty sound that emerged, almost against her will.

"Rrrr..."

"Very good, Julia," he whispered. "And now, open wide and

finish, 'aaaaaandalll.'"

And when her mouth opened, he brought his own mouth forward and cut off the sound, his tongue blocking hers from making all but the most primitive of noises.

She was boneless, her tight lacing and stays all that held her upright in his strong arms. She felt like she could have stayed there forever, until he pulled back.

"Randall," she whispered. His mouth moved down the bare expanse of her neck, across her bosom, and she found herself clutching his shoulders because he had eased his hands inside the front of her gown, his gloves making a susurrus against the satin of her dress. Then his thumbs were stroking her with small circular motions, the feel of the leather against her hardening tips an unbelievably erotic sensation.

"Randall," she whispered again.

"That's right, Julia," he breathed, "The real Randall Hawkins, not the pretend Rand Washburn. *This* is real—as real as our marriage."

He kissed her again, less gently this time, his mouth scorching hers as he brought the force of their shared passion to bear on her. She was the one who pulled back to glare at him, as she pushed his shoulders away and straightened up. He released her, but the look in his eyes made her wish she had the couch between them, instead of at her back.

"This is not a good idea, Ran—Lieutenant. If we are going to resolve our difficulties like civilized people, then we must act according to society's rules. Those rules do not allow unmarried women to go off to dark rooms with gentlemen! And despite your insistence, I am not at all convinced we are in fact married.

Your behavior offends me, sir!"

"I offend you, *Lady Julia*? Isn't it a little late for you to begin worrying about society's rules? After all, your father assures me you and your distinguished, aristocratic family can weather any scandal thrown up by rude Yankees. Perhaps I want to put it to the test."

"That *uniform* you wear offends me, Lieutenant Hawkins, for it reminds me of your mendacious ways."

"My uniform offends you? I can fix that, your ladyship."

He yanked his gloves off with his teeth and had his coat, vest, and cravat off before she could stop him, flinging them unceremoniously across a chair.

Randall stood there in his shirtsleeves, and while she'd seen him buff naked, there was something about seeing him in this state of undress that brought a throbbing low in her belly, and she moistened her lips.

Even in the shadowed room she saw his eyes darken.

"My uniform offends you? I'll show you what offends me."

He stepped in even closer, until she could see the faint dusting of hair at the top of his shirt, then the golden head bent over her wrist as he silently undid each tiny button on her evening gloves.

Her chest rose and fell with her rapid breathing. It was unbearably erotic, this slow, sensual dance they were doing, their breathing and the faint strains of the music from the distant ballroom filling the still air.

Randall peeled the gloves down past her elbow, his fingers trailing fire along the sensitive underside of her arm. He paused to plant a kiss where the pulse beat behind her wrist and her breath caught in her throat. Then her hands, the hands she'd been so careful to keep covered during her days back in civilization, were exposed to light.

He cupped them together in his own callused palms and planted soft kisses on each little mark and rough spot, the torn nail and the scraped knuckle. He licked at the base of her fingers where a callus had formed from the pressure of her cooking knives, and stroked his tongue along the healing burn from the pot of grits she'd grabbed too quickly.

"These are the hands of my Julia. My wife."

He looked up at her, his eyes blazing with green heat.

"My *wife*," he repeated. "Not the woman who hides her hands, and straps herself into corsets and boning and yards of satin. *Your* uniform offends me! I don't know that woman, the earl's daughter."

"And you did not marry the earl's daughter, did you?" She pulled out of his grasp and stepped back, the work-worn hands curled into fists. "You married Julia Cooper, the homeless orphan! How *you* must have laughed to think how easy it was to take advantage of a bastard tavern girl. She may not have had a choice, but I do! I am the daughter of one of England's leading families, and I have wealth in my own name, and a place in society. What exactly are you offering me?"

"I am offering you the same thing I offered in the woods, Julia. The protection of my name. I have a duty to you, and while my name may not mean much in the drawing rooms of London, it is respected here in the United States, and I know what my obligations are."

"Your duty? Your obligations? Forgive me if I'm not

overcome with warmth and passion at that declaration, lieutenant!"

"Oh, well if it's passion you want…"

He grinned, not the slow and easy one she remembered from Rand Washburn, or the polite smiles of Lieutenant Hawkins, but something sharper, hotter, and infinitely more dangerous.

The door, and safety, lay a few steps beyond her, but it might as well have been on the moon. She'd barely made a move before he had her in his arms again, one hand holding her hair, dislodging all the carefully arranged curls, while the other stroked down her back as he placed tender kisses across her neck and bare shoulders, on her face, across her eyes, at the corner of her mouth. He held her captive, but she made no further effort to free herself, only his mouth, and his skillful fingers coaxing her to stay.

The same fingers unfastening the hooks of her bodice as he was kissing her.

There was a mirror hanging on the wall, a convex reflector in a heavy gilt frame distorting their images. It was like watching someone else being undressed, even as she felt his long fingers brushing against her back, along the edge of lace on her camisole, and down over the stays of the fine French corset that nipped in her waist.

She blamed the corset for her breathlessness. Surely that was the explanation for her faintness as her dress puddled at her feet, the satin billowing out like magnolia petals floating across a pond.

Their distorted image in the mirror flowed together as his hands came around the front of her to cup her breasts, easing them out of the corset and into the cool air. His rough thumbs resumed stroking the nipples that tightened and darkened as his golden head dipped down, his breath searing the soft skin below her jawline, trailing kisses across her neck, moving purposefully lower, and she made a last attempt to regain control of the situation.

"What about those boots, and that swordbelt?" she said desperately.

She felt him smile against the top of the rounded breasts straining against his fingers.

"They come off if the corset and stays come off. I don't like your uniform either, your ladyship."

"No, I'll never get back into them!" she cried. "At least remove your sword!"

He raised his head and she saw his grin reflected in the mirror, the flash of white magnified into an erotic streak of lightning.

"Very well, the sword comes off."

He managed to undo the belt with one hand while the other kept her tight to him as he steered her, his body moving hers backward. She put her hands on his shoulders to steady herself as she came up against the sofa, heard the clatter of the scabbard hitting the carpet and buttons being undone, and glancing up at the sound realized he'd positioned them so she could still see the mirror.

Dear God, he intended her to watch as he made love to her. The thought made her already weak knees buckle further, but he was there, supporting her with one hand on her back, lowering her to the sofa while the other lifted the froth of lace and silk she wore beneath her full ball skirt.

"Why, Lady Julia," he murmured into her ear. "You are not wearing drawers and are out of uniform. How very naughty of you!"

"I fell out of the habit back in the woods. Now they only get in the w—Oh!" she gasped as he entered her smoothly, her own desire for him easing the tight passage.

She rose up against him, but he had her firmly in hand, soothing her with small noises, like a nervous mare being gentled. She eased back down.

"Good girl," he whispered, as he pinned her beneath him on the couch. He rested there a moment, inside her, their harsh breathing and the distant strains of music the only sound. She could feel him, all of him, inside her and touching every part of her, inside and out, until she was a part of him. He raised up on his forearms and looked down into her eyes, holding her captive as he began to move, the velvet beneath her back turning slick with sweat as he rode her. She looked away from his hot eyes and watched them in the mirror, the image wavering in and out of her blurred vision.

The tension rose in her, spiraling upward like hot embers from a pinewoods fire. She tried to resist being consumed by the conflagration, but it was all too much, so she let herself go, riding the waves of heat as his body moved against hers, their dance as old as time with its own musky scent and wet music, the anger and passion colliding into a maelstrom of sensation that overwhelmed them both. She heard his oath a second before he sank his teeth into the spot where her neck joined her shoulder and she curvetted against him, her own cry of completion muffled by the hand he placed across her mouth at the last moment.

"Shhhhh!" he whispered into her ear. "I hear voices."

"No, you can't go in there, ma'am." James Crane's voice came through the locked door. "A tomcat chased a tabby through there, and knocked over a lamp and a decanter, and it's just a terrible mess!"

"But I thought I saw Julia...oh..." said Lady Smithton. "Well. Carry on, lieutenant."

Julia turned so red she hoped they couldn't see the glow out of the windows, but Randall chuckled ruefully and said, "Good thing I knew you were a screamer, darlin'."

He'd called her darlin', missing consonant and all.

"Oh, Rand," she murmured, reaching up to touch his face.

He froze and grabbed her hand.

"Not Rand! Rand Washburn doesn't exist! I am Randall Hawkins."

He slid off of her and turned his back, gathering his clothes from where they'd been thrown, and she swallowed hard before rising to shakily step into her crumpled gown.

"Here, let me help you with that," he said, his warm fingers skimming up her back as he fastened the hooks, reversing his earlier actions. She said nothing but stared straight ahead and he must have read something of her mood, for when he reached the top of the hooks he turned her around and looked into her eyes, his own head cocked to the side.

"Now might be a good time to step out there, and tell your mother we are married and staying together."

"I have not changed my mind. I will be leaving in two days

for Savannah, where I'll catch ship for England," she said woodenly.

He grabbed her by her bare shoulders, and she wanted to step back because if there was heat before, now his eyes were blazing.

"Where I come from, husbands and wives are married 'til death do us part!"

"Where I come from, husbands and wives don't start their marriages on a lie. As you yourself reminded me, it's all been lies between us from the very beginning, and that is no marriage!"

"We have to do what is right and proper, Julia. Especially now. Your reputation is already at risk, and I suspect this interlude tonight will completely blacken your name, unless you come with me and formalize our marriage."

"So that was your plan!" She knew she looked disheveled and rumpled, but pulled her dignity about her and looked him in the eye. "You pulled me in here to ensure I would have to bend to your will? If you believe that, you do not know me very well. I will not make a decision based on your Bostonian notions of what is right and proper."

She picked up her discarded gloves and clenched them in her hands, free in the knowledge that she no longer cared who saw her blisters and calluses.

"You are a snob, Lieutenant Hawkins, wrapped in your mantle of righteousness and duty. Poor Julia Cooper! You would have expected her to be so grateful for being rescued from crime and poverty, welcomed into your American aristocratic family, that she would have always been there on sufferance, never a

320

true equal.

"I happen to like who Julia Cooper is. I also like who Lady Julia Delerue is. I can return to London and marry a marquess if I choose!"

His eyes narrowed. "Oh? Aren't you concerned that your marquess would accuse you of trying to pass off damaged goods? Or does your wealth and family make that little detail unimportant?"

"Get out of my way," she said in a low voice.

"Gladly, *your ladyship*," he said, stepping aside to let her pass.

Julia walked across the room, the longest journey she'd ever taken, and as her hand unlatched the door, she paused for a moment, turned and looked at him one last time.

"The reason I will not marry *you* is because you are not the man I want, Lieutenant Randall Hawkins."

His head snapped back as if she'd slapped him. But something in her voice seemed to give him pause.

"Who do you want, Julia?"

She just shook her head as tears swam in her eyes, and ran from him.

James Crane was gone when she stepped out into the silent corridor, but it wasn't empty.

Her mother rose from a chair where she'd been sitting. Julia took one look at her mother's face, then threw herself into her arms, silently crying from the bottom of her soul.

The countess led her daughter away to their waiting carriage. When the door to the room opened again, all was quiet and still.

Randall stood in the dark hallway and leaned against the

closed door, clutching his gear in his hands. He was still standing there when James found him a few minutes later.

"Don't say anything, James, please."

"Do you want to go get drunk?"

"Yes. But I'm not going to. For once, I'm going to sit and think things through without flying off half-cocked. I've got one last chance and I'm not going to let my temper destroy it."

"Now that," James said, "may be the most reasonable thing I have heard you say in ages, Lieutenant Hawkins."

CHAPTER 22

The day of their departure dawned sunny and fair, and Julia's spirits sank even lower. She'd sat home all day yesterday, pretending she wasn't straining to hear the sound of firm footsteps coming up the walk, Lieutenant Randall Hawkins demanding she return with him.

She wouldn't go, of course, but it still rankled. What kind of husband was he if he wouldn't keep trying to get her back?

But he wasn't her husband, was he? She kept insisting that was the case. If he gave up, and didn't come after her, she had only herself to hold responsible.

It was what she wanted after all.

Wasn't it? Hadn't she insisted she was *not* married to Lieutenant Randall Hawkins, the stuck-up Boston prig? After all, who wanted to be married to a man who constantly argued with her, and ordered her about, and didn't do everything she wanted?

She sank deeper into her funk at the thought.

Christine passed through the parlor, and frowned. "Julia Anne! If you are going to be ready to leave, pick yourself up and grab your bag. Sylvestre and the staff have done all the work, but I draw the line at them carrying you aboard."

"Yes, Mama." Julia sighed. She wondered how her parents would feel about her traveling to China on the next Delerue-Sanders run. Or somewhere else, far, far away.

Men at the docks were happy to take silver to row the Delerue family out to the countess' private yacht, *Tigress,* the schooner waiting to carry them to Savannah.

Julia sat silently, clutching her bonnet, her eyes trained on the massive walls of the fort.

"You can still change your mind."

Julia turned to her father and blinked her wet eyes, summoning up a smile.

"My mind is made up, Papa. It is better this way. Lieutenant Hawkins and I did not suit."

"And what of Rand Washburn?" her father asked in a voice solely for her ears.

Julia was quiet as the gulls filled the morning air with their cries, and it seemed as if she had not heard, but then she said in a low voice, "There is no Rand Washburn, Papa. He was as much a figment of my imagination as my pretend playmate when I was small."

"I remember her. Her name was Clarisse, and she was a French princess. You were the only one who could see her."

"Yes, but she was good company," Julia said with a smile. "Especially surrounded as I was by my brothers."

They sat in silence for the rest of the ride, the rowers singing a Bahamian chanty as they glided to the ship.

Julia climbed aboard with ease, then her aunt Suzanne was helped aboard and immediately left the family to lie down on her bunk. Suzanne was not a good traveler and they knew they wouldn't see her until they docked in Savannah.

Julia stood on deck as men rushed around her coiling ropes, hauling boxes, and out of the corner of her eye she saw her mother and father talking. He pulled a cheroot from his pocket, and her mother put her hand on her father's arm and said something that made him smile.

That was what Julia wanted. That warmth and tenderness, as well as the passion. For a while, out at the cabin, it seemed she'd found that. But not since. And maybe, never.

"Ahoy, *Tigress*! Prepare to be boarded!"

Julia rushed to the rail, heart pounding. A Revenue Marine boat was being rowed alongside, and standing in the stern, looking grim and purposeful, was a handsome lieutenant.

"Wrong lieutenant," Julia murmured to herself as James Crane climbed aboard.

"Now, this looks interesting," Smithton said.

Captain Jensen's brow furrowed as he stood alongside the earl.

"M'lord, if we don't sail now we're going to miss the tide."

Smithton took the cheroot from his mouth and turned to the captain. "Captain Jensen, I am surprised at you. Surely you do not mean to risk our being fired on by the Revenue Marine. These Americans are brash and, let us be honest here, largely uncivilized. Heaven alone knows what they might do if provoked."

"I understand, m'lord."

Jensen sighed, and directed the crew to stand by.

Crane was followed by Tompkins and Weaver, the former giving Lady Julia a small wave of his fingers, before his commanding officer spotted it and frowned at this insubordination in the ranks.

"I knew no good would come of having a revenue officer in

the family," Christine said as she stood next to her husband.

"There *is* no revenue officer in our family," Julia said through clenched teeth. "What are you doing here, Lieutenant Crane?"

James Crane looked at her, cleared his throat, and then pulled his glance away to the earl, a less intimidating visage.

"Captain Jensen, Lord and Lady Smithton, Lady Julia. As you know, I am authorized to board, search, and check the manifest of all ships within four leagues of the United States coastline."

"You have no reason to stop this ship!" Jensen said angrily.

Crane fixed him with a steely look. "The last British captain who refused to allow the Revenue Marine to inspect his ship was fined one thousand dollars."

"Pay him, Papa! It would be worth it to be rid of him!"

Smithton ignored this interruption and said with exaggerated patience, "You are supposed to be checking for goods smuggled *in* to the United States, lieutenant, not goods smuggled *out*. Besides, what is it you think we might be spiriting away from these shores?"

"We have reason to believe you are smuggling pickled possums out of the United States."

A stunned silence fell across deck.

"I am astounded you can say that with a straight face."

"Do not try to obfuscate, Lord Smithton! We in the United States know the situation in Britain regarding fine cuisine. After all, it is not like you are trying to smuggle possums into *France* now, is it? Pickled possums are a Florida delicacy, and I would not be at all surprised to find them showing up on the menu at Buckingham Palace. Perhaps you have heard about the proposed tariff on these items?"

"Lieutenant, there is no tariff on *outgoing* goods."

"We're making an exception for possums because of their beauty and rarity. Supply and demand, you know."

"Beauty and rarity? Good Lord, James, have you ever *seen* a possum in brine?" Julia said.

"Lieutenant Crane," Smithton said, examining the cheroot he rolled between his fingers, "does this action today mean you wish to stay with the Revenue Marine and, ah, not come to work for Delerue-Sanders?"

"Ahoy, *Tigress*!"

James Crane's sigh of relief was audible. This time, it was the right lieutenant.

No, it wasn't, Julia realized as she rushed to the rail. Rowing out to the schooner was not First Lieutenant Randall Hawkins, USRM.

The man pulling smoothly at the oars was dressed in butternut brown and a short jacket, with a broad-brimmed hat pulled down over his eyes. A rifle sat in front of him within easy reach as he shipped his oars and pushed the brim of his hat back off sun-streaked hair, looking up at the now crowded rail.

"Mornin', Mr. Earl, Miz Earl, and you, too, your worshipfulness," Rand Washburn called out cheerfully.

"His mind has cracked under the strain. Get me a rifle, Mama, and I will put him out of his misery," Julia said grimly.

"Now, now, dear," her mother patted her on the arm. "Let us not be hasty. Besides, I am entertained, and you owe me for the other afternoon's ennui."

"Mr…Washburn," the earl said. "What do you want?"

"Well now, I thought as how it's a mighty fine day to do some tradin'. An' I got me some goods here I'd be willin' to trade for a woman, seein' as how mine run off."

Smithton looked at the two women alongside him, one scowling, the other grinning, and said, "I have two here. Which one would you like?"

"Oh, now *that's* cruel," Lady Smithton said. "He is going to worry about which of us he offends."

"He has never worried about offending *me*," Julia muttered.

Washburn said, "I have to think on that, 'cause they're both mighty fine lookin' gals." He sat there in the gently rocking boat, scratching his stubbled chin, and then his face lit up. "I know! I want the one what can cook! I'll trade for her."

"That makes it easier. What do you have to trade?"

"Papa!"

"Let me come aboard and I'll show you," Washburn called out.

Captain Jensen looked at Smithton, who nodded, before turning to the gaping crew. "Back to work, you lubbers. This isn't a raree show!"

"Oh, yes it is," Christine said, *sotto voce*.

The earl looked at James Crane and the Revenue Marine sailors.

"Do you still need to examine the ship, lieutenant, or are you satisfied that all is in order?"

"I believe the situation here is well under control. You are free to hoist anchor and leave," he said, but he made no move to disembark.

"Lieutenant," Smithton said softly, bringing Crane's attention away from the rail and back to him. "I admire loyalty. See to it that the same devotion which almost cost you the factor's position today is brought to bear when you have that title."

"Yes, sir," Crane said with a nervous swallow. "Thank you, sir."

Rand Washburn was climbing aboard ship, barefoot and carrying a sack over his shoulder.

He gave the countess a wink, ignored the frowning Julia, and said, "Let's palaver, Mr. Earl."

"I am a modern man, Mr…Washburn. Perhaps you should, ah, palaver with the lady you wish to secure."

"He means you should be addressing me."

"If that's the way you want it, your ladyfulness."

Rand knelt on deck, and opened the bag.

"I got me a wedding quilt," he said, unfurling the rolled cloth. "Barely used," he added, looking at Julia. "It was made with love, and meant to be used with love."

She sniffed. "It is attractive enough, and looks warm. But I have high standards, Mr. Washburn. I don't come cheap."

"Now," Washburn said, drawing the word out for two syllables, "I never thought you was *cheap*, darlin'!"

"No, that is not what I mea—what else is in the bag?"

She raised her hand to make him pause, and looked behind her. Grouped in a semicircle around the couple were the Revenue Marine contingent, her parents, and those crewmembers of the *Tigress* who absolutely did not need to be somewhere else at the moment. Only Aunt Suzanne's *mal de mer* kept her from being up on deck in the audience, too.

"Don't you people have anything better to do?"

"No!" they chorused out, but the earl dragged his protesting wife away, and following his lead, Captain Jensen and Lieutenant Crane found someplace out of earshot for their men as well.

Rand Washburn grinned up at her. He was still on his knees at her feet. She liked it.

"Is there anything else?"

"Oh yeah," he said, without looking in the bag. "I got orange blossom scent, and lavender salve for a hard workin' woman's hands, and a 'broidered jacket to keep a gal warm in the winter. An' I got me a ring."

He reached into his pocket, and pulled out a delicate ring, and handed it to her. It was gold, and set with diamonds. It was a great deal finer than most Cracker wives would ever see.

Julia reached inside the neck of her dress and pulled out a thin gold chain. At the end of it was a man's ring, gold with a ruby inset. Rand's face lit up when he saw it.

"As you can see, Mr. Washburn, I already have a ring," she said with an arch smile. "But I have to admit, yours looks like a better fit for my hand."

"I got more to trade," he said in a low voice. "I got me a heart, in nearly new condition. It almost got broke, but I'm willin' to make a trade. If you give me your heart, I can give you mine, and I will be as true to you as the needle to the pole."

But before Julia could respond, he held up his hand to stop her from speaking, and rising to his feet, dipped again into his sack.

This time he pulled out a blue jacket with bars glinting on the shoulders, and a matching cloth cap with gold bands and the shield and anchor badge. He pulled off his rough Cracker garment, put on the standing collared jacket, and smoothing back his hair, added the cloth cap. Then he stood, a fraction straighter and taller than Rand Washburn, every line of his body shifting from indolent wastrel into firm command presence. The transformation was almost frightening in its completeness.

"Before you give Rand Washburn an answer, your ladyship," Lieutenant Hawkins said in crisp tones, "you need to be aware that I intend to pursue my case as well. You have stolen United States property."

"I don't have any pickled possums!" Julia squeaked. She wondered, briefly, if both Rand Washburn and Randall Hawkins were lunatics.

"No, not pickled possums, Lady Julia," Lieutenant Hawkins said. "You have stolen my heart."

He moved in closer, and took her hands in his, slipping Rand Washburn's ring onto her finger.

Then he tipped her chin up and looked into her eyes, his face Lieutenant Randall Hawkins's face, but his eyes were the warm green of a Florida palmetto in the sun.

"I loved being Rand Washburn. I admit it. I reveled in it, in being lazy, and crude, and free of duty and obligations, and just looking out for myself. Do you have any idea how easy it would have been for me to fade back into the woods and *be* Rand Washburn for the rest of my life? And then you came along and shook all that down to the foundations. I wanted to be Rand Washburn for *you*, for Julia Cooper, my smuggler bride, but I could not. Not and risk losing myself in the process."

"You should have trusted me!"

He shook his head. "That is easy for us to say now, now that we know the truth about each other. I had a commitment to my country. I had obligations far greater than the two of us, Julia. You did your best to convince me you were a smuggler, and I believed you. It was not a matter of trusting you, no matter how much I might care for you. If I had jeopardized the safety of the men under my command, and my sworn oath to the United States and the revenue service by allowing my feelings for you to overcome my honor and sense of duty, would I then be the man you want for a husband?"

Damn him, he was right. She blew her breath out. "No. You would not be the man I want if you would forswear yourself."

"As it was, I was trying to keep you safe while imagining the worst about my wife. To me, the marriage was always a valid marriage, for better or for worse. And for a while there, the worst appeared very bad indeed! I knew no matter how deeply involved you were with the smugglers, I would move heaven and earth to rescue you from them, and the law.

"I was willing to do all that not only because it was my duty to care for my wife, but because I could not imagine a life without you, Julia."

He leaned down and gave her a kiss, not caring that they were surrounded by interested parties. Shockingly forward behavior for a proper gentleman like Randall Hawkins, she thought. But she didn't mind, and kissed him back.

When he pulled his head back, he was smiling, a smile somewhere between Rand Washburn and Randall Hawkins, but all for her.

"Do you think you could come to love a stuck-up prig like

Randall Hawkins as much as you do that piney woods scoundrel Rand Washburn? I want to marry you, too, Julia."

She circled one perfectly polished brass button with a fingertip. The scales of the Treasury atop a fouled anchor glowed in the sunlight.

"Hmmmm…I have to admit, the stern and upright revenue lieutenant has a certain appeal. So commanding and forceful! Why, it would be very difficult for a girl to say no to *his* demands."

She looked up at him from beneath her lashes, suddenly clear on what she needed to do.

"I will marry *both* of you. Lieutenant Randall Hawkins and Rand Washburn. But on one further condition… I will spend summers with Randall Hawkins in Massachusetts, but I will winter with Rand Washburn at his farm in Florida."

Lieutenant Hawkins lips quirked at the corners. "I will answer for both of us then. That is satisfactory, but you understand, Lieutenant Hawkins may get posted elsewhere."

"So long as he takes me with him," Julia said. "And I expect Rand Washburn will be content to stay put in Florida and not go to Texas, if he does not have to work too hard and he has his comforts."

"There's just one comfort Rand Washburn needs, and she's right here."

Hawkins/Washburn pulled her into his arms for a kiss, and as her heart soared, Julia thought she was getting the best of this bargain, two men for the price of one.

"Ahem."

Julia broke off to see her parents had rejoined them, smiling at the embracing couple.

"It appears you two have worked out your difficulties."

"Wish me well, Papa," Julia said with a smile. "I am going to be married! Or stay married. We will work it out."

She leaned up and kissed her misty-eyed mother on the cheek.

"I could go with you to England, Mama, but Washburn's right. It is danged hard to get a good possum there."

"Do not worry, sir," Randall said firmly. "I will take good care of Julia, for I love her with all my heart."

"Very good, lieutenant," said Smithton. "Now you have finally said what I want to hear."

"We will wish you a *bon voyage* then," Randall said, moving back to the rail and his waiting boat, holding Julia by the hand.

"Not so fast," the earl said, holding up *his* hand. "My daughter will be properly married so that there is no question of impropriety. She will accompany us to Savannah to see her aunt off, and you may stay here and make arrangements for the church. When we return in a week's time, then you may have her, with my blessing."

"But...but we are already married!"

"That is an order, lieutenant."

"Dang!"

"You too, Washburn."

EPILOGUE

The Anglican Church on the Plaza—as Lady Smithton insisted was its proper name—was awash with light on a St. Augustine winter morning in 1843. The somber blue uniforms and black frock coats of the gentlemen contrasted with the bright tarlatans and striped silks of the ladies who filled the church for a much talked about event—the wedding of Lady Julia Anne Sanders Delerue to an American lieutenant in the Revenue Marine.

Robin was there, red-faced and sweating, because he'd insisted on preparing the wedding breakfast and was taking a break to dash over from Sanders House for the ceremony. He sobbed into a handkerchief, overcome with emotion, as Richard Cooper alternately awkwardly patted his back and favored the bride with one of his rare smiles.

Ma Ivey sat between her two boys, all of them slicked up and dressed in their Sunday best. Ma was right pleased to see two of her favorite people get hitched again, proper this time, and told the countess so when that lady thoughtfully provided Ma Ivey with a spit jar while she visited their home.

Randall Hawkins stood at the front of the church alongside James Crane and watched as his wife—or wife-to-be, depending on whom you asked—was escorted down the aisle by her proud papa. It was a good thing he had been able to arrange this so quickly. Much more waiting, and that scoundrel Rand Washburn would have carried the lady off back into the piney woods.

Julia came to him awash in Pomona green velvet, as bright as the greenery waving outside the open windows, her dimpled smile peeking through the veil that fell from the front of her bonnet. She carried a bouquet of orange blossoms and roses, and when she placed her hand in his, he clutched it tight and brought it up to his lips for a kiss. His eyes never left hers, telling her everything that was in his heart.

He'd captured his smuggler's bride and she was his, now and forever.

DARLENE MARSHALL

Aspiring authors are told "write what you know," but Darlene Marshall has to admit, she's never been a pirate. However, she is a semi-native of North Florida and loves Florida history and the area the locals call "the other Florida"—a land of rolling hills, along with giant cockroaches, fire ants, scorpions, lightning strikes, the occasional hurricane, and frog-drowning rainstorms. Only the strong (and the air-conditioned) survive.

Marshall is an alumna of the University of Florida and took up writing novels full time after selling her rock radio station. She's been a reporter and editor in television, radio and print. She loves science fiction, fantasy and romance, and tries to attend the World SF Convention each year.

You can learn more about Darlene by visiting her website:

http://darlenemarshall.com

*   *   *